BOMBSHELL

MEN OF SANCTUARY BOOK THREE

DANICA
ST. COMO

BOMBSHELL

After a volcanic one-night stand at a symposium in L.A., a demolitions expert finds herself partnered with her sexual nemesis, former Navy SEAL explosives expert turned local law enforcement officer. They butt heads during an FBI operation based out of Sanctuary, a paramilitary training camp well hidden in the wilds of New England.

Brian "Mac'" MacBride, sheriff of Catamount Lake, and Kailani "Keko" Holokai, owner of a demolition company as well as its lead explosives expert, create sparks of the wrong kind as they struggle to discover who paid a local recluse to build a special explosive device—the same type of device that killed Keko's father—and why.

How can they possibly solve what might be a national security issue, when they can't stand to be in the same room together?

The same bed? That's another story.

*To my brother, Marine scout-sniper,
retired, who still loves to blow things up.*

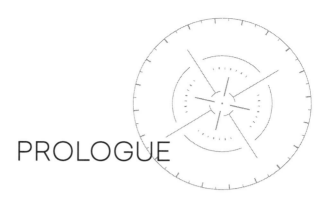

PROLOGUE

Sunday

JESUS JUMPED-UP CHRIST, I'm such a ho. When did I become a ho? What the hell was I thinking? Thinking? I wasn't thinking. My hoo-hah was thinking. And the man smelled like wintergreen, for chrissakes, and I love the scent of wintergreen. Jeez Loueeze, I didn't even get his name. Or his business card. Or his cell phone number. I don't know where he lives. Or, heaven forbid, if he's married. Shit, wouldn't that be a bummer. Then again, I'll never see him again—which is an even bigger bummer.

The only verbalization Keko Holokai recalled using the night before had been variants of "*Ooh, baby, do me like that again*" and "*Yess, omigod, yess, just like that.*"

Hand to her forehead, she moaned aloud at the memory.

The Demolition & Explosive Ordnance Disposal Professionals Symposium had ended. At checkout time, attendees scurried like centipedes when their rock is lifted. The Los Angeles International Airport overflowed with impatient crowds, the flights filled with hundreds of departing bomb experts.

Business class had been overbooked. Keko's choices were to wait another day, or move to economy class. Since her itinerary did not allow for the extra day, economy class won.

Being squashed in her window seat by a giant Hawaiian man, who took up both the center and aisle seats, who smelled sweetly

1

of frangipani, grated on Keko's last nerve. Not only did her head ache, but so did the muscles of her inner thighs—as well as other, more intimate body parts, which she refused to acknowledge.

To add to the physical and emotional turmoil, she'd discovered rug burns on her knees and elbows when she'd showered that morning. The sage-green capris would hide the knees. But, how to keep her elbows hidden, dress appropriately for Honolulu in late summer, yet not grab unwanted attention? She opted for dabbing a bit of liquid foundation on the red blotches, then prayed the stuff didn't get all melty in the humidity and rub off on her clothes.

The Hawaiian continued to needle her in his soft singsong voice. "Perhaps the next time you'll heed my advice, my little blossom. Would I ever give you *bad* advice?"

Trapped by his bulk, she couldn't even escape to the aisle.

"Makaha, my head is pounding off my shoulders and my gut is churning. Please, I beg you, shut your *poi* hole. Let me rest in peace. If you don't, I'm going to slice off your shiny black ponytail, then feed it to the sharks. You'll never go to the happy luau in the sky if the sharks eat your ponytail." As a curse, it wasn't bad for making it up on the spur of the moment.

He didn't miss a beat. "You're such a *malihini*." He thumped his chest. "I am Kamaka, the beloved one, not Makaha, the fierce. I'm just saying, the dude was like a total fox, totally buff, totally hot...but I warned you to slow down, didn't I? I tried to tell you that you *cannot* mainline Long Island Iced Teas like they're wimpy wine coolers, my little coconut. Did you listen? *Noo*, of course not. And poking him in his luscious manly chest because he didn't agree with you about the latest polymer compound to come from Navy Research was unladylike in the extreme."

"Makaha, you're a gay Hawaiian demolitions expert. Other than relying on you for fashion advice, or asking which wine to serve with dinner, why should I listen to you about dating? You haven't gotten laid in *how* long? A year? Two years? So, I swear to god if you don't shut your yap…"

"*Ooh*, girlfriend, that's harsh." Kamaka gave out a *humph*, then crossed his arms over his massive, aloha-shirted middle. "I'm just saying…"

Keko slid the puny airline pillow from behind her head, plastered it against her right ear to muffle the sound of his unwanted words.

Kamaka ignored Keko's rudeness. "Kailani, darling, as I was saying, if that big spectacular stud *really* gave your poor neglected hoo-hah the workout it so richly deserved—and I am *so* totally jealous—then I don't see what the problem—*oof!*" Her elbow caught him in the gut. "Damn, girl, you are a mean bitch!"

She glanced at her watch. "In just over five hours, I must deal with my mother, and I have no desire to *deal* with my mother. Why must we visit now? We could be heading to Massachusetts and home sweet home. I could crawl into the comfort of my own nice soft bed, instead of winging it over the Pacific."

The packed jetliner shuddered as it rose to a higher cruising altitude. Her stomach lurched. "You let me worry about my hoo-hah. Now, *please* be quiet so I can get some sleep."

Kamaka shifted his bulk to get more comfortable, squashing Keko even more. "Honolulu's airport is just over five hours from LA, girlfriend, but at least a dozen hours from Boston. So, we're already halfway there. Good planning on Grandmother Iekika's part so you can visit the family in Maui for a few days.

"As far as seeing your mother, we already know she likes me more than she likes you. She *misses* me; *you*, she tolerates. And because we both know if you're already in Maui and don't show up for Aolina's new gallery showing *and* in enough time to dress appropriately, she'll send her squad of flying monkeys to snatch you up by your hair."

"Makaha, please don't assault me with logic right now. I need recuperative rest. You're taking unfair advantage."

But she couldn't sleep. Closing her eyes didn't pose a problem. The difficulty surfaced when she couldn't blank out the previous night's images of the tall man's stunning hazel eyes. Or the feel of his incredible physique, naked, perfectly aligned against her body. Or her hands tangled in his thick, toffee-colored, sexy, Hugh Grant mop of hair as his mouth...*ahh, sweet holy livin' hell.*

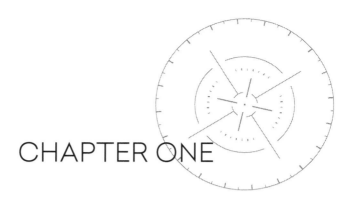

CHAPTER ONE

Monday

"CHIEF, OLD MAN Smitty seems to have come up missing."

Deputy Joe Collins tossed his hat on his boss's desk. "He didn't make his usual grocery run, missed his Friday baked lasagna dinner at the Hungry Bear Café. You know how he feels about Bertie's lasagna. Folks are worried about him."

Sheriff Brian MacBride rolled back his chair, stretched his legs, massaged his temples. Jet lag had kicked his butt after the West Coast conference, but he admitted that other achy body parts weren't technically due to jet lag.

Those aches were due to the exotic emerald-eyed wild child with shiny, waist-long black hair, who first accosted him in the hotel lounge over a difference of opinion about a new polymer compound. Then, she damned near fucked him in the elevator.

By the time they'd reached the door to his suite, her little black cocktail dress had slid up her thighs; her shapely legs wrapped around his waist. His hands had cupped her firm ass cheeks as her sleek arms slid around his neck.

The heat in her kisses had made him weak in the knees, which definitely interfered with his ability to swipe the key card to open the damned door to his rooms. It hadn't helped matters that after her first hot kiss, his cock stiffened enough to shatter shagbark hickory nuts. He'd never actually been jumped by a woman to be her boy toy for the night.

Then there was the tattoo.

Sometime during their hours-long romp, Mac had impatiently slid the *Welcome, Dear Guest* fruit basket off a side table, then lifted his partner's sweat-slicked body to the polished table top. Just the right height for his heavy, straining cock to slide into her tight, passion-engorged pussy. Again.

By the glow of a reading lamp, the mirror over the table reflected the intricate lines and eddies of bright greens and blues and golds etched into her skin. Colors swirled throughout a mythical phoenix that erupted from a bed of orange flame and red embers.

The bird of legend came alive as its owner writhed in Mac's arms, from the unfurled wingtips that reached from one slender shoulder to the other, to the crested head at the base of her neck, to the magnificent tail that ended just above the crevice of her perfect ass.

With a heavy sigh, he shook himself from his reverie.

"Joe, give Abigail O'Connell a call, will ya? Can't hurt to have our trusty game warden keep a sharp eye out for Smitty."

"Aye, aye, chief." Collins glanced at his boss. "Not for nothin', but you appear to be suffering from a severe case of Monday morning black-ass."

Monday morning black-ass, indeed. I need about twelve hours of uninterrupted sleep on a soft bed in a nice cool, dark room, not go chasin' after some loony old man who's probably out drowning worms at his favorite fishing hole. Mac shifted in his seat, groaned quietly to avoid attracting additional attention and more remarks.

I can't believe I didn't ask that black-haired fireball for her name, or get a freakin' phone number, or a business card, or something, anything. I'm so out of practice. Then again, the cover of the airline ticket sticking out of her purse said Hawaii, which is about as far as one can get from Maine. Not likely to run into her in the produce section of the Sugarhouse Farm Market on Snowshoe Street, in beautiful downtown Catamount Lake.

"Let's get this over with." *And maybe keep my mind off other things.* He sighed, rose, stretched, cracked everything that needed cracking. He checked his service piece and ammo, lifted his hat from the peg, then settled it firmly on his head.

"C'mon, Joe, grab your cover. Let's go visit the worrisome Mr. Smith to see if he's at home."

He tossed his deputy the keys. "You drive."

Bernie Smith lived about half an hour from the village of Catamount Lake, over hill and dale and into the deep woods.

Mac appreciated Smith's woodworking talents, how the man had attached several well-built wooden structures to the main cabin, which was more like a story-and-a-half log ranch house. The entire collection of buildings ended up shaped like a large U.

Mac knew the old man had his storage buildings, workshops, and other accoutrements arranged so he didn't actually need to go outdoors for days at a time, during the worst of the brutal Maine winters. Even Smitty's stash of firewood stayed dry and neatly stacked inside an attached garage-like building. *I'm good at organizing my stuff, but I could take a few lessons from the old codger.*

Bertie of the superb lasagna said that Smitty had lived in the city of Augusta with his wife, a kindergarten teacher. They'd never had children, so when pneumonia took his Elsa five years before, Smitty had made a permanent transition to his woodland hunting retreat. Except for his regular Friday sojourns into town, he had only the wildlife for company. He seemed to prefer it that way.

Deputy Collins piloted the big, black SUV along the woodsy roads. Mac leaned back against the headrest, tried unsuccessfully to close his eyes. The trail's overgrowth grew thicker while the ruts cut deeper as they drove on. His planned power nap proved impossible. If it wasn't for his seatbelt, the sheriff would have been airborne.

"Damn, Smitty needs a bulldozer out here, plus about a hundred tons of gravel, just for starters."

Collins chuckled as he negotiated the truck around huge downed trees with exposed roots. "Tells everyone he prefers his privacy. Says the rough road keeps the riffraff out."

"Yeah well, privacy he has, the old goat. We'd better find him rocking on the front porch. I have no intention of searching any deeper into the freakin' woods without dragging out the ATVs."

Smith's old but serviceable Jeep Cherokee could usually be found parked in the courtyard framed by the horseshoe-shaped footprint of the buildings. No vehicle in sight.

Mac stepped out of the SUV, stretched his aching body. "Hello the house!"

Nothing.

"Smitty, it's Sheriff MacBride. Hello!"

Still nothing.

He tried the front door. It was not locked. He pulled his piece, motioned for Joe to do the same. "Check the interior. I'll go 'round the back." Joe nodded.

Mac knew that every room was accessible by a maze of interior corridors and doors. He circled the buildings, inspected the outer doors and windows for signs of vandalism. All the doors of the surrounding buildings were securely locked. Tough to tell if any footprints were fresh; they all looked dusty.

The facility appeared tightly buttoned up—except for the front door.

Going around to the front again, he climbed the three stairs to the porch, walked inside the main residence. Everything looked neat and orderly, as if the old man just stepped out for a moment. Mac met Joe in the living room.

"Boss, looks like a rifle, fishing pole, and I'm assuming a tackle box are missing from the racks in the mudroom. No disturbances, no signs of trouble. But it doesn't make sense that the front door was unlocked when he's so particular about security everywhere else. I got as far as his bedroom."

"Check the other quarters anyway. I'll finish nosing around here."

The townsfolk might shake their heads at the thought of the old geezer living like a hermit in the woods, but everywhere Mac looked, Smitty had everything organized, everything in its place. Definitely not a hoarder. The dwelling held a citrusy scent, like the old man used orange furniture polish on all the wooden surfaces. Mac perused the gallery of photos on the mantle over the big fieldstone hearth in the living room.

There were photos of Smitty and his wife at various times through the decades of their long marriage. In the wedding photo, Elsa had been an absolute stunner, a real Gibson girl, as Mac's granddad would say. But most of the photos were snapshots of Smith and his buds during their military days.

Mac leaned forward, toward one of the larger framed photos, a group shot—

The screen door slammed.

"Boss, *whoa*! Don't touch anything in here. Stick your hands in your pockets, then follow me. You really need to see this." Joe, usually steadfast and unflappable, sounded shaky, looked pale.

"What's up?"

"Trust me. Ya gotta see it to believe it."

When they reached the front porch, Joe handed the sheriff a Kevlar flak jacket, then slid into his own. He tossed Mac a pair of latex gloves. He'd already pulled on a pair.

"Joe, why am I—?"

"Come around to his workshop by the rear entrance. I opened it from the inside. And don't touch a damned thing, gloves or not."

***

Tuesday

It took the FBI field office in Massachusetts a surprisingly short time to get a bomb squad wagon with an Explosives Ordnance Disposal team to Smitty's cabin.

Mac yawned widely, then stepped out of his SUV into the morn's early light, unwrapping the sleeping bag from around his body. It had been his turn to keep a fuzzy eyeball on the place until the Fibbies arrived. The autumn temperature had dropped overnight, low enough to cover the truck with frost.

A tired looking man in a rumpled gray suit approached.

Mac stuck out his hand. "Catamount Lake Sheriff Brian MacBride. Call me Mac. Didn't know you boys were anywhere in the vicinity."

"Special Agent in Charge Will Chandler, Boston field office." The agent gave a half-assed grin as he shook Mac's hand. "We weren't in the vicinity, exactly."

He turned deliberately, took in a panoramic view. "Then again, is any place up here actually in the vicinity? Got the call to reroute to moose heaven before we returned to domicile."

Mac threw the agent a questioning look.

"Don't ask."

Mac shifted uncomfortably where he stood. "Be right back. There's a tree callin' my name."

When he returned, he'd straightened his uniform, ran his fingers though his hair in lieu of grooming. "So, what's your take on this little cottage enterprise?"

Chandler handed him a large container of coffee, pointed to the creamers and sugar packets in the center of the cup carrier. "Honestly? I haven't seen a setup this neat and organized outside of Quantico. What did you say this guy did for a living?"

Mac dumped three packets of sugar in his coffee instead of his usual two, needing the quick sugar fix added to the caffeine. "Retired, as far as I know. Thought he'd been with the Army Corps of Engineers or some such, before he gave it all up to hunt, fish, and play Dan'l Boone. After a few beers, Smitty's been known to spout off about blowing up bridges, moving mountains of rock for roadways, stuff like that. Never stepped outside the law. No reason for me to do a background check."

A deep swallow of coffee had Mac feeling somewhat renewed. "According to the locals, he owned the property, built the cabin, used it for the aforementioned hunting and fishing trips during the seasons. Each year for decades, he expanded the buildings, did more work on the place.

"Moved here permanently after his wife died. That was probably about five years ago, about the time I left the SEALs then landed up here. Don't see much of him except on Fridays, when he does his weekly errands in town, then heads to the diner. Churlish on occasion, but never a problem."

"Churlish?" Chandler chuckled as he scrolled through screens on his handheld satcom unit. "Hold the phone. Check this out. He was an engineer all right, but not exactly the bridge-building kind. Explosives Engineering Specialist in our own United States Army. Interesting."

He flipped through more screens. "Instant intel. Ain't technology grand. Looks like Bernard Smith could build or defuse just about any explosive device on the planet. Meritorious medals out the whazoo, all sorts of commendations for putting his life on the line for the good ol' U. S. of A. Looks like his health took a nosedive after 9/11—he spent time at ground zero. Medical discharge not long after. *Hmm.*"

As MacBride opened his mouth to respond, a Special Agent Bomb Technician in full gear trudged up. He pulled off his helmet to suck in clean mountain air.

"We have an issue." He looked pointedly from Chandler to Mac.

"Take it easy, I'll vouch for him."

"Yeah, well, I don't know too many guys who are going to have clearance for this." The SABT looked at his feet, shook his head. "Sheriff, I understand you were a SEAL explosives specialist, right?" He waited for Mac's nod. "You're familiar with the Larsson case?"

Another nod. Mac's expression changed to a thoughtful squint as he recalled the details. "John Larsson, demolitions specialist. Killed in a freak bomb blast a few months ago. Sporadic intel chatter at the time suggested it was an al-Qaeda op, but no one came forth to take credit for the job. The bomb signature was not previously identified. Appeared to be a timer within a timer."

"Yeah, well, it might be identifiable now." The agent had the attention of both men. "We won't be sure until our squints check the photos and get actual samples back to the D.C. lab, but the components look familiar. The timer on the Larsson device had a peculiar set up. That's why I remembered it."

Chandler shook his head. "The next question: what was our little ol' bomb maker doing in the middle of moose country Maine, followed closely by who ordered the device to be built? So far, his profile does not point to a man who didn't love his country."

Mac headed for his vehicle. "People's politics have been known to change. More to the point, where is the bomb maker himself, so we can ask him those self-same questions? I need to call this in, get an APB out on Smith."

He glanced at Chandler's man. "Your secret is safe with me. The last thing our little town needs is a bomb panic during the height of the fall tourist season."

Thursday

Two days later, Game Warden Abigail O'Connell left a brief message on the sheriff's satphone. *"Meet me at these GPS coordinates ASAP."*

An hour later, Mac, O'Connell, Collins, Deputy Medical Examiner Thomas Blake, and Jack, the M.E.'s assistant, stared at the raggedy human remains at the bottom of a cliff.

"Are you sure?" Mac gazed up the nearly vertical rock face. He directed his question toward the M.E., but he didn't particularly care who answered.

Abigail responded immediately, shifted her stance. "Yeah, it's him. Even with the scavenger damage, that's him. His hair, his clothes, his old military ID in the front vest pocket. He mentioned a time or two that he still had all his own teeth, so Army dental records should do the trick. Or maybe DNA testing?" She turned to the M.E. "Right?"

"The identification and autopsy will be complete, Abigail, not to worry. Mr. Smith's death was probably accidental, considering where the body came to rest. Landing at the bottom of a hundred-foot rock face would account for the skull trauma and broken cervical vertebrae, but I certainly won't rule anything out until I do the postmortem examination.

"Can't be certain until the bugs attached to the remains tell their stories, but he probably died the same day he went missing. Thankfully for us, he landed in the shadow of the cliff. With the temperatures dropping, the remains stayed cool enough to delay decomposition. Now, all of you need to skedaddle. Inspect your accident scene while I get to work on our victim." The M.E. motioned for Jack to haul over the body bag and unfold it.

When they reached their vehicles, Abigail turned to Mac. "We have a problem. Or, rather, you have a problem, since this is your jurisdiction."

Mac cocked his head, raised an eyebrow. "I can't wait to hear this."

"I found Smitty by following crow sign. They were circling overhead, which meant something died on the ground. That makes sense. What doesn't make sense is that I didn't find his Jeep."

"Really."

"Really. But I *did* find his hunting rifle, fishing pole, and creel."

"So, what's strange about that? We surmised fishing stuff was missing from his cabin, as well as a rifle."

"Yeah, well, I would have expected the rifle and fishing gear to have fallen close to Smitty's point of impact. *If* he slipped off the mossy edge of the rock face."

"Abby, I already have a blasting headache. I've been chewing aspirin like Jujubes. Where are you going with this?"

"Mac, work with me here. Smitty had his favorite fishing spots. His body is at least half a mile from the nearest water source. He's nowhere near where he usually parked his Jeep when he fished, or even when he hunted.

"I'd run into him every few weeks, so I have a fairly good idea where his favorite stompin' grounds were. No Jeep between here and there. As a matter of fact, no Jeep anywhere. Now check out the markers I laid down for his rifle, rod and creel, and backpack."

She pointed to an area about forty feet from the body, where several yellow plastic crime scene markers had been placed within a corral of crime scene tape.

Mac was relieved to see that she'd secured the vital elements as soon as possible, but not surprised. O'Connell was a hell of an officer, even if she wasn't one of his.

She swept her arm in an arc, from the position of the body to the nearest of Smith's belongings. "There's no way those items should have landed so far from his body, *if* they went over the edge when he did. The ground is too soft for any serious bounce and ricochet effect. Nothing seems damaged. Animal activity could account for some movement of the backpack and creel, if they'd contained food or fish, but I'd hazard a guess that coyotes or foxes didn't move his rifle or fishing pole."

He had a feeling his headache was about to get worse. "Shit. Anything else?"

"Yeah. There are tire tracks near the top edge of the cliff, but they're not his. Then they disappear in the pine needle ground cover. Since his Jeep isn't anywhere to be seen, I'd be making tire casts before the tracks are lost due to weather or animals walking over them.

"Care to make an educated hypothesis?"

Abigail gave half a headshake. "Best guess? Either he flung them over the edge, then jumped to his death—highly unlikely— or his gear ended up being tossed over the edge after he was pushed. Or thrown."

Her blue eyes flashed. "Mac, I'm thinking our accident wasn't an accident."

"Damn it to bloody hell, Abby. We don't need this right now, with tourists bustling in and out and all over for leaf-peeping and craft fairs."

"I know. I know."

She leaned against her Sierra's hood, kept her voice low. "I didn't want to say anything in front of Blake that might influence his investigation, not that I think he'd do anything less than his usual best. I'm just saying, I think this whole scene is hinky. It looks staged."

Mac was about to climb into his truck when he caught a peculiar scent in the air.

"Abigail, what is that smell?"

"Ya gotta be more specific, chief."

"Sort of sweet, like perfume." He turned toward her, then sucked in a deep breath. "Are you wearing perfume?"

"No, not me. I don't wear perfume when I'm on the job. Screws with the wildlife."

She closed her eyes, sniffed the air like a beagle. "That's wild honeysuckle. It's all over the damned place. Grows like a bushy weed. The flowers have mostly died off by now, but you should smell it when it's in full bloom. Why?"

"No reason. Reminds me of something, but I can't recall what at the moment." He straightened up, scanned the woods.

Abigail nodded. "Research has proven that scent can be the most potent time machine."

Time machine. Good explanation. Then he got it, as a tingle crept up his spine. The last time he'd smelled honeysuckle, his bristly cheek had rubbed against the soft throat of the ebony-haired beauty in his hotel suite. She'd laughed, said the stubble tickled. He'd slid down the length of her body to see what else he could tickle. *Damn.*

"Mac, you okay?"

"Yeah, no worries. Just tired." *And frustrated. Why did Green Eyes take off before I could find out her name?*

"Well, don't be too tired to call me if you or Blake come up with anything interesting."

"Will do."

Abigail paused as she opened the door to the Sierra. "Hey, I hear the Three Musketeers are back."

He grinned. "You heard right."

Yes, they're back, so I can set Lucian on my mystery woman's trail. Before I lose my mind.

Evening fell by the time Mac caught a break to call Special Agent Chandler.

Chandler picked up on the second ring. "Good timing, Sheriff. I planned to contact you in the morning after I grabbed a couple hours of shut-eye."

"Let me know how that sleep thing works for ya."

Chandler snorted. "I'll be sure to do that. I've had about enough of sleeping upright in the seat of a moving vehicle. Anyway, confidence is high that the signature of the bomb components has the same characteristics as the device that took out John Larsson. The good news is that the top expert on that particular device—the only expert—will be landing in Boston."

Mac heard Chandler shuffling papers. He could imagine the chaos of files that probably covered the agent's bed at the CataLodge Hotel. His desk occasionally looked the same way.

"*Ahh*, here it is. Damn, either my penmanship is really deteriorating, or my eyesight is finally history. I already know my brain cells are gone. And the phone connection wasn't the greatest. Sounded like K-something Holo-something. I'm guessing it's Kyle Holloway, maybe."

"Anyway, Holloway apparently worked closely with Larsson. Our D.C. office didn't have a chance to divert him, so he and his second-in-command are winging their way to Boston from the West coast as we speak. State Police will snatch them up when they land at Logan, then toss them on a red-eye shuttle. They should arrive at the Catamount Lake regional airport in the wee hours, morning after next."

"That's the soonest they can get here?"

"Yep, that's it. They're civilians, not government employees—until we know what's going on, we can request, not order. They'll be arriving in Boston on their regularly scheduled flight, but they had two stops in between.

"We've been chasing him across the country, always half a step behind. Hey, count yourself lucky, we're picking up the tab on this one. Larsson had gone independent, but he was still one of ours. One of the good guys. We want whoever targeted him, and we need to know why. Give Holloway all the cooperation you can, then let him do his job."

Mac cleared his throat. "Something you should know about Smitty."

Chandler sighed heavily over the phone connection. "I'm not going to like this, am I?"

"Probably not. It sure fucked up my day. Our game warden found him. Well, found his body. She doesn't think it was an accident. I agree with her. My deputies processed the crime scene without our input, then reached the same conclusion."

Chandler kept silent for a moment. "Shit. Number one, how reliable is the game warden? Number two, can she keep her thoughts to herself?"

"You won't find a better investigator. She doesn't miss much. Neither do my boys. And their sense of discretion is absolute."

"When will your M.E. be finished?"

"He said best estimate, a couple or three days. We usually deal with out-of-control vacationers who party too hard. Occasional break-ins. A domestic disturbance or two, usually beer-induced. Tourists who get lost in the thick woods and mountains. Homicide is not a problem up here—which is why I accepted this job. The M.E. should be able to give the body his undivided attention, but he won't leave any stone unturned. He's good. Really good."

Chandler sighed. "I suppose we shouldn't get all sorts of nuts until he finishes his report."

"Works for me. Sweet dreams, Chandler."

"Bite the big one, MacBride."

Mac grinned as he disconnected.

Friday

The next morning, Deputy Collins cocked his head after Mac finished relaying the news.

"Let me get this right. The Fibbies are babysitting *our* bomb in *our* jurisdiction. We're parking our butts on the sidelines over Smitty's corpse, which is probably a homicide and also within our jurisdiction."

"Yep, appears so." With a heavy sigh, Mac headed out of the office into the fresh air and sunshine, turned toward the Hungry Bear Café with its always-fresh high-octane coffee.

And I've been awake all night, haunted by recurring memories of having had the hottest sex with the hottest woman any red-blooded man could ever imagine. So, suck it up and deal with your disappointment, partner. I'm fresh outta sympathy.

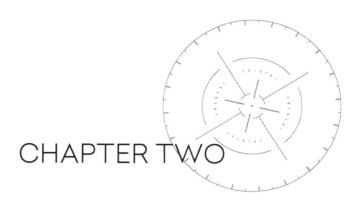

CHAPTER TWO

Saturday

WHAT WOULD HAVE been a five-plus-hour drive to Catafuckingmount Lake from Logan International in Boston was only a quick hop by plane. Keko was convinced it took longer to load their luggage than the time they actually spent in the air.

Including the pilot, copilot, and flight attendant, the total passenger list of the sky shuttle boasted five. The FBI had apparently put a rush on their trip. As soon as they touched down at Logan, the State Police ferried them to the waiting puddle jumper. They were damn near catapulted back into the air.

Keko copped a squat in the single-seat row, while Kamaka spread comfortably across both seats of the two-seater row. He snored. She checked files and made notes on her laptop. An occasional glance through her window gave her visions of the Monet-like effects of the fall, as hints of yellow, orange, and red leaves mingled with the still lush green of the north country.

Which means the tourists, the leaf peepers, will be coming out in force.

She finally sat back in her seat, closed her eyes. *Could it be true? Did the Fibbies actually identify the bombmaker responsible for Dad's death? In omigod Maine, for chrissakes? What self-respecting terrorist would hide out in Maine?*

19

The bomb signature had been truly unique, the mechanism so sophisticated that once armed, it couldn't be disarmed. John thought they'd disarmed it; so had she. Seven minutes later, after she'd vacated the post-office building where the device had been found, the rearmed device erupted in a Vesuvius of shrapnel that shredded John into bloody bits of nothing recognizable.

The range of mourners paying their last respects at her dad's funeral had impressed Keko. High-ranking military officials. Members who represented all the armed forces. His retired SEAL team members. Leaders and representatives from other countries who owed thanks to John, in part, for their peace and prosperity.

Keko's mother refused to leave her artists' colony in Hawaii, refused to attend the memorial with the "black angels of death" in attendance. Those black death angels included her daughter, a demolitions specialist who followed closely in her father's footsteps.

Keko had come to terms with being a disappointment to Aolina Hualami years before, so she ignored good ol' mum's refusal to attend the memorial service. She had her father's remains cremated—what they could gather of his remains—as he'd wished. She placed the urn with his ashes over the mantelpiece in the living room.

Every evening before bed, she settled herself in what had been her dad's favorite wing chair, then poured two fingers of his favorite bourbon, Old Fitzgerald 1849. No more, no less. Then she shared the day's events with him, while listening to Garth Brooks sing *The Dance*.

John Larsson would rest for eternity in his black faux Ming dynasty urn, embellished with fire-breathing, golden-scaled Chinese dragons that seemed to undulate in the hearth light. She thought he'd like that.

I'd certainly tell him about this trip. She hadn't yet had a chance to acquaint him with the story of her encounter with the man in L.A. She wondered if the incident was something she should share with John's spirit. She decided yes, she would. She thought he'd understand.

In a few moments, the transport would bounce along the regional airport's weeds-in-the-cracks runway that she could see looming under the shadow of the descending plane. When the warning bell dinged, Keko repacked her gear, leaned across the narrow aisle, swatted her second-in-command in the arm.

"Rise and shine, Makaha."

He corrected her automatically. "Kamaka."

"Yeah, whatever. Shake your sorry ass awake."

He lazily waved a hand in her direction. "Be gone, evil spirit."

His sparkling black eyes closed again.

Podunk definitely described the little regional airport. Since they were the only passengers, the lone luggage attendant unloaded their bags and equipment onto the cracked tarmac. He left them standing there, then went about his own business.

The crisp chill in the air crawled along Keko's exposed arms. *Damn, it had definitely been warmer when we landed at Logan to make the transfer. My jacket would be useful, if it wasn't crammed into my luggage.*

Inside the terminal, Keko took possession of a wheeled luggage rack to transport her equipment, her single roll-along suitcase, plus Kamaka's pair of oversized, nearly-florescent fuscia bags with their fancy tandem wheels.

Really. How many aloha shirts, Hawaiian shorts, and pairs of size fourteen Birkenstock sandals does one fat man need to survive a trip from Massachusetts to Maui and back?

Keko found the ladies' room, took care of the most pressing issue. Then, desperate for caffeine, she cruised past the few store-fronts, found them all gated and locked. *Damn, nothing open yet, not even a damned vending machine for coffee.* As she rolled the luggage rack toward the only lit check-in kiosk sign, she vaguely noticed a tall LEO, a law enforcement officer, leaning on the counter.

The body language of the woman standing next to him indicated an open flirtation was in progress. The woman's perfectly creased, mocha pants suit looked very expensive, as did her leather-trimmed, four-wheeled rolling luggage.

Still jet-lagged and cranky from the L.A. to Honolulu trip—plus the twenty-something-hour return flight from Honolulu to Boston, by way of Minneapolis and two other airports that she couldn't even identify—she suspected the counter-leaning womanizer was probably their ride to Catamount Lake.

Shit. Really? The woman was well-dressed, certainly. But it stopped there. *Did anyone other than NASCAR groupies do the platinum-blonde poufy-hair thing and the Ford Mustang Blue eye shadow these days? Crap. Then we get stuck with a backwoods Lusty Lothario who's permitted to carry a side arm to add to the excitement.*

As she and Kamaka moved closer to the kiosk, Keko caught a better look at what appeared to be thick, wavy Hugh Grant hair that barely touched the officer's crisp khaki uniform collar. The only time she'd seen such lovely, sexy, unruly hair that same color had been—

Mac heard a strange, gasping sound. He turned away from Pepper Hunsacker to investigate the noise. Next to a large Hawaiian man who looked vaguely familiar, half-hidden by the mound of bags stacked on the luggage trolley, stood a petite beauty whose hair hung to her waist like a shiny black waterfall.

She stepped around the trolley. Came to a rock-solid halt. Stared at him. Her emerald eyes opened wide enough to mimic Garfield the cartoon cat.

Wearing a sleeveless button-down vest in some dark-red shiny fabric, hip-hugging black capris with a thin silver chain around her naked waist, and black high-heeled sandals, she was a knockout. Sexy enough to cause any greeting to catch in his throat. Competition enough for Pepper to utter rude, catty comments under her breath.

As he struggled to focus on the improbability, Mac's cock recognized the slightly-built woman immediately—followed a millisecond later by the rest of his body. The brain finally checked in, third out of three.

Dear Jesus sweet Christ in heaven, it's her! The sex-crazed nymph, the girl with the emerald-green eyes and the phoenix tattoo. How the blue livin' hell...?

The woman didn't say it aloud, but he had no trouble reading her pouty crimson lips. She mouthed the words, slowly and clearly: *Oh fuck.*

Her Hawaiian companion smiled broadly at Mac. "Yo, dude, it's you. Far out."

She elbowed the big guy in his well-padded ribs, but did not break eye contact with Mac. "Please tell me you're not MacBride. I beg you."

The Hawaiian glanced at her, shook his head sadly. "Have I taught you nothing, my little coconut? Don't beg—it's tacky."

Pulling himself into professional mode, Mac stepped forward, offered his hand. "Sorry to disappoint. Yes, ma'am, Sheriff Brian MacBride of Catamount Lake, Maine. Just Mac will do. If the FBI kidnapped or coerced you, if the State Police shoved you into that plane to send you here, then yes, I'm your ride." His brain zoomed into the pleasure zone. *Oh, baby, yes, please ride me. Again.*

From the look on her face, he didn't think she would return the welcoming gesture. To her credit, she reached forward to shake his hand. Her small hand grasped his firmly, without hesitation. The lightning crackled in his brain when their skin touched. He was sure his heart bumped out an extra beat or two.

Their hands still connected, Mac felt a slight squeeze from her fingers. He also caught the woman's subtle eyebrow lift and barely perceptible head tilt. *Aha, yes, Pepper.* Pepper Hunsacker stood there, observing them intently. He knew from experience that the word *secret* was not in Pepper's vocabulary. He released the woman's hand, then turned toward the blonde. "I'm sorry. Miss Hunsacker, would you please excuse us? Official business."

"You expect *me* to leave? Well. Really." Obviously annoyed, she glanced out through the glass doors. "Anyway, my car is waiting. Sheriff Mac, I'll see you in town."

After petting his arm possessively, Pepper stalked off without another word, her luggage wheeling smoothly behind her.

Now, back to his visitor. *Oh yeah, there it is. The scent of honeysuckle. As if I had any doubt.*

She offered a modicum of civility. "Thank you, Sheriff, for maintaining our anonymity, and for providing transportation."

"When the FBI makes requests that aren't really requests, we hear and obey." Since she still didn't offer, he had no choice but to ask. "Now that we're alone, I assume neither of you is Kyle Holloway."

She blinked at him. "Who?"

He stared at the woman, then shook his head to rouse himself out of the mental haze still covering their brief time together. "Never mind. And your name is...?"

She handed him a business card from a pocket secreted in her sexy vest. "Keko." Then she angled a thumb toward the large Hawaiian. "My comic relief here is Kamaka."

Mac read the card twice, turned it over, read the card again, then stared at her. "Kailani Holokai, Larsson Demolitions? As in John Larsson?" He flipped back a page in his notebook. "I have a message that refers to a Mr. Kyle Holloway."

He must have butchered the pronunciation of her name, enough to get a giggle from the Kamaka guy. He soldiered on. "We were never...ah...formally introduced in L.A. Are you the office manager for Larsson Demolitions? I don't mean to be rude, but we really need your lead explosives expert, and quickly."

He turned toward Kamaka. "You must be—"

The big guy held up both hands in surrender, took a quick step backward. "Whoa, boss. Don't look at me! I get my ass in enough trouble all by myself. Man, I like you, so I'm giving you fair warning: piss her off at your own risk."

In a manner Mac remembered all too well, the little fire-ball invaded his personal space, jammed a slender finger against his chest.

"*I* am your expert, Sheriff." *Poke.* "*I* represent Larsson Demolitions." Another poke. "I'm *not* a freakin' secretary!" *Poke poke.* "Why the hell did I attend the conference? What did you think, that I decided to troll a convention center chock-full of powder monkeys to search for suitable husband material?"

Kamaka could barely control his mirth, obviously at Mac's expense. "*Ooh*, sheriff, dude, you are so righteously busted."

Mac couldn't prevent a sigh as he shook his head. "Ma'am, it's too early in the morning. It's been a bitch couple of days. I haven't had anywhere near enough sleep or enough coffee. I'm not tracking real well at the moment." He massaged his temple, felt a headache coming on. "Exactly who are you?"

Kamaka laughed outright, a big booming sound that echoed through the high ceiling rafters of the nearly empty terminal. "You're on a roll, dude. She likes *ma'am* about as much as she likes being mistaken for Mister Kyle Holloway."

Keko whacked her companion's arm with an open hand, which obviously didn't phase the big man. "Will you shut your *poi* hole?"

Her lips tightened. She addressed Mac directly.

"Kailani Holokai." She drew out the syllables. "My fa—I worked with John Larsson as a senior crew chief. He called me Keko, which proved easier than going through the whole pronunciation thing each time. So, there you have it. In a manner of speaking, I'm your man."

Mac took a hard look at her. "We all knew John, either in person or by reputation. Nothing, not even scuttlebutt, about a Keko. Nothing about a Kailani. Nothing about a woman working on any of his teams."

Keko of the slender sexy body shot back a glare of her own. "John worked on such high security projects that only a few people knew about me—or the specifics of any members of our crews. I would greatly appreciate your assistance in maintaining our confidentiality. We all look alike in helmets, facemasks, and hazmat suits. Just think of me as one of the short guys."

His groin stirred. *She could never be mistaken for just one of the guys, even a short one.*

Then she mumbled something that sounded Hawaiian.

Kamaka clucked, shook his head. "Oh now, *that* was naughty."

She crossed her arms under her marvelously firm breasts in a definitely confrontational posture. "Did you actually *know* John Larsson?"

Mac looked away, took a moment to collect himself in the face of the red-hot bedroom memories.

"Yes, I did know John, as a matter of fact. SecNav called him in as advisor on a SEAL mission of…some sensitivity. We had an issue. John bailed us out. Showed me things I'd never seen before, amazing tricks. He saved lives during that op. Probably saved me and my team." He stopped himself, pulled in a deep breath. "I…we…admired him greatly." He faced her squarely. "I'm very sorry for your loss."

The light apparently dawned in her brain at the exact moment the thought pierced his.

"That's why—" she began.

"—the demolitions conference. I try to keep up, " Mac finished.

He recovered quickly. "But you were flying to Hawaii, not Boston. I wasn't snooping, but I saw part of your ticket."

"Family obligation." Keko left it at that.

Kamaka prodded Keko out of the way, steered the luggage trolley toward the doors.

"Well, kiddies, this has been a real gas, but yours truly is practically fainting from hunger. I've had nothing to eat except a few peanuts and teeny tiny pretzels. I need sustenance. Real sustenance."

Keko turned away from the sheriff, followed her wingman. "Bullshit. You could survive a famine of at least six months' duration. I swear, one more cheddar bacon burger, and the post office is going to assign a separate zip code just for you."

Kamaka shook his head slowly. "You're a harsh, bitter woman, Kailani Holokai. And soon, you'll be a harsh, bitter, *old* woman."

"Bite me, *Ma-ka-ha.*" She drew the word out, snarked at the big man.

"*Ka-ma-ka.* And you wish I would. Maybe just a little nibble. You know what they say. Once you go gay, there's no other way."

He blew her a kiss.

She flipped him the bird.

Mac shook his head, slapped his palm against the metal wall button that swung open the doors. *And these are my experts. Great. Just what I need, preschool kiddies battling between themselves.*

They headed for a big black SUV parked in the no-parking zone, the vehicle emblazoned with SHERIFF on the side, bold gold lettering across a white circle. He slowed his stride, which gave him the opportunity to observe the sexy sway of Keko Holokai's trim hips as she marched down the sidewalk. She was obviously still in a foul frame of mind.

Oh yeah, it's her all right. He closed his eyes for a moment, savoring the memory. *It's her, with the incredible tattoo of a fiery phoenix rising from the embers and ash on her naked back.* Now, with her clothes on, the phoenix's tail feathers peeked out from the bottom edge of her vest, as well as the top of her waistband. The wing feathers shot out from the armholes of her vest as the unfurled wing tips crept along the outer edges of her shoulders.

And I'd remember that perfect ass anywhere. Hooyah.

"Do you want to eat first, get settled first, or head out to the site first?" Mac had pulled up in front of the police station, about a block from what looked like the town square. He let the truck idle.

Keko glanced at him from the passenger seat, hoped he didn't notice. Not only did he notice, but her body swore the sparkle in his eyes promised good things to come. Her hoo-hah remembered how good he'd been, which left her poor sex to twitch and tingle. *Now is so not the time for this. Can he really be the MacBride?*

"The site first." Her voice sounded firm, businesslike. At least, she hoped it did.

From the back seat, Kamaka whined. Actually whined.

The sheriff looked in the rear view mirror. "Sorry, friend, we don't have fast-food joints around here. However, there is a great diner two blocks down the street, the Hungry Bear Café. An easy walk. Open 'round the clock, good food, reasonable prices. Put it on our tab."

He handed Kamaka his business card. "You can come back here to the station, make yourself cozy until I return. Or, catch a ride out to the site with one of the Fibbies. They're sharing the last vacant suite at the CataLodge Hotel. The other motels are full. Autumn tourist season. The FBI guys are working in shifts to cover Smitty's place. Or—"

"Diner works for me." Kamaka slid his bulk out of the SUV with surprising ease, then headed toward the Hungry Bear, seemingly oblivious to the slight chill in the air. "Catch ya later, Boss Lady."

Just like that, he was gone.

"What's with the names?"

Keko cocked her head. "Excuse me?"

"Your buddy's name. It changes."

"Ah." She faced front again. "Translated from the Hawaiian, *Kamaka* means beloved, adored, venerated. You get the idea. He's very proud of that. His parents were older, so he was the last born of that generation. They followed the ancestral custom of not using a surname. His passport and driver's license actually state Kamaka Kamaka, because he needed a last name for ID—he didn't feel like dealing with *Kamakawiwo'ole.*

She sighed. "He believes that makes him doubly blessed."

"And…Makaha?" He bungled the pronunciation.

"It translates to fierce. He hates the name, insists that it's harsh and messes with his good karma."

"So, you do it…"

"Just to bust his coconuts."

"Uh-huh."

His arm still draped over the back of the seat, MacBride turned his attention to Keko. *All* his attention. At his clearly lascivious glance, the tiny hairs on her arms prickled in remembered passion, as did the hairs at the back of her neck. *Oh man, this is so not going to work. Three thousand miles between here and our assignation, yet fate steps in and plays us. Some joker god is having quite the giggle at our mortal expense.*

"Now that your coworker's made his choice, I am totally at your service. What would you like me to do for you?"

It was a loaded question, dripping with innuendo, and they both knew it.

He released his seat belt, turned to face her, the fabric of his slacks pulling tight over his muscular thighs. "You were gone when I woke. You didn't need to leave, you know. I hadn't planned to kick you out of my hotel suite. I thought we'd have a nice, leisurely breakfast together, perhaps become better acquainted— maybe even exchange names. You flew the coop, which left me no way to get in touch with you."

Oh God, he's going for it. Shit.

His alpha body posture made her feel very vulnerable, naked. She wasn't familiar with the feeling, and she didn't like it.

"Kamaka and I had a flight to catch." The excuse sounded lame, even to her. *Please let him drop it.*

"You didn't even leave a note, a business card, anything, on the night stand. Nothing pinned to your pillow."

She bit her bottom lip, something she hadn't done since she was ten. Words wouldn't come.

"You don't want to discuss this, do you?"

A wave of relief rolled through her. *Oh, thank freakin' heavens.* "No, I don't."

29

"Husband? Boyfriend? Ex? Stalker? Just so I know how we stand."

"None of the above." *And we're not standing anywhere, friend.*

Keko read the bald desire in MacBride's eyes, almost gave in to the same yearning that ramped up in her body. Her nipples—the little traitors—immediately perked to attention. Afraid to look down, she was sure the peaks were attempting to push through the rich satiny fabric of her vest. She *knew* what he looked like out of uniform. The memory of him panting in her ear, his hot, thick, hard flesh sliding into her wet, overheated… *Oh, no. No way. This shit needs to stop. Now.*

MacBride brushed a wave of thick, gorgeous hair away from his eye.

Oh dear God, he's killin' me here. Her sex throbbed and dampened, and with that last throb, she nearly came. A smidgen of squeak escaped her lips. She swallowed. It took all the control she had to keep her hands still, and prevent her voice from cracking.

"Will you take me to the site, please? I need to see the device, put together a report for the FBI. I haven't been home or had a good night's sleep in nearly two weeks." She realized how whiny that sounded, but the words were already out there. *And I need you to go away. I need you to leave me alone before this becomes too complicated for words.*

He actually bowed his head. "As you wish. The FBI finished processing the house and buildings. You can use the indoor plumbing facilities, and they've stocked the kitchen. No one will starve."

She'd faced forward again, but at his comment she glanced sideways. "Why didn't you tell Kamaka there was food available at the cabin?"

Mac didn't bother to hide the smile as he fastened his seatbelt, then put the truck into gear. "I would have gotten to it. He didn't give me the chance."

And you didn't see fit to stop him from leaving, either.

She guessed, as the crow flew, Smitty's place wasn't all that far. It was the condition of the secondary and seasonal roads—more like barely widened, twisty game trails—that made the trip arduous and time-consuming. MacBride stopped apologizing after the first few minutes. The silence dragged on, as neither chose to be the first to break it. She refused to bring up their very recent association.

Keko did her best to enjoy the scenery. At least, to do whatever it took *not* to look at her driver. *Not* to notice the tousled look of his thick, tawny hair. *Not* to observe how well his heavy shoulders filled out his tailored uniform shirt. *Not* to glance at the khaki fabric that pulled tight across his hard thighs. *Not* to see how Top Gun he looked in mirrored aviator sunglasses.

She didn't understand what was going on in her brain and her body, the physical reactions being the worst of the two problems. Never, not ever, not even once in her life had she reacted to a man the way she reacted to MacBride.

They'd both arrived late to the last day's lecture at the convention, then took the only seats available among the hundreds of attendees. They'd been stuck at the back of the large room; he was seated a row ahead of her and to the left. Too far away for her to read his nametag.

Since it had been her first time out as the principal of Larsson Demolitions, she'd worked hard all week to keep a low profile: dressed in conservative tailored pant suits, hair held in a low ponytail by a silver clip, simple low-heeled pumps. She'd concentrated on business. With the fine-looking man sitting just at the edge of her peripheral vision, she had a difficult time following the printed handouts. She lost her focus while only half-watching the videos and Power Point presentations.

During a coffee, juice, and snack break, she'd overheard his plans regarding the night's activities. All she'd managed to do during the afternoon's programs was to calculate the time it would take her to clean up and *wow* him in the lounge.

As the new title holder of Larsson Demolitions, she'd been off to a rough freakin' start.

Keko tried to pace in front of the workstation, but there was only enough room to take baby steps in any direction. When she could no longer avoid it, she stared at the twin sister of the explosive device that took her father's life. Stared at the device that nearly took out her and Kamaka. Her skin tingled, but this time it wasn't in a good way. *Must be my Spidey senses, telling me to run for freakin' cover.*

In the end, her professionalism saved her. John had always handled the front end stuff, approved the contracts, dealt with their clients. Keko worked behind the scenes, and preferred it that way. By pretending this was just another job, by being sure her notes were accurate and concise as her father had taught her, she hoped she could get through the day without breaking down. She needed to remind herself that her dad couldn't pick up the pieces if she screwed up.

The buck stops here. It's all my responsibility now. Hooyah!

The FBI agents on site were polite and efficient. They'd been told she was the expert, so they expected her to be skilled in her field. She appreciated their professional demeanor, which helped her do the job. Interested, obviously appraising glances came her way, but none of the agents actually hit on her—which came as a relief, considering her already knotty sheriff problem. Maybe their boss, Special Agent in Charge Chandler, had warned them off; he seemed like a fairly upstanding guy.

After scoping out the explosive device and the workshop, Keko jotted down her first impressions. Then she pulled herself together, left the shop, weaved her way through the maze of buildings.

Let's get a feel for the old man who built highly sophisticated bombs in this backwoods hideaway.

Deputy Collins eventually delivered Kamaka to Smitty's lair. The big man took a calculating look around the shop. Then he took a quick sniff of the C-4. "Smells funny. Wrong color, too."

Keko nodded. "I agree. Looks like it has almost a pink tinge to it, doesn't it?"

"Could be."

"In any event, I can't identify the manufacturer. Any thoughts?"

Kamaka checked the cabinets, looked through the supplies. "Not yet. Lookin' at the other material and equipment, all high quality, I'm wondering why someone went to the bargain basement of demo suppliers for the C-4. It isn't on any list with which I'm familiar."

She shrugged. "Possible, I suppose. That would explain why I can't place it. The FBI took a stick of the stuff to run tests down at their lab in Quantico. We'll see what they find."

"Don't need Time-Of-Flight Secondary Ion Mass Spectrometry to tell me there's a problem." Kamaka tapped his nose. "Over three hundred olfactory receptors. *This* tells me something isn't right. Best mass spec in the world."

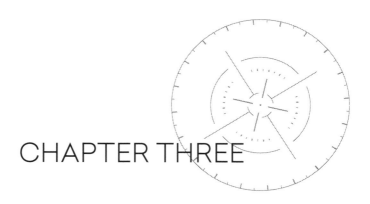

CHAPTER THREE

Saturday evening

SHERIFF MACBRIDE ENTERED the workshop, took a wide-legged stance, thumbs hooked in his web belt. "Ms. Holokai, we have a logistical snag with housing everyone."

Damn, he looks good enough to... She shook off the memories. "What's the problem now?"

"Between the autumn leaf-peepers and craft-fair tourist season gearing up and the Fibbies spread out trying to keep a low profile, there are no rooms available. The next real town with lodging is about an hour away."

Kamaka perked up. "And maybe has a Mickey D's?"

Keko cut Kamaka off before he could salivate over the possibility of his next McAngus Burger. "So, now what? Do we commute?" Exhausted, she didn't want to hear that no beds were available. "Can we sleep here? I don't take up much room, and I'm good with the sofa or love seat."

"Sorry, three FBI agents stay on site to protect the premises. One sleeps, two stand guard."

"Protect the site from what or whom, exactly? Rampaging moose? Crazed raccoons? Squirrels with night vision goggles and Uzis?"

MacBride hiked his belt, settled his holster. "Ma'am, with a federal agency taking first seat, it's not my call. I live to serve."

Oh yeah, I just bet you do. "There you go again with the ma'am thing, Sheriff. So, what choices do we have? Do we stay, commute, or leave it all in the hopefully capable hands of the FBI so we can grab a ride back to Boston?" *Please say we can go home now.*

He shifted his stance again. "I made a suggestion to Special Agent in Charge Chandler. He agreed. Good friends of mine have a lodge not too far from here. I crash there when I have time off, babysit the place when they're away. And check on the cat. They just arrived home from an extended visit, offered accommodations for you and Kamaka. An SUV will also be placed at your disposal."

"And who are *they* to whom we owe for such generosity?"

"Adam Stone and Lucian Duquesne, Marine sniper-spotter team. Well, scout sniper and spotter, retired. They own Sanctuary lodge and training encampment. Their woman, NCS Special Agent Lorelei Randall, is currently on medical leave for injuries sustained during an aborted assassination attempt in the line of duty. Since Lorelei is now pregnant, medical leave will probably slide into maternity leave." He reacted to their expressions of puzzlement. "The situation sounds complicated at first, but it isn't really all that bad."

"*Their* woman? Assassination attempt?" Kamaka's round handsome face lit up. "*Ooh*, intrigue. I love it already."

The security at Sanctuary's main gate proved impressive, but was totally overshadowed by the view of the lodge as the sheriff's vehicle broke out of the tree-lined drive. The majestic log edifice appeared to be patterned after the massive ski lodges in Colorado's snow country. Beautifully landscaped multi-level gardens in a full array of fall flowers surrounded the buildings. A series of large, impressive outbuildings spread out to the left of the wide parking area, then disappeared into the trees.

While Keko gawked, she didn't realize that MacBride had gone around to the passenger side. He handed her out of the vehicle, then escorted her up the wide stone stairs to a pair of massive multi-paned glass doors. Too tired to care, she ignored his hand as it maybe-nearly-almost caressed her arm.

The big doors swung inward before MacBride could ring the bell. They were met by a stunning woman with a luxurious mane of crinkly blonde hair, gorgeous brown eyes, and a superb tan. A mint green middy shirt and white shorts showed off her trim, toned body.

Keko stared. *Pregnant? No freakin' way. Not and look that good. Must be another woman who's pregnant.*

"Welcome to the Fun House." The woman accepted a quick peck on the cheek from MacBride, then she linked her arm with Keko's, led the way through the foyer and into the great room. "Glad you decided to stay with us. Mac, do something useful. Find the boys."

The sheriff obeyed without question, took off immediately.

Keko made a complete turn before she came to a standstill, wide-eyed and slack-jawed at the magnificent interior.

In the huge space, a half-dozen seating areas, each formed by a collection of heavy leather furniture, were arranged on richly-patterned Oriental area rugs. Two staircases, one on either end of the great room, led to rooms on the second floor gallery. A tremendous fieldstone hearth on the main floor dominated one wide wall.

The woman made a sweep of the interior with her arm. "Don't let all of this throw you. It may take a time or two to get oriented, but you'll be okay. There's the eat-in kitchen, butler's pantry, laundry, guest bathroom, library-den, and formal dining room. Go through the etched glass doors behind the far staircase, and you'll find the indoor pool pavilion. Through the far set of pavilion doors at the end of the pool is the entrance to the underground training center. Feel free to make yourself at home."

Keko was overwhelmed. "This is Sanctuary? Have we been kidnapped by insane survivalists? A cult?"

"*Nah*. I asked the same questions," the woman chuckled, "except my list included axe murderers." She held out her hand. "Special Agent Lorelei Randall, currently on leave from the National Clandestine Service. The guys are wandering around here somewhere. We've been visiting, so they're glad to be back in their own playground. No matter. We can begin introductions without them. Incredible tat, by the way."

"Thanks. I tend to forget it's there." Keko took the hand Lorelei offered, shook it firmly. "Keko Holokai, Larsson Demolitions. And Kamaka, my second."

Lorelei and Kamaka bowed their heads to each other, which in other circumstances might have seemed theatrical. For those two, Keko thought it worked.

"Okay, you have choices. There are three empty guest rooms upstairs. Two, if Mac hangs out with us."

Keko felt a chill zoom up her spine at the thought of MacBride being domiciled only a door or two away. They hadn't been safe from each other in a seven-hundred-room resort hotel. How could they bed down so closely, and still keep their hands off each other?

"*Um*, does he hang out here frequently?" *Please say no, please say no, please say no.*

"Often enough. He's good company, and the three boys play nicely together in the same sandbox. We also have twelve efficiency cabins; each sleeps as many as nine—I guess in the old summer camp days, each cabin slept eight kids and a counselor. The cabins are self-contained."

Kamaka raised his hand. "Cool! An adventure. I'm good with a cabin." He grinned broadly, winked, wiggled an eyebrow like a villain from a silent film. "Miss Keko, share a cabin with me? We could snuggle, keep each other warm and toasty."

Before Keko could respond with a smartass remark, Lorelei held up her hand. "No, Miss Keko is *not* one of the guys, therefore, she is *not* staying in a cabin, with or without you. No snuggle bunny for you, unless you want to sleep with the cat. Keek stays here with me, like civilized people. You lose, fella."

"Who loses?"

Keko's jaw dropped again.

Tall and gorgeous, a GQ fashion model strolled up behind Lorelei, wearing a black, muscle-hugging, sleeveless T-shirt that showed a Marine tattoo on each hunky bicep. The smooth, slinky motion of his torso and trim hips reminded Keko of a black jaguar, the action embellished by snug black jeans. Long, blond, Fabio hair swayed, loose and silky, as he moved. Mustache and goatee were short and neatly trimmed, hazel eyes sparkled. He wrapped his arms around Lorelei, leaned forward to kiss the top of her head. "What's up, sweet cheeks?"

"Lucian, mind your manners. We have visitors. Since the Fibbies have taken over the town—again—Mac delivered guests to us for safekeeping." A smooth hand gesture indicated their guests. "Keko Holokai, John Larsson's daughter. Kamaka, Keko's wing man. Folks, this overgrown beach bum is Lucian Duquesne, Marine spotter, retired."

Chills ran down Keko's spine. And not the good kind.

"B-b-but how did you know about my f-f-father? N-n-no one is s-s-supposed to know." *Who the hell* are *these people?*

Lorelei's smile could have peeled the grumpy off the worst curmudgeon. Keko trusted her instantly. The feeling of intense panic kicked down a level, maybe two.

"Not to worry," Lorelei responded, leaning back into Lucian's wide chest. "You're safe here. We're family. The first thing you need to learn, the most important thing, is that there are no secrets at Sanctuary. Mac mentioned your name, Lucian commenced digging." She pointed toward the right on the second floor gallery. "I call it the Death Star Comm Center—nothing escapes without first being investigated until it can no longer stand."

She covered Lucian's hands with her own, sighed when he kissed her ear. "Lucian is our own mad intelligence specialist, aren't you, baby?"

"The mad part is accurate enough." The new voice nearly echoed, sounded as deep as a cavern.

Keko stepped back involuntarily. *Whoa, holy shit, big dude in the house!* MacBride and Lucian were tall and superbly fit, Kamaka was super-sized all over—but this guy radiated total awesomeness. In a snug blue Moosehead Ale T-shirt tucked into faded jeans, she reckoned he had to be every inch of six-foot-four. His jeans were extra faded over his heavy thighs—and over the noticeable package at his crotch. He fit the image of Magnum, P.I., right down to the sharp blue eyes outlined in stunning black lashes, black wavy hair, and full, black mustache. His muscles had muscles. The guy exuded a blatant aura of total testosterone.

"Keko Holokai, Kamaka, meet Adam Stone, retired Marine scout-sniper. And yes, although I am loathe to admit it, his bark *is* as bad as his bite."

Lorelei freed a hand and placed it on Adam's broad chest, an oddly sensual gesture. He didn't kiss her, but his body language made the situation abundantly clear. *Back the fuck off. She's mine.*

"Hey, baby. Mac brought guests to stay with us. No rooms at the inn."

"FBI?" His tone sounded as rich and smooth as the twelve-cylinder Jaguar XKE that Keko had inherited from her dad.

"Of course. We were just discussing room assignments."

Kamaka spoke up. "Like I said, I'm good with a cabin, Miss Lorelei."

Keko tried to read Adam Stone's expression as he sized up her Hawaiian. She failed.

"Look, honestly," she added, "we're low maintenance. No need to fuss. I can bunk with Kamaka. We live together. Wait, that didn't come out right. He shares my father's house with me." She felt heat in her cheeks. "My house. He stays at my place, y'know, like housemates." *Oh man, this is not going so well.*

"No way, Keek. You'll bunk in the room next to mine." Lorelei turned in Lucian's arms, pointed up to the gallery level. "Left to right. Adam's room, guest room, your room, my room, Mac's room when he stays over, Death Star room, Lucian's room. Each has its own bathroom, so you have complete privacy. All the comforts of home."

"That's very generous, thanks. So, *hmm,* Sheriff MacBride might stay here?" *I hope that wasn't too flippin' obvious.*

"Possibly. Probably, since he's already here." Lorelei looked around. "Speaking of Mac, where is he?"

"He's in the exercise room. He delivered your message, stripped down, started pounding the heavy bag before I left him," Lucian shared.

Keko felt uncomfortable. "Does MacBride know about my dad?"

Lucian shook his head, his silky blond mane flowing around his shoulders. "Just Lorelei and Adam. Our friend Garrett knows, but he dug up the intel independently, then we compared notes. Over-the-top clearances from every branch of every government—he won't say anything to anyone."

"There you go, Keek, everything is under control." Lorelei slid gracefully from her lover's arms. "Lucian, we need lemonade and maybe some sort of snack before dinner. Any of your wonderful cookies left?"

She turned back toward her guests. "Kamaka, the cabins all have names. Take cabin number one, The Pine. There are cases of bottled water in the lower kitchen cupboard. Fresh bedding is in the linen closet next to the kitchen area. You're on your own as far as housekeeping, I'm afraid.

"You can stock upon snacks when you're in town or hit up Lucian's stash, but you'll eat here with us. Adam does breakfast, Lucian handles lunch, the boys alternate cooking dinner. Meals at six, noon, and six, roughly speaking. Feel free to raid the kitchen any time you wish. Lucian usually whips up some sort of snack or dessert."

A huge grin nearly split Kamaka's face. "Miss Lorelei, I can help. I know how to cook." He folded his arms over his sizeable girth. "And I'm good, too. Just ask Miss Keko."

Keko nodded. "Oh yeah, our boy is quite the chef. He can conjure up an entire luau all by his little lonesome. What he can do with pork, coconut, and pineapple nearly defies description. Oh, and don't forget fresh fish and seafood. He's brilliant."

41

"Noted. We'll put you to work, big fella." Lorelei laid a gentle, caressing hand on Adam's heavily-veined forearm. "My darling man, I believe you're up for chef duty for supper. How about something simple, like cheddar burgers, and perhaps a nice green salad?"

Kamaka's countenance lit up again, then he grinned, broadly. "Cheddar burgers? Maybe with bacon? Real bacon? All right!"

Before Keko could stop her, Lorelei snarked, "What, you think I can't do real bacon?" Then she pasted a pretend scowl on her face.

Keko shook her head, pantomimed sadness. "Lorelei, you said the magic words. Cheddar bacon burger. You now have an adoring slave. Forever."

She turned to Kamaka. "Before lemonade and cookies, let's sort our luggage, then get everything where it needs to go. C'mon, Pineapple Man."

Keko and Lorelei settled, snugged into a corner of the great room with mugs of steaming chamomile tea and a plate of Lucian's sugar cookies. Kamaka lounged across from them. Keko reached for another cookie. "Where'd the guys go?"

Lorelei stretched out on the sofa, got comfortable. "Adam and Lucian returned home with too much nervous energy to burn, after dealing with the necessity of behaving themselves at the Duquesne family insane asylum—so, they whomped the snot out of each other on the wrestling mats downstairs, in the training complex. Assuming no real blood was shed, they showered, dressed, then planned to meet MacBride in town to blow off more steam. He went home to shower and change, declining to participate in the organized mayhem on the mats. He'd already massacred the heavy bag."

Keko admitted to herself that she felt relieved as soon as she knew MacBride had gone. She needed time to process all that had happened since she landed at the airport. A rumble that seemed to be coming from inside the house suddenly jerked her out of her MacBride mindset.

"What the—"

Lorelei didn't even look up from petting the cat. "Not to worry, it isn't an earthquake. Adam's moving his much-beloved truck out of the garage—the thing should probably be housed in an aircraft hangar, just to deal with the size of the beast. Ford F-450 Super-Duty Super Cab," she recited. "Dual axles, dual five-inch chrome exhaust stacks—just in case they need to cross high water. It's a guy thing."

Relieved that what she'd felt hadn't been an earth tremor, Keko settled back in her comfy chair. "Believe me, I understand about guy things."

Kamaka finished his tea. He rose, turned, bowed to his hostess. "Miss Lorelei, sorry to beg off sampling what passes for night life in the Cata-whatever Lake town square, although the Hungry Bear place is actually very cool. Chrome, neon lights, swivel stools at the counter if you don't want a table. Awesome cheddar bacon burger, perfect crispy fries, unsalted. What *is* a catamount, anyway, and why does it have a lake?"

Lorelei stretched out on one of the sofas, her feet propped on a pillow. The little calico cat nested on the woman's belly—a belly not yet showing the slightest indication of a baby bump.

"A catamount is a mountain lion, a cougar. Legend says that a couple of hundred years ago, there was a huge boulder on a tiny island in the middle of the lake that resembled a snarling cougar. I haven't been here long enough to see it firsthand, but that's the story.

"Kamaka, I feel like I'm putting the dog out before bedtime by sending you to rough it. We have plenty of room—you don't need to bunk out in the cabin. Even the cat stays in at night. Since we seem to have somehow acquired a cat." Callie purred under Lorelei's hand.

"Miss Lorelei, it's not a hardship, believe me. Rough it? The cabin is twelve-hundred square feet, kitchen, bathroom, gang shower, my choice of nine beds, satellite television. It even has heat. My previous apartment was six-hundred square feet and there were always weird people hangin' out. Present company excepted, of course. Not that I'm complaining, Miss Keko, boss lady." He grinned. "*Aloha po*. Good night. See you in the morning."

Keko waggled her fingers. "*Aloha po* to you, too. Sweet dreams."

Lorelei's eyes followed the big jovial man as he disappeared. "What's his deal?"

"What do you mean, his deal?" The cat switched allegiances, hopped to Keko's lap. "Hey, critter, how do you know I even like you?"

"Trust me, she doesn't care, as long as you pet her. I mean, the dude is a screaming queen, yet well-schooled and well-spoken when he's not spoofing people with his homeboy Island dialect. An expert in explosives and demolition, hangin' out with a single, presumably hetero, woman. Seems an odd combo, that's all."

Keko felt her hackles rise in defense of her best friend. "You have a problem with Kamaka?"

"Are you kidding? Hell no, he's a hoot. I already love the guy to pieces. Lucian is all right with him, but I'm not sure about Adam. Our alpha lad may take some finessing." Lorelei grinned. "Which could be fun."

"I don't know how you do it," Keko muttered. "I can't manage to keep any one guy for more than thirty seconds, let alone two men forever. Plus a career? Plus a baby on the way? Damn." Keko frowned at the pushy cat, who cared not at all about Keko's personal issues.

"Believe me, relationships and motherhood were not even penciled in on the short list that had been imprinted on my government-issued brain. But Adam and Lucian? Kismet. Destiny. It's tough to explain. I guess the simple version is that each of us complements the others. I lived alone quite comfortably, worked my ass off at my job, gave my all to the FBI, the CIA, then to the NCS. Now, I can't even contemplate being alone again. Not ever."

Lorelei rubbed her still-flat belly. "Seeing the guys with a baby should be a laugh riot. After visiting North Carolina for a couple of weeks, surrounded by the insane antics of his lunatic family, I know Lucian will be a natural. His thundering herds of nieces and nephews adore their Uncle Lucian like nothing I've ever seen before. He even changes diapers like a pro, forms his own assembly line."

She laughed. "Adam, not so much. He'll need to work on his parenting skills. But he's so happy about us, about the baby…" A liquid shine highlighted Lorelei's soft brown eyes. "So happy."

Keko felt a lump in her throat, found it difficult to respond to such honest emotion. She finally managed a weak smile. "I'm beat. Sorry to be the party pooper, but this tired camper is headed for bed. And thanks again for putting us up in your home. This place is truly awesome."

"Hell, I'm right behind you as far as bed goes. I'm glad you like the digs, but I can't take any credit. The boys told me that they upgraded the outbuildings when they bought the place, but kept all the original architecture. They extended the scope of the outdoor facilities, had the firing range installed in the underground training area. One of Lucian's sisters, Julia the Designer, handled the entire interior. The guys even have a housekeeping service and a landscaper. I could get to be a seriously lazy bitch."

Lorelei stood, brushed the last of the sugar cookie crumbs from her lap. The cat jumped ship once again, launched off Keko's lap to search out any morsels.

"Besides, are you kidding about putting me out? Having another woman in the house in the midst of this hotbed of male hormones—you're doing me a favor. Plus, with Kamaka here for protection, the two Musketeers felt comfortable enough to leave for the evening. I actually get to stretch out in my own bed with no big hard bodies squishing me. For a few hours, at least. Not that I'm complaining, but after our trip to the Duquesne family's madcap central, I've had my fill of people for a while. Forced togetherness can be a trifle wearing on the nerves for someone like me, happily raised an only child. Nighty-night."

As exhausted as she was, try as she might to clear her mind, Keko couldn't settle after slipping between the layers of cool, crisp sheets. *I'm an only child, too.* Yet, she heard the happiness in Lorelei's voice, felt the aura of contentment that surrounded the strikingly beautiful Special Agent. Lorelei's men—her lovers—not only adored her, but it was obvious they truly cared for her. They didn't spoil her, exactly, but they did cosset their mate and mother-to-be. Lucian seemed the caregiver of the trio, and no doubt, Adam's role was the protector. There would be no saving whoever tried to harm his woman.

Their woman.

Damn, how does Lorelei balance the best of all worlds? I can't even balance my freakin' checkbook.

Keko pounded her pile of pillows into a comfortable mound. She finally relaxed enough to slide into lullaby land, surrounded by the ambient glow of the starry starry night sky, shining through wide windows and overhead skylights.

She had no idea how long she'd been asleep, when loud grunts and groans echoed through the lodge, followed by the pissed-off yowl of a cat.

Now what? Keko slid into her robe, grabbed the Smith & Wesson .38 revolver from her panty drawer.

Lorelei beat Keko to the gallery railing, a Walther PPK hanging from her hand. She hit a light switch, glanced over the railing—then pointed down to the illuminated great room. "Keek, I think you need to deal with this one."

Keko pulled her robe tighter, leaned over the railing as far as she could without falling.

"Oh, for fuck sake. Kamaka, *please* put the nice Marine down. Don't break him or they won't let us stay."

Kamaka had Lucian in a bear hug from behind. For all his considerable strength and skill, Lucian could not break free.

Like a big lazy lion, Adam leaned against the doorjamb between kitchen and great room with arms and ankles crossed. "He caught Lucian bringing up the rear."

The Hawaiian, all six-foot-five of him, didn't even break a sweat while Lucian struggled. "I was scoping my last recon, y'know, Miss Keko. Heard someone sneaky-sneaky 'round the back. Not sneaking so well—made enough noise to wake the ancestors. Normal people use the front door in their own house, right?"

Kamaka looked up. "Sorry, Miss Lorelei. I think I scared your cat, maybe a little bit."

"Yeah, well, the cat's on her own" Lorelei groused. "You for sure scared the blue livin' shit outta me!"

Keko felt the heat creep to her cheeks. "My fault, sorry. After my dad died, I persuaded Kamaka to move into the main house with me. He always does a last perimeter check before he feels comfortable enough to bed down for the night."

She thought Lucian's skin color didn't look so good. "Kamaka, let Lucian go. He's turning blue."

When the big Hawaiian didn't move, Keko gave him The Look. The *squinty-eyed, cocked eyebrow, I'm going to beat you to a bloody pulp with a tire-iron or die in the attempt* look. Like the five-foot tall, hundred-pound Keko could force Kamaka-the-man-mountain to do anything. "Don't fucking a-well make me march down the freakin' steps, fella! Drop the Marine… right… this… minute!"

With a dramatic sigh, Kamaka unlocked his massive arms. Lucian sucked in a huge gulp of air as his feet hit the floor.

"Keerist on a fucking popsicle stick. *Damn.* He about broke both my elbows and all of my ribs." Lucian moved his shoulders and arms experimentally, checked for damage.

"Shit, may have cracked something." Lucian glanced over at Adam. "Ah'm here ta tell ya, hoss, that boy is some kinda wicked strong. Strong like a freakin' tank. And by the way, bro, thanks for the assist."

Adam shook his head, mustache drooped, expression sad. "Duquesne, ol' buddy, you're beginning to worry me. This is the second time you've been taken captive. In our own home. The first time, by a woman half your size. You're losin' your edge, boy."

"Fuck off, Stone." Lucian continued to test body parts to make sure they were functional.

"Fellas, enough with the mutual admiration society. I've had all the excitement I can deal with for one night." Lorelei glanced at the wall clock. "For one morning."

She pointed at her men.

"Your own beds tonight, boys." Patting her belly, she added, "Junior and I need restorative sleep."

Keko agreed with the back to bed comment, although she didn't need to warn anyone that she intended to sleep alone. Sadly, she didn't have any suitable candidates lined up to share her space, and the one who would volunteer in a New York minute had trouble written all over him.

"Kamaka, promise to play nicely with the other children so I can go back to sleep." When the big man didn't respond, she arrowed a lethal glare at him. "Well?"

Kamaka grinned up at his boss and best friend. "Promise, Miss Keko."

Before Keko turned back to her room, she watched the man mountain gently pat Callie on the head as he headed for the kitchen and the back door—again. "Sorry, cat. Next time, stay out of the way."

Keko shook her head at the conundrum that was Kamaka, then headed to bed.

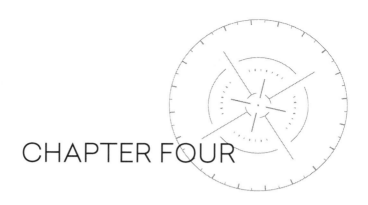

CHAPTER FOUR

Sunday morning

AFTER A QUICK breakfast with Kamaka, Keko grabbed up her map. "I'm heading out to Smitty's camp. Are you coming with me, or staying here?"

Kamaka popped the last piece of bacon in his mouth, talked while he chewed. "Staying here. If you can handle the stuff at the cabin, Lucian said I could use his programs and the big screens this morning. Did you see all the intel toys Lucian has? Outstanding! He and their buddy Garrett from GMG will go through the FBI results with me, the stuff that Agent Chandler forwarded to us."

Keko had laughed aloud when Kamaka modeled the black Darth Vader helmet he'd found on a wall-to-wall shelving unit in the comm center, which was stocked as well as a computer super-store. Shaking her head at their silliness in the midst of potential death and destruction, she left the boys to play with their toys.

At Smitty's, Keko examined the explosive device components more closely. The agents had nicknamed the bomb The Larsson. The label caused Keko an emotional twinge every time some-one said it, but she knew they meant it as a sign of respect for a fallen comrade. Since she'd been introduced as Keko Holokai, the agents were unaware she was the only surviving Larsson. She intended to keep it that way.

The apparatus of the device had been laid out with great precision on the workbench, apparently in preparation for assembly. It was a complicated piece, with redundant fail-safes.

Yeah, fail-safes. A terrible term for ensuring the bomb detonates, regardless of what we do to shut down the mechanism. A terrible term to underscore the certainty that people will be killed, maimed, or mangled, despite our best efforts. Fuckers.

Keko photographed and diagrammed every circuit, every component, every tiny screw and length of wire for her own files, even though she was sure the FBI had completely processed the scene.

Special Agent in Charge Will Chandler finally arrived, showed her what they had so far. Gentleman that he was, he even presented her with a whole-grain pita pocket stuffed with chicken-pecan-white-grape salad and yogurt dressing, from the diner in town. They sat in Adirondack chairs on Smitty's front porch and ate.

"I don't know how you people sit on these blasted hard seats. My ass falls asleep." Chandler shifted again and grunted to prove his point. "This situation doesn't make sense. All our file data, all our interviews with locals, indicate Smith wasn't the type to work with insurgents against his own country. He seemed like a dyed-in-the-wool patriot, always had been. Lied about his age to enlist in the Army when he was fifteen, got caught, had to wait until he was legal. The guy was a hero. I don't see him being a turncoat. That dog just won't hunt."

Keko sipped from her water bottle to clear her throat before speaking. "Sorry, Agent Chandler. I can only help with the device—I'm not very good at profiling. That was my...that was more John's forte."

"Sonofabitch. I'm sorry, Ms. Holokai, this must be torture. We get so wrapped up in the who-done-its that we forget how personal this is to you."

Keko fought the tears, but one managed to slither down her cheek anyway. "Thanks. He was...like...a father to me." *And I miss him so much, sometimes I can't breathe.* She tried for a smile when he patted her hand, but they were both uncomfortable with the emotions.

"I'm fine. Really. It's just that it's all still too new. I will, however, suggest you run any theories past Kamaka. His insights border on frighteningly accurate, and his brain is hardwired like a computer."

He grinned at the portrayal. "I'll take him up on that. Great tat, by the way."

Keko had worn a backless, sky-blue halter top that allowed the brilliantly inked tattoo to be viewed in its entirety when she had her long hair pinned up. Which she'd done, to prevent any stray hairs from contaminating the components. "Thanks."

Chandler excused himself, headed inside the main cabin to confer with his men; Keko returned to the shop. She had several lengths of wire under a lighted high-powered magnifying lens, when she heard a knock against the doorframe, presumably the agent announcing his return.

"Chandler, there's something about the composition of these wires—"

Before she could turn, strong arms wrapped around her. Before she could react, she caught a faint, barely there aroma, the sweet woody scent of wintergreen. Her heartbeat instantly kicked up spikes on the chart.

"Damn it, MacBride, what do you think you're—"

"*Shh.* Hush, Ms. Kailani Holokai Larsson, explosives expert with the incredible tattoo and who smells like wild honeysuckle. I did my homework. It took some digging, then Lucian verified so I didn't ask the wrong people the wrong questions. You're the real deal. Impressive. John Larsson's daughter. No one knew. Imagine that."

"The real deal?" she snarked. "Is that right? Is that what I am? You are *such* a jerk. Let me go or I'll…"

He refused to stop what he was doing. "For instance, I know that both your names derive from seafarers, from the sea, from the sky. You're a water baby, with the strength of the oceans." He pulled her against him, her back to his front, his muscled arms holding her captive as he nuzzled the black hair she had trapped in a mother-of-pearl barrette shaped like a leaping dolphin.

"Damn, baby, I missed this," he murmured. "I missed you, Kailani-of-the-sea. I didn't know how to find you. I've been going crazy trying to dig up a lead, any lead. Why did you jackrabbit out of L.A.? Why bail out in such a hurry? Those were the best ten hours of my entire life! God, it feels so good to hold you again."

She struggled in his arms. "I said let go of me or else—"

"Or else what? You'll take sexual advantage of me? Again? Wrap your legs around me. Again." He shifted to pin her with his groin, sandwiched her against the sturdy workbench. "Little hellcat."

She felt his erection through his uniform trousers, his stiff cock pressing against her. Damn it all to hell, her sex heated to flash point so fast any hint of common sense flew out the window. A traitorous groan escaped before she could prevent it. *How the hell does he manage to light my fire at freakin' warp speed?*

His hands on her shoulders, MacBride tried to turn her to face him.

She resisted. "No. This way."

His body stopped pushing against hers. "What?"

"I said, take me this way."

"Baby, you know you're a crazy women, right?"

"That's possible. Do it now. Quickly. Before someone walks in."

MacBride hesitated, so she rubbed her ass slowly, sensually, against his solid arousal.

"Now or not at all, sailor boy."

"I'll sailor boy you." With little in the way of finesse, he shoved her shorts and panties to her ankles. She heard his zipper as he released his cock to press against her, as lusciously hard and thick as she remembered. Leaning forward, his mouth brushed her ear, whispered, "Forget sailor boy. I liked it better when you cried *ooh baby* as you came on my dick. And came. And came."

He reached between her thighs and fingered her. "Damn, girl, you're already wet for me."

"Stop talking!" She nearly hissed in her frustration, unable to disguise the raw naked yearning in her voice, pissed off at herself for falling victim to his presence and the aura of his sexual heat.

She heard him rip open a condom packet; two seconds later, he'd buried his lubricated shaft into her hot flesh. Her hot, *needy* flesh. Once again, he stretched her to the limit, that delicious burn as perfect as she remembered.

MacBride pulled back enough to slide his arm around and under her pelvis, reached her clit with long strong fingers, as the tender petals of her labia unfolded and clung tightly to his shaft. He rolled the bud between forefinger and thumb, then sharply tapped his fingertip against the nerve bundle above the hood of the swollen nub. Again. And again.

"*Omigod, sweet Jesus*, whatever you just did, do it again, I'm right there, baby, I need to come on your cock, oh god, I missed this, missed you…" *Oh, damn in diamond dust, did I just say that out loud?* She wriggled her hips against him. *Maybe he didn't hear me. Maybe he's too busy. Maybe…oh shit, oh sweet Christ!*

He slid his hands under the sides of her backless halter top so he could reach her high firm breasts, kneaded the stiff points of her nipples. Then reached down, rolled and flicked her clit again.

With no pillow to muffle the sound, she thrust her forearm against her mouth to keep from screaming his name as she came. His orgasm burst free a few seconds later, as the walls of her throbbing pussy gripped his shaft. He grasped her waist, pumped into her until there was nothing left except the harsh sound of their hoarse breathing.

Head down, Keko rested her elbows on the workbench, while she willed her pulse to slow. *Great, now I'll have splinters, as well as rug burns.* Her hair had worked free of the barrette, which had disappeared. Long, black strands draped across her back and shoulders, fell forward over her breasts.

MacBride carefully pulled out, disposed of the condom, used hand wipes from a container hanging on the wall to clean each of them as well as possible. He found the plastic bag from her lunch in the trash basket, stashed all evidence of their encounter.

Keko pulled up her panties and shorts. "Leave everything. I'll toss it later."

MacBride attempted to hold her again, but she wouldn't turn, wouldn't raise her face. The heavy curtain of her hair hid her expression. *I am such a ho.* She couldn't look at him.

"Sheriff, you'd better go before Chandler, or one of his agents, decides to check on my progress."

"Now I'm the sheriff again? Keko, I can't leave you like this."

"Like what? I'm fine. We'll…talk…later."

"Keko, baby—"

"MacBride, will you leave?" she snapped. "Please?"

"You could call me Brian."

"You could go away."

"Okay, maybe just Mac?"

"Just go, dammit! Get out!"

When she heard him leave, she heaved a huge sigh. She retrieved the barrette from the floor, smoothed her hair and clipped it back, leaned against the table to regain her bearings.

What's wrong with me? Am I brain dead or something? Bar Barbies had lined up to check him out at the lounge in L.A. He shamelessly flirted with the Junior League woman at the airport kiosk. He's gorgeous, he's hung, he has skills, he's a player. What are the chances that this will end happily ever after, like Lorelei and her lovers? No chance in hell, idiot. No chance at all. I should finish up here, hop back to Boston with Kamaka. End of story.

Chandler returned about ten minutes later. From the concerned expression on his face, she must have looked dreadful.

"Ms. Holokai, I understand you're bunking in the lodge at Sanctuary. Sheriff MacBride must have received a call; he left in a cloud of dust before I could ask him to give you a lift. Anyway, one of my men can ferry you to the lodge if you're not up to driving and finding your way through the woods. Why not call it a day, grab some shut-eye? After bouncing around the country, I'm sure you're jet lagged, and there's nothing here that can't wait until tomorrow. Our squints in D.C. are *still* working, and there are more of them than there are of you. You can't do it all in one day."

"Agent Chandler, please call me Keko. Y'know what? I'm not even gonna pretend to argue. You're right. I'm jet lagged, working on a headache, and I can't think straight. Something bothered me about the wiring assembly, but I can't remember what. I'll take a fresh look in the morning."

And my pussy is still pulsing and throbbing from MacBride's attentions, and I can smell his sex in the air. It's making me nuts, and I need to get away from here. She wondered if Chandler picked up on the pheromones that must be swirling around the room like crazed hummingbirds.

"All right, Keko, call me Will. Leave this puzzle until tomorrow. Let's go 'round front to the courtyard, instead of weaving through the labyrinth of rooms and doors. I'll grab one of my boys to play chauffeur."

⌖

Keko walked into the Sanctuary lodge through the entryway that opened into the great room.

Choosing the light-blue leather grouping, she huddled in an overstuffed wing chair, arms around her knees. She wasn't quite ready to go to her room.

"Overwhelming, isn't it?"

Lorelei must have come up from the training center. Her mass of hair cascaded from its high ponytail. Sweat soaked her sports bra and the waistband of her gym shorts. A towel was wrapped around her neck. She looked lean and hard and fantastic.

"Which part?" Keko felt like a helpless child again.

55

"The whole package. The lodge. The camp. The isolation. The men." Lorelei moved the calico cat, then parked on the edge of the sofa. She wiped droplets of perspiration from her face with the edge of the towel.

"All the men, not just mine. Everyone is military, ex-military, or some sort of law enforcement or security. They live hard, they play hard—sometimes they die hard. None of them are exactly housebroken. We're just back from visiting Lucian's people, so the camp isn't in full swing. If you think it's tough now, wait until the clients show up." She grinned. "Then it's a real party. The clients don't stay here in the lodge, but it's still Testosterone Central at Sanctuary."

Keko shook her head. "How do you do it?"

Lorelei shrugged. "Honestly? I like it. More to the point, I need it. Training hard, strategizing, the investigations, the assignments—they charge me up like a Tesla coil."

She draped the towel over her shoulder. "Frankly, it took coming to terms with Adam and Lucian for me to admit that I'm an adrenaline junkie. I crave the action, crave walking along the sharp edge of the knife. Why should men have all the fun?"

She left, then returned with two tall glasses of iced tea and a plate of macaroons. "Lucian makes the tea, fresh. Nothing like a good ol' Southern boy to brew up real sweet tea like his mama taught him. The caffeine and sugar will either knock you on your butt, or keep you wired for three days."

She took a long drink, then winked. "Yup, that'll keep ya goin'. Mostly sugar-free lemonade for me these days, because of the baby. This will be my special treat."

Settled back against the cushion, Lorelei turned a hard look toward Keko. "You're a demolitions expert, your father's daughter. It's totally a man's world. If you don't mind me asking, where's your mother through all this?"

Keko stretched out her cramped legs; the cat abandoned Lorelei to settle on Keko's lap. "Story is that my folks met in California where my dad was stationed. By all accounts, they hit it off like the rocket's red glare. But as soon as Mother realized that the SEALs—and not she—were his life, she pulled up stakes and flew back to Honolulu. Pregnant with me."

"Then what?"

"Hawaiian families are totally cool and loyal to a fault. Family is family, everyone helps everyone. A total support system. In Mother's case, she traded in her own family—me—for a place in the art world. She's an incredible painter and sculptor of primitive art, hugely talented. When I was a baby, she foisted me on grandparents, aunts and uncles, cousins. Anyone who would keep me for a while so she was free to work. Don't get me wrong, I wasn't abused or anything. Very loving people cared for me. Everyone except my mother."

Keko had to look away for a moment, rein in her emotions before she could continue. "But I wanted my father; he was my hero. He visited as often as he could. They told me that when I was about five, I raised such holy hell after Dad left—wouldn't eat, wouldn't drink, screamed bloody murder for days until I couldn't speak—the family gave up. Grandmother Iekika intervened and had my father called home on emergency leave. Apparently, Mother handed him sole custody. From what I overheard when no one knew little ears were listening, she never shed a tear."

Lorelei gave Keko a measured look. "Sounds like a cold-hearted bitch."

"Wow, tell me how you *really* feel." Keko managed a small half smile, then shrugged. "I guess so, and she still is. On the rare occasions when I'm forced to be in her company, I always feel like I'm five again. That I'm an annoying inconvenience. I don't know why she periodically feels my presence is necessary—that's where we went after the L.A. conference concluded, to see her. She never acknowledges me as her flesh and blood, so it can't be for the mother-of-the-year vote. She likes Kamaka better."

Her expression sobered. "I may have grown up with rough, tough, powder monkeys for playmates, but I couldn't have been more cared for and protected. Dad did his best to have women around for the female influence. Mrs. Wiggins was my nanny until I turned thirteen and became, even by my own admission, totally obnoxious."

She grabbed another macaroon, turned it over in her fingers as if she was sorting out what to do with it. She took a bite, washed it down with iced tea.

"Twin sisters, neighbors of ours, were kidnapped right from our high-security private school yard. The bad guys tried to force their dad, a *compadre* of my father, into doing something highly illegal. Marine Force Recon found the girls. They were alive, but barely. Seems the kidnappers did not intend to honor their end of the bargain once they got what they wanted. The end result? Marines, 12. Bad guys, 0. Dad had me homeschooled after that. I knew what had happened to Annabelle and Annalee—so I never complained about my situation again."

"So, no social life? No dating? No going out with the girly girls to the mall?"

"You're kidding, right? Boys braved the house only once, and then they ran in the opposite direction as fast as their feet could carry them. Girls my own age thought I was totally weird. Creepy Keeky, that's what they called me. Creepy for short."

Keko got her voice under control, embarrassed to realize she was still affected by the memories. "No friends with normal names like Brittney, Ashley, Samantha, Allison. My pals were Eight-fingered Jack, Powder Burn, TNT, Scarface, Freak, Sweetcheeks—don't ask about that one—Fireball, Screw Up, Ash Kisser, Flame Out. Dad had three full crews, so I'll spare you the rest. Then he imported Kamaka, who earned the moniker, Tiny Tim, for obvious reasons. At least Kamaka was closer to my age, and Hawaiian." She cocked her shoulder. "I'm *hapa haole*. Half blood."

Lorelei shared a flake of coconut with the cat, who couldn't decide whether or not it was edible. "If you don't mind me saying, you seem to have a great fashion sense—how did that happen?"

A heavy sigh resulted. "Don't laugh. When tomboy garb no longer suited, when a clean pair of jeans or coveralls, new work boots, and a *Rock On* T-shirt no longer worked for evening wear, my dad was absolutely clueless. The guys in my crew bought me girly magazines. Not girly as in porn, girly as in fashion."

Lorelei laughed. "I'm surprised you didn't end up looking like a street walker or an exotic dancer, with the guys giving advice."

"*Nah*. Read Cosmo, Elle, Vogue, Glamour, the whole lot. I studied clothing lines, practiced doing makeup in the privacy of my room, stuff like that, until I passed. Oh, and I do keep Victoria's Secret, secret."

"And none of the crew members hit on you?"

Keko felt her face grow warm. "And cross my father? Not likely. Actually, the guys, especially the older guys, were very protective. They said that when I wasn't working, I should look classy, not trashy. So, that became my motto. Class, not trash."

"Sounds like boatloads of fun. So, what's with you and Mac?"

Keko choked on a macaroon. "I beg your pardon?"

"Look, I don't know Mac that well, but I know him well enough. He's a good guy. Smart, dedicated. Single, to my knowledge never married, a straight shooter. The air fairly well strums with tension when you two are in the same room. Or maybe that's brimstone." Lorelei grinned. "He's been a freakin' basket case since he arrived home from the conference. Is that your doing?"

I'm so not in the mood for this. I can't even sort it out for myself. "Lorelei, not to be rude or anything, but I'm really whupped on my ass. I need a warm shower and a big soft bed. Could we maybe continue this discussion another time?" *If we ever discuss it at all.*

Keko couldn't decide if Lorelei's expression mirrored confusion or righteous conviction.

"Sure. What about supper?"

"Not hungry, thanks. If you would let Kamaka know I'll chat with him in the morning? Oh, I left Lucian's SUV at Smitty's place. One of Chandler's men gave me a ride. Will told me to call him in the morning for a lift."

"Uh-huh. No problem. G'night."

"*Aloha po*."

CHAPTER FIVE

Sunday evening

"KEKO ISN'T COMING down for supper?" Mac nearly spilled his drink at the kitchen table, then tried to regroup, attempted to appear unconcerned. "She went to bed already? Is something wrong? Is she okay?"

"Calm down, Galahad." Lorelei passed the salad bowl to Kamaka. "She's fine. Apparently, your explosives expert was so exhausted that she nearly fell asleep at the workbench, almost face-planted on the components. Chandler had one of his boys bring her home."

Lucian perked up.

"What did she do with my truck? Plowed it into a tree or boulder or something?" Then he grinned at Lorelei. "Oh, no, wait—that's your technique for parking a motor vehicle."

Adam snorted, and nearly grinned.

Lorelei shot her lover a seriously squinty-eyed glare. "Duquesne, watch it. I know where you sleep. I even know *how* you sleep. As I was saying, Chandler thought she was too tired to drive, so the Fibbies are guarding your precious truck at Smitty's. She'll need a lift to the site in the morning."

Kamaka helped himself to another thick pork chop filled with pineapple and apple bread stuffing. "That's no lie. Miss Keko hasn't gotten much sleep lately, just a couple of power naps in the air while we crisscrossed the country. As a matter of fact, she hasn't had a good night's sleep since, well, let me think…since the conference. For some reason, the workshops really wiped her out."

Mac saw Adam perk up at the news. *Aww, crap.*

"Conference?"

Kamaka nodded. "Yeah. Demolitions and explosives symposium. Out in L.A. We continued on to Honolulu, bopped out to Maui, returned to Boston by way of air terminals I can't even pronounce, then hopped the red-eye from Logan to here."

Mac didn't miss the sly smirk the Hawaiian sent his way. *Did Keko tell her big buddy about our liaison? Does she tell him everything?*

Lorelei poured another lemonade. "Mac, isn't that where you were, the explosives conference in L.A.?"

"*Uh*, yeah." He stuffed a cheesy Brussels sprout in his mouth.

"Are you staying out here tonight? Your room is made up."

If Mac didn't know better, he'd swear Lorelei shot him the same smug look as Kamaka. *What the hell was that all about?*

He hadn't planned on staying over, but why not? "Sure, I'll stay. Tomorrow is my day off, anyway. Joe Collins has the ball. I'll let him know I'll be out here if he needs me. Should give Chandler a call, too."

Usually enjoyable, the after dinner coffee and chitchat in the great room seemed to drag on forever. Mac watched the minute hand crawl sluggishly around the large-faced, antique train station clock on the far wall. A small fire, not one of Adam's usual pyrotechnic affairs, blazed cheerfully in the hearth.

Kamaka had long since departed for his cabin, more than pleased when Lucian broke into his personal stash of snack food. And shared.

Lorelei looked classy and comfortable in a soft blue sweater worn over a long flowing blue and cream skirt. The waist-to-hem buttons were undone to mid-thigh. Sitting on the sofa with her legs stretched out on the cushions, she appeared serene as she stroked the little calico cat on her lap—the cat that had moved into Sanctuary while the three lovers were away.

Adam and Lucian looked edgy. Sensual anticipation rippled in the air, like sun's rays bouncing off hot pavement, and Mac guessed the trio would end up in Adam's bed tonight. After all, they'd spent a couple of weeks at the Duquesne farm in North Carolina, where the men needed to be on their best behavior—or Lucian's mama would have thumped them until they remembered their manners.

Mac's room sat next to the comm center, the farthest unused bedroom from Adam's. While the trio didn't overtly partake of sexual excesses in front of their guests, it was impossible not to hear the sounds of wild passion coming from behind closed doors.

Keko's room is only two down from Adam's. Not far enough. Mac stood, yawned, and stretched. "Everyone, dinner was fantastic as usual. Thanks again. I'm knackered, I'm heading up."

Lorelei moved the cat, shifted onto one hip, crossed her legs. Her actions were seductive, whether she meant them to be or not. "G'night, Mac. Or, as Kamaka taught me, *aloha po*. See you in the morning. When you go up, would you be a dear and hit the light switch on the wall next to Adam's room? We're not ready for bed yet. I'd like to enjoy the fire."

When he reached the gallery level, Mac glanced down at his hosts. Lucian had already settled next to Lorelei. His hand slid up her naked thigh where the gauzy skirt fabric had fallen away. Adam slouched in his chair like a big jungle cat and stretched his thighs wide, which emphasized the bulge behind the zipper of his cargo pants.

By the look on her face, Lorelei noticed, because she licked her lips.

Oh yeah, fun and games about to commence on this fine night. Mac clicked off the remote switch for all the lamps in the great room.

As he passed Keko's room, a strip of light from under her door indicated she was still up. He knew that Lorelei's room separated Keko's from his room, with no connecting doors between.

In his own room, stretched out on his bed, he remembered when his life at Sanctuary really began. Even though he'd begun attending classes and training sessions at the camp shortly after he left the SEALs and arrived in town, it hadn't been until the following year that Adam and Lucian felt comfortable enough with Mac to initiate him into their *ménage a quatre* lifestyle. Not as their third with two or more women, but by vouching for him, by introducing him to men and women who enjoyed playing as singles, couples, or in small groups, at a classy, private club.

He agreed with his friends' life-long decision never to play too close to home. So, when he sought female companionship, a quick phone call to Lucian, who acted as cruise director, set up an evening's entertainment about two hours away from the quiet hamlet of Catamount Lake, away from Sanctuary. After a couple of years enjoying the life, the men had fallen into a comfortable routine that worked remarkably well for the three bachelors.

After the abrupt arrival of Lorelei into the fold just a few short months ago, neither Adam nor Lucian strayed from her side, effectively ending their liaisons away from home.

It had been a shocker to Mac when Adam and Lucian showed up at their private club, Outlandish, with Lorelei on their arms. Lorelei was so comfortable with her men that she accompanied them to the sex club for an occasional dinner, their meals always prepared by a top-notch chef. The guys didn't wander through the club as they had in their previous lives, and no one dared approach Lorelei with her Marines in such close proximity. And she always dressed like a totally sexy, sensual siren. Other men looked at her with obvious envy, but knew enough to admire from afar.

On those rare occasions when Mac desired company on his own, he'd pack an overnighter, his kit bag containing condoms as well as lubricants and a variety of sex toys, then head for the club. He was always mindful of a tenet Lucian taught him: *Be ready. One never knows ahead of time what the ladies might request.* He couldn't stop a grin at the memory.

Then, when all was quiet and peaceful and the world was good, along came Kailani Holokai Larsson to disrupt Mac's orderly existence. And he liked order, a holdover from his SEAL days, which were not too far behind him. Order, control, knowing how to react in any given situation without conscious thought, had kept him alive. From their first glance across a crowded lecture hall, to the lounge, to his hotel suite, it had been Keko, and only Keko. As Linda Ronstadt had belted out, *just one look, that's all it took.*

Indeed, when Keko showed up, his well-ordered life had flown right out the window.

Mac finally lost the battle with his conscience and cat-footed to Keko's room. The strip of light had been extinguished. When he tried the knob, he was rewarded with an unlocked door. He heard her rustle in her bed.

"Lorelei? Is that you?"

"*Shh*. Not Lorelei. Just me." He pitched his voice low. With the large windows and wide skylights common to all the gallery rooms, it wasn't difficult to find her in the ambient illumination. He took her by the hand, gently pulled her out of bed.

She resisted. "So much for privacy in a house full of Marines and CIA. What the hell do you think you're doing?"

"*Shh*. Quiet, please. Come with me."

"Why should—"

He placed a finger against her lips. "It's urgent. C'mon."

Soft moans sounded, barely audible from the great room, as Mac pulled Keko along. When they reached his room, he quietly closed the door behind them. The only noise was the metallic click as he engaged the lock.

"Now, do you want to tell me what's so freakin' important that it requires abducting me from my bed? And what's going on downstairs?"

He pulled her close. "My best guess would be that our hosts and hostess are becoming reacquainted after their travels, and they haven't reached a bed yet. Now, regarding your abduction. It is of the utmost urgency that I feel you in my arms again. I can't do my job because of you. Can't keep my mind on work because of you. My universe is in full tilt because of you."

How could he tell her that the image of her face was forever etched in his mind? The image of her face, her body, as they had appeared in the soft lamplight of his L.A. hotel suite. As he spent more time with her, he also saw the resemblance: in the daylight, she mirrored John Larsson's handsome Nordic facial features and bright green eyes. *She cocks her eyebrow just like John did when he was annoyed. Must have gotten the hair and skin coloring from her mother.* The combination of coal-black tresses and emerald green eyes, highlighted by golden skin, hypnotized him.

"All right, you've lost your fucking mind, sailor boy. Why should—"

His mouth silenced hers. They finally came up for air. "Since L.A., all I think about is you. Holding you, touching you, fucking the daylights out of you until there are no orgasms left, until we melt like ice cream on hot bricks."

"And the SEAL waxes poetic."

The next kiss lasted longer. Tasted sweeter. Felt hotter.

"Can't help it," he murmured against her neck. "I haven't been able to think straight since you left my bed. I get an instant hard-on whenever you're around. Hell, I get a hard-on every time I just imagine us together. You cast some sort of spell on me, didn't you?"

She tried to pull out of his arms. "It didn't seem to be a problem at the airport when you were coming on to Miss NASCAR bouffant blonde with dock bumpers for boobs. Look, buddy, I'm going back to my room. I'm too tired to think about you right now."

He ran his thumb along the smooth underside of her jaw. She whimpered at the pleasure of his touch; his cock twitched at the soft sound. "Baby, don't think. Just do."

"MacBride, where do you think we're heading with this?" She pulled away from him. "The woman you met at the conference wasn't me. She doesn't exist. She was an aberration. Consider her a temporary figment of your imagination. I don't come on to men like that. I never drank so much at one time in my entire life, and sure as shit never will again. Sport sex and one-night stands aren't my thing. She's not who I am. I don't do casual spur-of-the-moment flings."

"I know."

"How could you know? How could you *possibly* know? We spent one night together, as incredible as it was. And me—no better than a female lounge lizard, a ho, only I didn't ask for money."

He pulled her closer again, unwilling to break contact. "I *know* because you are the most honest and reactive woman who's ever been in my bed. No game playing. You were warm and funny and incredibly high-energy sexy, and you played my body like a virtuosa. The feeling of having you under me, of being inside you, defies description. I couldn't get enough of you. I still can't."

"Fella, I hate to state the obvious, but you were thinking with your dick. Then *I* was thinking with your dick." Leaning her forehead against his chest, she wilted and sighed. "The problem is, it's a wonderful dick."

He ran his hands from her shoulders to her waist. "Look, Keko, I don't know what brought us together across an entire continent, but it must mean something. Kismet. Destiny."

"MacBride, I heard those words once already, from someone who seems like a normal adult. I doubt if it's meant to work its magic twice. What it means for us is that we were sex-starved lunatics in the right place at the right time, with the stars and planets in perfect alignment. When we were in each other's arms, the sky trembled, the earth moved. Now it's back to business as usual, playing with things that explode."

"Play with me," Mac chuckled, "and I'll certainly explode. Are you still a sex-starved lunatic?" Before Keko could respond, he shucked out of his T-shirt, jeans, and briefs. He lifted her so she could wrap her legs around his naked hips, her arms draped over his shoulders.

"You like this position, as I recall." His cock stood at attention as its head prodded her panty-clad pussy. "I know I do."

He lowered her feet to the floor, stripped off her undies and satiny baby-doll top. Reaching into his kit bag, he had a condom out and was sheathed before she could react. Settling on the edge of the bed, he lifted her again, brought her to his lap. "Are you ready for me, baby?"

With his hard member knocking at the door to paradise, Keko shifted to a better position with her knees braced on the mattress, then carefully mounted up. As she slid her snug sex down his shaft, he thought he would pass out from sheer ecstasy before she managed to engulf only half of him. "Sweetheart, you are *so* incredible."

Keko twisted her hips to seat him deeply inside her body. She twisted again, then nibbled at his nipples with her teeth and lips after she laved the hard nubs with the flat of her warm tongue.

"Oh *fuck*! Baby, stay still. Dear god in heaven, stay *very* still. If you move like that again while you're playing with my nipples, I'm gonna explode in about two-point-three nanoseconds like Fourth of July fireworks."

Not only did she move, but she rode him hard, like he was an eight-second bull that couldn't unseat her.

As he thrust up, she twisted down harder, wrapped her arms around his neck, pressed her small, firm breasts against his chest. She mashed her mouth against his; he felt her breath hitch the same instant her pussy went wild. His hands on her ass cheeks pulled her even more tightly against him.

She threw back her head and cried out his name.

"MacBride!"

CHAPTER SIX

Monday

KEKO POWER-WALKED FOR about two-hundred yards down the parkour trail, then eased off a bit.

What does he expect from me? Pronouncements of love and devotion? More kismet? More destiny? Keko was fairly sure the concepts that worked so splendidly within Sanctuary for Lorelei and her lovers didn't usually work as well in the real world. *I have a solid business. I'm into my job. With Dad gone, our people depend on me to keep their lives going smoothly and their bills paid. I have Kamaka, and we make a great team.* She was smart enough to know their liaison wasn't a permanent solution—Kamaka deserved his own life, not to spend his time babysitting her. Until then, the symbiotic relationship worked for both of them.

More a treadmill gal than a runner, Keko strolled along the two-mile path with an unintended walking buddy. Apparently, the cat had decided Keko needed company. A dog would run ahead, make giant circles, sniff out everything of importance until he was exhausted. The cat simply followed at Keko's heels, meowing pathetically, tail held high with its tip twitching.

"Look, critter, you can go back to the lodge if you're that miserable. Go chase mice or something. No one is forcing you on this march."

The cat responded with another dismal *meow*.

Keko had grabbed a couple of protein bars, headed out the back door before anyone else woke. When she'd padded through the great room, a woman's sweater and long skirt were hanging off the back of the sofa. She wanted to be out of the lodge before anyone else was up and moving—she wasn't sure she could pull off ignoring what would surely be Lorelei's satisfied look at breakfast, after hearing the sounds of pleasure throughout the night from her hosts and hostess.

She also didn't want to deal with her new friends' awareness of what had transpired between her and MacBride throughout the night and into the wee hours of the morning. Could she meet Lucian's and Adam's knowing glances at the kitchen table, after they most likely heard her howl like a she-wolf while she'd been impaled on MacBride's cock, writhing in unbelievable rapture?

She'd lost count of how many orgasms MacBride had teased from her, had drawn from her very soul, but she knew he used up four condoms. At least four. His dick was like the Energizer Bunny.

The couple had finally collapsed in each other's arms from sheer exhaustion. Wrapped in his embrace, she couldn't remember being lost in such a feeling of complete satisfaction, of well-being, of belonging, at any other time in her adult life. It was a new sensation; she wasn't sure how to handle it.

The guy totally rings my chimes. So, what's the problem?

Keko had awakened in a panic when she realized the sun had broken through the gray light—and she was still in MacBride's bed.

MacBride looked so comfortable she hadn't wanted to disturb him. Never having awakened in the morning with a man in her bed—or had ever been in a man's bed after the break of dawn—she was unfamiliar with the protocols. *How does one avoid any early morning drama?*

With the lightest touch, she smoothed back the wave of heavy, toffee hair from over his closed eyes. Reacting without thinking, she brushed his forehead with her lips. *He makes it so damned tempting to crawl back into bed with him.* A quick shake of her head didn't clear the cobwebs, so she grabbed her scattered garments, then slipped back to her room.

After a quick rinse, she pulled on running shorts and sports bra, grabbed a hoodie, tippy-toed downstairs. She took a long gulp of orange juice, pulled on her sneakers, stuck two protein bars in her bra, then snuck out the back door. The cat snaked between her feet, nearly tripping her at every other step.

She walked past Kamaka's rustic lair without incident. In stand-down mode, once he zonked out, he usually slept like the dead.

It had been a long time since Keko had enjoyed the outdoors for its own sake. A light breeze swirled under and through the tree canopy, the leaf colors having only recently begun to turn. The morning brought a refreshing chill to the air. The light wind carried so many scents—from fresh and clean to heavy and earthy, sometimes almost exotic. Neither her sneakers nor the cat's soft paws interrupted the sounds of nature all around them. Bird song, crow caws, squirrel chatter, all continued unabated. Keko felt comfortable in her skin, blending with the surroundings.

No wonder Lorelei doesn't want to return to D.C., and Adam and Lucian are so content here. Sanctuary, indeed. Such a perfect place to raise their children. The ideal playground for children also proved to be the ideal location for men to train for the cruel realities of combat in its infinite forms. The irony wasn't lost on her. She wondered, for the briefest moment, at the cosmic injustice of bringing even the smallest touch of mankind's violence to such a haven of peace and tranquility.

Such thoughts had niggled at her since her father's sudden, brutal death. Yes, he built explosive devices, for a myriad of reasons. Yet, how many people had he ultimately saved by deconstructing similar devices? How many lives had he spared? How many families around the world had been left whole, untouched by senseless tragedy on their own turf, because of her dad? He had the ability, then taught her the skills needed to disassemble bombs meant for nothing other than death and destruction, whose sole purpose was to commit more and more acts of terror.

Without any sense of false modesty, Keko knew she was proficient at her craft. Side by side with the big boys, she worked on, worked with, built, and dismantled explosive devices. She'd been called out to crime scenes. To scenes of terrorist bomb threats, both real and imagined. She could handle firearms and ordnance with the best, was proficient in the arts of self-defense.

If truth be told, her favorite assignments were building deconstructions. Bringing down a huge structure in the space of the building's own footprint, or laying down a structure exactly where it needed to go, never ceased to thrill and amaze her. And she'd proven brilliant at calculating the numbers and placements of the explosive charges. Even the veteran powder monkeys were impressed, and learned to trust her judgment.

Keko had never been on a battlefield, never ducked live ammo during a firefight on foreign soil, but she'd been well-trained, knew the drills. Knew how to take care of herself.

Fully aware that he could not dissuade his headstrong daughter from following in his footsteps, John Larsson did the best he could—he taught her how to stay alive.

Lorelei's words stayed with her. *Did Lorelei have it right? Am I an adrenaline junkie, too? Is that my problem? Do I need the constant challenge of fear and excitement to keep me centered? Do I need to be kickass jacked-up to feel alive? Is that why I can't survive a serious relationship? What mortal man could compete with a locker full of explosives? Regardless of the situation, I know my crew will never let me down: no man left behind. No woman, in my case. Abandonment is not an option. Most people can't say the same about romantic entanglements.*

In Keko's experience, many military lifers, law enforcement officers, firefighters, search and rescue personnel, professionals who lived on the edge, became addicted to the intensity of their professions. They needed that spark of danger, the threat of peril, to keep the juices flowing, to keep them feeling vital, necessary, alive. She was sure that extended obsession, at such high levels, accounted for the number of infidelities, divorces, broken homes. For such men—and women—partners and teams became, out of necessity, closer than family, closer than spouses.

Keko had begun to keep notes, just out of curiosity. Of the Larsson crews, the only married guys were newcomers. In the first twelve months, newbies either left the job as being too physically and emotionally demanding, or their wives left them for mates who led more normal lives. It wasn't a scientific analysis, but it gave her an idea of how the mop flopped in her little corner of the world.

Why can't MacBride leave the relationship as it is? Isn't incredible sex between us enough? She considered that. Did MacBride fill the physical gap for her, so she didn't lose total contact with her humanity?

Then again, mix former military and current law enforcement with two demolitions experts—that recipe could prove volatile. Keko saw trouble on the horizon, there was no doubt. *Where could this possibly lead?*

Well down the length of the parkour trail, she stopped, stretched, perched on a wooden railing to the side of the path. The cat sniffed the granola when it was offered, and plainly indicated such fare wasn't worth consuming. Keko ate the protein bars, then tucked the wrappers in the pocket of her jacket for later disposal.

"Cat, normally I would agree with you, but it's better than picking nuts and berries in the woods, or checking out carcasses for signs of freshness. Call me silly, but I prefer granola to mice." Keko gave the creature a look, shook her head. "Great, now I'm talking to a cat."

"You could talk to me, but the cat is probably more entertainin'."

The cat spit, yowled, then ran. Keko yipped, jumped off the railing, fell into a crouch as she spun toward the masculine voice. Her right hand flew to her hip, came up empty. *Oh, that's just great. I left the lodge without a sidearm. Damn it all to bleedin' hell.*

A tall, lean, muscled man stepped silently from behind a huge pine. An older man, his long, graying braids held back by a red bandana. His blue plaid shirt was as faded as his worn jeans. His scuffed boots had seen better days.

The sun had weathered his nut brown face, leaving crow's feet and deeply etched lines. Still, she thought he must have been a handsome man in his younger days—was still handsome in a rugged way—his American Indian features square and chiseled, with high cheekbones. His black eyes were clear and bright, alive.

Keko's hands flew to her chest, as if the gesture would calm her racing heart. "Who the hell are you?" she nearly shrieked. "FBI? Undercover? Sonofabitch! Wear a bell around your neck or something. Saints in a freakin' sidecar. You coulda sent me into freakin' cardiac arrest."

"Nah, not one of those guys. They're too noisy, like buffalo in the bush. You woulda heard 'em."

He took a moment to look her over. His glance was casual. Not threatening. At least, she didn't think he appeared threatening.

"Bobby Black Crow, Army scout, retired." He kept his distance, didn't move close enough to offer his hand.

"Yeah, well, Bobby Black Crow, retired Army scout, you scared the goddamned shit outta me." Her hand still over her heart, she hoped her pulse would eventually slow down in the next half century or so.

"Yep, that seems to happen. Especially with you women."

"*Us* women? Did you pull this stunt on Lorelei?"

He shook his head, hooked his thumbs behind his carved leather belt. "Hell no. She's crazy, that one, and she's armed. That female woulda shot me dead, then skinned my sorry carcass before it hit the ground."

"Then what are you doing out here? Are you a friend of Adam's or Lucian's?"

"We know each other."

The adrenaline still spiking, Keko took an aggressive spread-legged stance, fists parked on her waist. "Okay, look, Mr. Black

Crow. You scared the crap outta me and I'm in no mood to play twenty damned questions. Since you obviously decided knocking on the front door wouldn't work for you, exactly what the hell do you want?"

"Feisty little thing, aren't ya. Kinda like a blue jay with young'uns in the nest. Not so much what I want, more like what your friends need ta know. Tell your man there's been someone hangin' around Smitty's place, just outta sight of the FBI. He'll want to know. He can pass it on."

"My man? I don't have a man."

"The sheriff. MacBride. He's a good one, spoke up for me at my hearin'. So did those two Marines. Only got community service for poachin'. Of course, I was huntin', not poachin', but the law didn't see it that way."

"Why the hell did you say MacBride is *my* man?"

"Just be sure you tell him."

"But what made you think…?"

Then, just as quickly as he appeared, Bobby Black Crow vanished into the woods with the stealth of a fox. His words trailed behind.

"You're fresh outta his bed. I can smell him all over you."

Mac had been awake when Keko left his room. He played possum to see what she would do. Grabbing her and pulling her back under the bedclothes with him would have been his choice, but she seemed determined to sneak away. *If she was so hell-bent on leaving, why did she brush the hair away from my eyes?* Why were her warm, soft lips so tender when she kissed his forehead? *Damn, she's an exasperating woman.* A vibrant, headstrong, sexy, but still exasperating woman.

He'd been serious about someone only once in his life, serious to the point of marriage. But what he felt for Keko was different, stronger. He always joked that his brothers had better luck with the ladies—although he did admit that the MacBride boys made a striking quartet when they cruised their favorite hometown watering holes and eateries.

"I swear, you're the bane of my existence," his mother would say—repeatedly—when they'd all reached their teens. That led to the boys happily tormenting their mom by referring to themselves as Banes One, Two, Three, and Four. Mac was Three.

However, even though they made her crazy, their mama couldn't hide the love and pride in her voice. *Her boys.* Their father would just smile, shake his head, then return to his sacred workshop to build beautiful things for their mother.

Down in the kitchen, Mac stepped aside so Adam could whip up breakfast. Lucian brewed the coffee, set the table, then parked out of the way to suck down the caffeine he appeared to need.

Lucian gave Mac the hairy eyeball. "Boy howdy, chief, you're not lookin' so good. Definitely rode hard, put up wet."

"Yeah, well, Golden Boy, you should check the mirror before casting aspersions on others." Mac held out his mug for Lucian to fill.

Lucian poured. "*Ooh*, big words this morning. Did you hear that, hoss? I'm casting aspersions."

"It means you made a rude and insulting remark, Luce. Not fishing for trout." Adam turned back to the stove.

"Hell, I knew that." Lucian pulled out another chair, rested his feet. "I'm just sayin' it appears to have been a lively night all the way 'round. An observation, that's all."

Already in a mood, Mac's back stiffened; he sat up straighter. "Duquesne, if you have something to say…"

"If Duquesne has something to say, he'll keep his sweet, sexy, Southern boy mouth closed until the caffeine reaches his brain and the little gray cells kick in. Won't you, darling?"

Lorelei strolled into the kitchen, sidled up to Adam for a quick kiss, then settled on Lucian's lap. "Hayseed."

Lucian wrapped his arms around her, nuzzled her ear. "Heartless wench. There's no call to be takin' the sheriff's side. He's only a guest. I live here. I'm special. I have privileges."

"Mac is not a guest. He's a friend."

Lorelei kissed her blond Adonis full on the mouth. "Here's one of your privileges. Now, hush up, be a good boy, and brew up a nice cup of special lemon tea to perk up your exhausted woman."

Sliding off Lucian's lap, she settled on his chair as soon as he rose to put the water on to boil. Lucian refused to use the microwave to brew tea.

Since Lorelei had arrived rather abruptly at Sanctuary months earlier, Mac never ceased to be amazed at how these three people ebbed and flowed around each other, like water in a tidal pool. As individuals, they had great energy—yet they still merged well. More than amazed, he suddenly realized jealousy was rearing its ugly head. He wanted what his friends had. *Why can't I get through to one half-Hawaiian woman I want so bad that my soul aches?*

Lorelei rested her elbow on the table, her chin propped up in her hand. "So, are you going to ask her?"

All three men swung around.

Lucian found his voice first. "Is who going to ask whom to do what, exactly?"

She pointed at Mac. "Is he going to ask Keko to move in with him?"

Mac forgot what he was doing with his coffee mug halfway to his mouth.

Lorelei reached over, took his mug, set it safely on the table. "Are you going to continue to mope like a love-struck kid, or are you going just come out and ask the girl?"

From the look on Lorelei's face, Mac knew better than to deny it. He'd been caught out, fair and square. "Damn. Is it that obvious?"

"Been there, done that." Lucian pulled out another chair and settled, so he didn't disturb his mate. He'd been enamored of

Lorelei from the first moment he saw her—while she'd still been unconscious.

Mac rested his head in his hands. "Man, I don't know if I can take another beating."

Adam usually avoided such discussions, but must have felt the need to say something. "She isn't Caroline. That ship sailed."

Lorelei perked up. "Caroline? Who the hell is Caroline? What did I miss?"

"Let's not go into this, all right?" Mac retrieved his mug, took a long pull. He didn't notice whether the coffee was hot or not.

Lucian wasn't about to cooperate. "His fiancée."

At Mac's harsh glare, he amended the comment. "All right, his ex-fiancée."

"Wow, how did I miss that?"

"It was years ago. Many years ago. Before your time."

"And…" Lorelei's eyebrow cocked.

Mac gave a defeated sigh. "You're not going to let this rest, are you?"

"Not hardly. Out with it."

Lucian grinned. "Mac, old buddy, you might as well get the thing over with. Trust me. She doesn't give up until she roots around like a truffle hog and unearths all the gory details."

Adam grunted his assent.

Lorelei made herself comfy, wrapped her hands around her tea. "Lucian, baby, later we'll discuss exactly why your thought processes associated me with a truffle hog, but I'll let it go for now."

Lucian reached over, took her hand, kissed her fingertips. "Good truffle hogs are prized in Europe."

Lorelei retrieved her hand. "Uh-huh, I see. Prized in Europe. Mac, this hasn't gotten you off the hook. Spill."

"Nothing much to tell. Caroline, my fiancée, bailed on me before the wedding."

"How long before?"

Mac couldn't prevent the curse that escaped.

Lucian kicked in. "Bubba, you might as well spill it now, or she'll hound you until she squeezes every last little detail out of your hide. Trust me. We saw her in action at Mama's. She held her own in a houseful of Southern women. Our sweet baby took no prisoners, showed no mercy."

Adam nodded. "It got ugly."

"Damn." Mac took another swig of his coffee. "I was stationed at the Naval Amphibian Base in Coronado, had already extended my enlistment. Caroline and I had been seeing each other on and off for about a year, any time I reached the motherland between deployments. We seemed solid. She said she was okay with the SEAL thing. I finally asked her to marry me.

"I'm thinking a simple on-base ceremony with a Navy chaplain and a couple of witnesses. No, that wasn't good enough. Nothing would do for Caroline and her folks except a huge, white dress wedding. They could afford it, so I finally caved, went along for the ride."

He ran his fingers through his hair so it resembled a bird's nest. "I brought Caroline home to meet my family—my mother, father, three brothers. I thought it was odd that they didn't seem to warm up to her, especially our mom, but no one interfered. Whatever I decided to do was okay with them, as long as I was happy." He stopped, glanced at Lorelei for a reprieve. It didn't happen.

"I had no idea what it took to bring off a big-deal wedding. Our group stayed at a ritzy hotel for nearly a damned week to get through all the wedding nonsense. It was the day before the ceremony. The booze had been flowing freely, so Caroline had been fairly sozzled before and during dinner.

"After dinner, I thought she'd disappeared to take a nap before the evening's festivities. I wanted to ask her something. To this day, I can't remember what was so bloody damned important. There was a communicating door between our rooms. And, well…"

He stopped again. "I walked in on my fiancée. And my brother. Naked. Wrapped in each other's arms. Tongues down each other's throats."

The guys knew the story. Lorelei sat back, finally stunned into silence.

"There was the obligatory 'it's not what it looks like' bullshit from Braedon. Rather than pound anyone into pulp and end up in jail, I left the hotel. Walked along the beach until the sun came up. When I got back, Caroline and her parents were gone, along with her very expensive engagement ring and all the wedding gifts. So was my brother." He cleared his throat. "That night was the last time I spoke to either of them."

"Dear sweet Christ, Mac, I had no idea." That was probably as close as he'd get to receiving an apology from Lorelei for digging into his past.

"I left the SEALs when that tour was finished. I'd stayed close to my Navy recruiter. He came to me with a list of possible employment opportunities in the law enforcement sector. I hooked up with the gig up here. Took my tests, aced the job. End of story."

"And your brother?"

"Braedon? Don't know, don't care. I speak to my folks, and my other two brothers. It took them a while, but they finally learned not to bring him up in conversation. That's it, in a nutshell."

"Does Keek know?"

"No. Why should she?"

"Mac, I'm—"

Talk ceased abruptly when they heard the buoy bell on the back door clang twice, to indicate the door had opened, then closed. The cat strolled into the kitchen with the nonchalance only a feline can manage, tail straight up in the air, then made a beeline for Lorelei's lap.

Adam placed a platter of thick French toast coated with slivered almonds on the table, accompanied by a large ramekin of his homemade raspberry honey butter. He settled in a chair. "Clever cat. Opens and closes doors."

"Yeah, well, teach the clever cat to be a better watchdog, will ya?" Keko walked into the kitchen behind Callie, pulled out a chair, slumped into it.

Mac, touchy after his confession to Lorelei, didn't bother to hide the agitation in his voice.

"What's wrong? Where did you go? Why did you leave the lodge without telling someone?" *Someone like me, someone who thought you were still in your damned room. What was wrong with staying in my bed?* "Did you at least take a sidearm?"

"Okay, Columbo, just why would I need a bodyguard or a weapon when we're surrounded by security central? Or, perhaps you'd prefer to glue a GPS chip to my ass?"

Mac ignored her sarcasm—although the GPS chip idea seemed plausible—then turned terrier. "Keko, what happened?"

"Some dude named Bobby Black Crow scared the hell out of me, that's what happened."

Adam and Lucian rose the same instant as Mac.

Lorelei placed the cat on the floor, stood as well, held her hands up. "Hold on, boys. Let's find out what happened before you charge down the warpath with guns blazing."

Mac leaned toward Keko, hands flat on the table. His pulse revved up, his muscles twitched for action. "Did he threaten you?"

"No, of course not. Nothing like that. He told me to give you a message."

Lucian exhaled in relief, returned to his seat, threw in a question. "Which *you*, exactly?"

"MacBride. Although I suppose you all need to hear it. Mr. Black Crow said to tell Sheriff MacBride that he found signs that someone's been hanging around Smitty's place, just outta reach of the Fibbies. He said you should pass it on to whoever needs the intel." She looked like she had something else to say, but pursed her lips together before more words escaped.

"You should also know that the three of you boys are on Black Crow's short list of good guys, in case you ever wondered." Keko gulped a mouthful of coffee from Mac's mug, made a face. "Yuck, no milk."

She turned to Lorelei. "He also said that if he ever pissed you off, you'd field-dress him before his carcass went cold."

Lorelei sat down again, retrieved the cat, laughed until tears fell. "Is that what he said? Good to know."

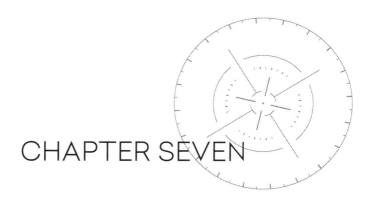

CHAPTER SEVEN

Monday, late morning

"I THOUGHT YOU were driving me to Smitty's. I don't recognize these roads." Keko considered her statement. "Not that I've been here long enough to recognize much."

Neither of them mentioned any discussion that might have been spoken over breakfast. The tense mood continued after MacBride volunteered to drive her to Smitty's.

She grabbed the *oh-shit* handle over the passenger's side door, although she'd already made sure her seat belt was securely fastened. MacBride maneuvered the big truck with care, but the ruts were unavoidable.

MacBride finally spoke, but he seemed distracted, like he had something else on his mind.

"I need to stop by my place first, grab fresh clothes. I didn't plan on staying at the lodge last night. Usually carry a duffle with a change of clothing, but forgot to repack my kit. It's not much of a detour. Didn't think you'd mind."

"Since I seem to be a captive audience, I suppose not." Keko realized she sounded snarky. "Thanks for the ride."

MacBride grunted.

Despite the bumps and ruts, the trip provided enough visual interest to prevent her from staring at him. The woodlands and meadows eventually gave way to small neat houses surrounded by small neat yards, enclosed in fences made of small neat white pickets or slender peeled-log posts.

They pulled into the driveway of a log-and-stone ranch house with a porch that wrapped around the front and left side. On the right, an enclosed breezeway connected the house to a three-car garage.

Logs. Stone. Big garage. Definitely a guy thing.

That the yard and the flowering borders were orderly, trimmed, and free of weeds came as somewhat of a surprise.

Not such a guy thing.

MacBride must have noticed the direction of her glances.

"Don't get all excited. I'm not Harry Homeowner. I pay a high school kid to take care of the property. He's a real go-getter. Has his own little landscaping business that he handles after school, plus weekends."

She felt heat rise to her cheeks over his mindreading skills.

"I figured it wouldn't do for the sheriff to live in a dump like trailer trash. Community spirit, hiring a local teen, and all that."

"I see. Well, it looks very nice."

He shifted the SUV into park. "Care for the short, guided tour? It will take only a few minutes to pull my stuff together."

She hesitated for a split second, but he caught it.

"I thought you might like to see how bachelors live"—he sounded testy— "who don't own a massive lodge on thirty-five hundred acres."

Surprised, she turned to him. "Thirty-five hundred? As in, three thousand, five hundred? Acres?"

"Yep. That's how much ground Sanctuary covers, at least at the moment. Adam plans to expand. There's a tract of five thousand acres butting up to their property, and probably more is available. I'm sure they'll buy it up."

"Yikes."

"Exactly." He walked around to the driver's door. "So, are you coming in?"

This isn't a good idea. I know this isn't a good idea. I may trust him, but I sure as shit don't trust myself.

"Okay. Sure. Of course."

He unlocked the front door, then led her into a surprisingly bright interior. With an open floor plan, the large living room sported autumn colors based on a deep cream background, mostly reds and browns with splashes of gold here and there. Gold-and-cream-striped drapes covered wide windows. Autumn harvest area rugs were scattered on the floors. The deep red leather sofa, love seat, and side chairs surprised her.

"Nice job. This place looks great." She meant it. The house radiated comfort and warmth.

"I can't take credit. One of Lucian's sisters, Julia the Designer, took pity on me. Begging and groveling on my part finally persuaded her."

Keko laughed. "I can't imagine you either begging or groveling, but apparently whatever you did worked."

"Updated kitchen and bath, three bedrooms. Nothing fancy, but it's home."

"Three bedrooms?"

"Yeah. Master bedroom, guest room, office."

"May I see?"

He looked surprised, but his features lit up. "Yes. Of course."

The office was masculine, with dark woods, chrome, and glass, cabinet-style file drawers, built-in bookshelves. It was surprisingly neat and organized.

The guest bedroom had more browns and greens than the living area, with a wide leaf-and-vine motif area rug anchoring the king-size bed. On all the walls, soothing watercolors of sunlit ponds and subdued meadow scenes balanced the heavy colors.

"Well done. Really. A calm room, peaceful."

The master bedroom could have fit two king-size beds with ease. To Keko's surprise, soft shades of plum, orchid, and fuchsia dominated the room. Area rugs in patterns of darker plum and black covered sections of the wide plank floor. The furniture was plain, Shaker style, in black.

"Oh, wow. This is awesome. Lucian's sister did—"

Keko turned toward MacBride to finish her comment, only to be pulled into his arms.

Oh crap, I knew better than to get out of the truck.

"MacBride, I don't think this is…"

"See, there you go again. Thinking. You think entirely too much." He leaned down to kiss her, captured her mouth with his own. Like smooth chocolate, she melted against him. "That's it, baby, let your body think for you."

He always called her *baby*—she'd never been *baby* to anyone before. From his lips, she decided she liked it, which made it tougher to stop anything he planned to do. "I have work waiting. So do you. Important work."

"And we both have good people on the job. They can do without us for a bit longer."

A soft groan escaped her throat as his hand slid down to the V between her thighs. *Damn it to hell, how does he do this to me?* Her legs spread wider without her brain kicking in; her hand pushed his fingers tighter against the clothing that covered her sex.

"*Omigod*, MacBride, whatever you do, don't stop." She pressed forward against his hand. *Please don't stop! I need you.*

He did stop, though, long enough to peel the clothes off her body, then lift her onto his high bed. He stripped quickly; his clothing landed in a pile next to hers. He joined her on the wide, deep mattress.

When their skin touched, she spread wider for him, but he lay beside her instead. She arched against him. "Come to me."

"*Shh.* Let me take care of you."

He aligned his body next to hers. His right hand began to play her like a precious viola, his fingers stroking, touching, caressing her torso until she lifted her hips to urge him to go further, faster.

"Easy, baby, let me take my time. No need to rush."

Her eyes closed, her neck arched back. She moaned.

He slid his hand between her thighs, into her warmth, her wetness. Rather than penetrate her, he trapped her labia between his fingertips and palm. Rolling her flesh, he gently tugged at the lips of her pussy, first together, then separately.

"MacBride," she panted, "you're driving me crazy. Do something!" She writhed, tried once again to entice him to mount her.

"Slow down, baby. All in good time."

He moved away, stretched far enough to reach the drawer of the nightstand. When he returned to her, his fingers were slick with lubricant. She groaned and spread for him, anticipating—but he held back. Using slow circular motions, his fingertips spread the lubricant from the top of her mons to the tight rosette of her ass. Without entering her, his fingers danced over her hypersensitive skin, sliding between the crevices of her labia and buttocks.

Disappointed, she grabbed his hand, tried to direct him back to her pussy.

"Not yet, baby. You're not ready."

"For fuck's sake," she nearly howled with frustration, "I am *so* ready!"

"Not yet."

When she whimpered, he finally plunged his fingers into her, alternating the number of digits as he slid in and out with maddening slowness.

She clutched his arm, tried to force him to fuck her faster.

"Is that what you want, baby? Harder and deeper? Tell me."

"Oh yeah, yes, please, *yess!*"

He covered her sex with his palm, massaged her in firm circles, then penetrated her with two stiff fingers as deeply as her body would allow.

Keko moaned and writhed, grabbed his hand, pumped her hips. "Oh god, yes, do that, bring it, bring it, *kee-rist in heaven I need to come!*"

He pumped into her, alternating with two and three fingers, gently twisting his hand as he pleasured her. His mouth sought and found her breasts, her nipples. He suckled her softly, then with more vigor.

"MacBride, damn it, I'm gonna come, I'm gonna…"

"Not yet, baby, we're not done yet." He pulled his fingers away, to her cry of frustration, then, without warning, turned her over onto her stomach.

"What are you…?"

He reached between her thighs from the back, worked his fingers into her pussy again. She immediately pumped her hips against the mattress, against his hand. *So close, so close…*

He moved away and returned with the bottle of lube, dripping the wonderful slippery stuff down the crevice of her buttocks, down to her pussy. Working his fingers deeply, he then pulled them out so he could massage her with his closed knuckles.

"Fuck, damn it, MacBride, I need you." She was nearly sobbing. "You're making me crazy! I need your cock now, baby, *now!*"

"Oh yeah, you'll have a cock." He pulled her hips up so she was on elbows and knees. "You'll have it, baby."

She felt him move around again, then he massaged more lube on her warm sex. He spread her labia with one hand; she felt a hard blunt object against the opening of her pussy. She didn't know what it was, just knew that it wasn't his cock. She became quite still as she tried to get a grip on what he was doing.

Before she could give voice, the crown of the dildo slid into her, followed by the shaft. He slowly pushed the entire length into her, then held it still until her flesh adapted. The different sensation coerced her, and she was *so* close to the edge. She began rocking her pelvis, carefully, signaling him to thrust the dildo in and out.

MacBride knelt behind her as if he would take her doggy style, but continued to fuck her with the firm, flesh-like toy. He reached under to fondle her breasts and nipples, which made her wriggle and writhe beneath him.

Her voice deepened from whimper to breathy. "I want you, MacBride. Give me your cock. You promised."

"I will, darlin', I will."

He shifted again, reached under her hip, pumped the dildo into her with his left fist. He pressed his thighs tightly against her. It took her a moment to realize that he'd gone from smearing the slippery lube along the crevice of her buttocks to pressing a fingertip against the rosette of her ass. He didn't offer discussion or wait for permission—already impaled with the dildo, her body slammed her brain into overload as his finger pushed fully through the tight ring of flesh.

"Oh my god, MacBride, you're making me nuts!"

"I'm giving you what you asked for, sweetness. I'm giving you my cock."

With that, he removed the dildo, replaced it with the tip of his condom-sheathed member. He guided the shaft with his hand until he lined up his cock head, then plunged into her until he hit bottom. Her earthy groans followed, which spurred him on. He reached around and under, tweaked her clit, rubbed and rolled the flesh.

She moaned. "Don't stop baby, I'm so there!"

"Not yet, darlin' girl, not quite yet."

She growled, arched her back like a cat, then pressed back against him. "Yes, *now!*"

He slowed the tempo of his thrusts, pulled nearly out, before pushing deeply once again.

She felt the coolness of the lube dripping between the cheeks of her ass. Without changing his rhythm, he worked a finger into the puckered flesh. That broke her concentration, but she didn't pull away. Heartened, he pressed deeper. She met the pressure and pushed back, caught up by the strange new feeling.

MacBride removed his finger; she felt a broader object press against the sensitive opening. He pulled his cock halfway out of her pussy, worked a blunt shaft into the virgin flesh of her ass—she realized it was the dildo, a slender, but fully man-sized, phallus. She tried to relax as her body responded. Her pussy was screaming for the attention of his own hot cock—he must have felt her. With a smooth move, he pierced her deeply with the dildo, then buried his own shaft into the depths of her pussy.

Keko screamed as her orgasm launched her to an alternate universe, one in which all sensations, all meaning, were centered in the maelstrom happening in the center of her physical and emotional being. Her muscles contracted like springs recoiled; her stretched flesh burned with the fullness of the dual penetration. *Heaven help us all, don't let this end!*

Mac leaned forward, then buried himself in her hot, oh-so-tight channel. He used the flat of his hand to press the dildo deep as his cock pressed deeper. Their cries echoed as she came again, drawing him into absolute nirvana with her. He remained deeply entrenched as she continued to writhe against his encompassing arms, her pussy throbbing and pulsing and clutching.

Finally, after the last throb and pulse and clutch was wrung from her body, breathing absorbed all Keko's remaining energy, as the air roared in and out of her lungs.

MacBride carefully pulled out, then gently withdrew the dildo from her tingling, burning flesh. He laid her down on the mattress, briefly left the room. He returned with a warm wet face cloth and a towel, then gently cleaned her nether regions, patted her dry.

Keko was too limp, too spent, to move a muscle as MacBride spread a blanket over her body. She thought he'd left the room, but that impression was more a feeling of something essential missing than a certainty.

In a doze, she heard a gurgling sound from another room. She had no energy to speak of, and felt too comfortable to turn an ear in that direction to identify the noise. Sure that MacBride would handle whatever it was, she sighed, then burrowed down.

He returned shortly with a cup of something that smelled suspiciously like hazelnut cream coffee. She groaned in complaint as he piled pillows behind her so she could sit up, then covered her again with the blanket. Somewhere between making love and making coffee, he'd pulled on a pair of drawstring sleep pants.

As if it had appeared by some sort of magic, she stared at the mug of steaming coffee, a fat dollop of whipped cream floating on the surface. She called up enough energy to lift an eyebrow at him.

MacBride held the mug under Keko's nose, let her breathe in the scent. "I cheated. Keurig coffee machine. K-cups. *Voila*, fresh coffee every time. Don't you dare tell the guys I drink flavored coffee. I'd never hear the end of it."

She managed a half-assed grin. "The stuff of which blackmail is made."

Mug in hand, she took a sip. The sigh of contentment was unintentional, but he looked relieved at her reaction.

He sat next to her, his weight barely making a dent in the mattress.

"Are you all right?" He lifted her long hair, placed the black waterfall behind her shoulders, smoothed it with the back of his hand.

Her eyed closed in response to the extremely sensual manner of his touch.

"I'm not quite sure at the moment. I think so." She avoided meeting his gaze, not knowing how else to respond. *Wow, I am so definitely a ho! And a kinky ho at that! Who knew? My hoo-hah knew. How can this man read me so well that he knows what I want, what I need, even before I do? Ooh, baby, this is totally new ground for me, but I like it!*

He stroked her arm. "Y'know, you don't need to leave."

She raised herself up, slithered along the bed, sat at the edge of the mattress next to him. "I have a job to do. So do you."

"I know. I wasn't proposing we shirk our duties. But you could come home, here, to me, instead of haring off to Sanctuary every night."

Her spine stiffened, immediately. "What, and be waiting in the foyer with your pipe and slippers, with a hot meal on the table? Maybe quit working, be a stay-at-home girlfriend? A Happy Homemaker wannabe?"

Mac reared back a bit. "Hey, whoa, I wasn't suggesting anything of the sort."

Intellectually, she knew he hadn't suggested it, but her reaction was still immediate. And uncharitable.

"That's good to know. Other than not fixing a hot meal—lack of opposable thumbs—a Labrador retriever would work just as well for you."

"Keko, I didn't ask you to become a *hausfrau*. Didn't even imply it."

"Sorry. Sometimes words just fly out of my mouth, instead of keeping them to myself. It's a really bad habit." *But I need to set down ground rules, fella, before you think you can domesticate me.*

He moved to stand in front of her, gently took her face in his hands. "Baby, there's no reason you can't say what's on your mind. No need to censure your words around me."

"Yeah, well, you may come to regret that statement."

"I doubt it." He rubbed his thumb along the underline of her jaw, which provoked more throbs from her achy sex.

"I was serious about you bunking here. In the guest room, if that would make you more comfortable. Give us some alone time, get to know one another."

Keko slipped off the high mattress, found her clothes, dressed. "It would be rude to just bail out of Sanctuary. Lorelei seems to like my company, imagine that. And then there's Kamaka."

"Baby, I'm sure Lorelei and Kamaka can manage fine on their own." He picked up his clothes, began to dress. "At least think about it, okay?"

Ahh, a way out. "Of course. I just need time to consider my options." *But do I really want a way out?* She slipped into her shoes. "We'd better get to Smitty's before someone sends out the Mounties."

MacBride sent a quirky grin her way, . "A bit too far south for Mounties, but I suppose you're right."

He pulled her into his arms, kissed the top of her head. "Promise me you'll think about staying?"

She laid her cheek against his warm skin. He hadn't buttoned his uniform shirt; his tawny chest hair tickled her face. *Mmm, sweet wintergreen.* "I said I would."

"Promise?"

At his persistence, she pushed back. "Look, I already told you that I would. Besides, no one knows how long the Fibbies are going to be here. Chandler said he and his crew will probably be ordered to pack it in, wrap it up, head on out, by tomorrow. Makes sense. They already took samples of everything they needed. Kamaka and I haven't really added anything of substance to their knowledge base. Yet."

"You could stay longer."

"Look, you have a high-profile position in town. I have a business in Boston to run. Larsson Demo has projects on hold until I land back home. Don't forget, Kamaka and I have been away from the shop for going on two weeks. I left Eight-fingered Jack in charge—who knows what I'll find when we get there."

"You're the boss, you can delegate. Can't Kamaka—"

She backed away, her hands pressed against his chest. "MacBride, enough! I have work to do. Either take me to Smitty's, or I'll call Chandler for a ride."

As he locked up behind them, Keko shook her head. *Why the hell does he insist on wrecking a good thing?*

⌖

Mac was frustrated. *She can't hide all the damn time.*

Since arriving at Smitty's place, Keko had avoided him. She'd holed up in the living room of the cabin with Special Agent Chandler, scrolled through screens on his laptop showing the current results from the lab in Quantico.

The FBI team appeared ready to bail. That left Kamaka for company in the workshop, until the Fibbies packed up the last of the evidence, which included all the bomb components and specialized equipment that Smitty had neatly organized in a bank of secure cabinets.

93

Mac parked on a folding chair. "Kamaka, any more thoughts on the discoloration of the C-4? I've never seen it before, but these days I'm not always up on the latest. That's why I attended the conference, to tune up. We don't even have locals who dynamite fish ponds, if you can believe that."

Kamaka was checking samples under a surprisingly good-quality microscope he found stashed beneath a dust hood in a cabinet. "*Nah*, dude. I'm still working on the wire coverings. All the wires are the same gauge, have the same thickness of plastic coating—except the white wires. The covering on the white wires looks like it came through an imperfect extrusion process, resulting in either too much or too little plastic along the length of the wire. In some places, it's actually bare, which could result in a short along one of the circuits."

"Someone never heard of quality control, that's for sure. I wouldn't wire up a reading lamp with this stuff. Chandler said Miss Keko had been exhausted, said she couldn't remember what bothered her about the wires. I'm betting this is it."

Yeah, and I'm betting that our little sexual interlude over the workbench before she took off for the lodge probably didn't help the functioning of her brain, either.

"There's an odd smell to the C-4 that I can't identify, nor can Miss Keko. Neither the color nor the odor are traditional detection or identification taggants. I'm hoping our friends in Quantico come up with a trace on its origin. Those dudes have *über* cool lab toys."

Mac straightened up. "Not for nothing, but I gotta ask. What's with the *Miss* Keko and *Miss* Lorelei? I can't believe those two tolerate the girlie-girl titles without flaying the skin off your bones for being either a chauvinistic prig, or an ass-kisser of the first magnitude."

Kamaka chuckled. "It's meant as a sign of polite respect, as I was taught by my mother and grandmothers. Too much trouble to translate honorifics from Hawaiian each time."

He stood, straightened out his back. "Plus, it's fun to annoy people who might be hangin' around. They aren't sure if one is being deferential or being a totally sarcastic sonofabitch."

Mac grinned. "You devious bastard."

"Exactly. That's why Miss Keko loves me."

Without fanfare, Keko stuck her head around the corner of the workshop door and surprised both men. She shot a look at MacBride, her expression tight, obviously not in the mood for any bullshit. "We need to talk. When and where?"

MacBride jumped into the deep end without hesitation. "I'm on third shift tonight, midnight to eight. My place, tomorrow, noon, lunch?"

"Fine." She turned to Kamaka. "I'm leaving here in a few minutes. Need a ride?"

"Yes, ma'am, boss lady. Just give me about five minutes to finish this."

"Fine. Meet you in front." Without another word to Mac, not even a glance, she left.

Kamaka didn't take his eyes off what he was doing at the microscope.

"Sheriff Mac, I really don't like to climb into anyone else's business, and avoid it when at all possible. However, I think you should be aware that I've known Miss Keko up close and personal for a few years now, and I've never—repeat, *never*—observed her in her current stage of flip-out."

"Her current stage of flip-out? Is there a translation that goes along with that?"

"Chief, she's been a totally flipped-out chick since you hooked up in L.A. Never saw anything like it. She usually won't give guys the time of day. She doesn't date—or, at least, hasn't in years. She gets like totally in their faces when we're on a job and she thinks they're not taking her seriously. Like she did with you in the hotel lounge about the Navy's polymer stuff. But after you, all bets were off, man. Her mind was blown. She totally left the reservation, dude."

Mac felt the heat rise at the back of his neck. "Okay, so you know about that."

Kamaka finally turned to him. "Know about it? Damn, I dressed her and did her makeup, she was such a nervous wreck. I gave thanks to all the Island gods that you didn't meet each other until the last day of the conference. Otherwise, the paramedics would have needed to administer intravenous fluids by day two."

The flush moved from the back of Mac's neck to his face, which hadn't happened since he'd been about six and his aunt pinched his cheeks for the first time. "I see."

"Dude, get with it. Keko and I, well, we're best friends. Like best girlfriends. BFFs. We share everything."

"Good to know. I'll keep that in mind."

Kamaka lifted an eyebrow. "Don't get stuck on stupid. She's had a rough time since her dad died, so you might consider cutting her some slack."

"So, as her best, *uh*, girlfriend, what would you suggest? I'm doing my damnedest to get through to her, but it's like pounding my fists against a stone wall."

"Miss Keko has issues, man, long-term issues. She usually doesn't see guys socially—when she does, it's over before it begins. She's her own worst enemy. Don't push her, or she'll leap to the defensive like a boxing kangaroo.

"I'm trying to convince her to take a few extra days at the lodge after the Fibbies leave, told her that she needs some time for herself. After John died, she took only one day off—for his funeral. And Miss Lorelei is really no-shit enjoying the boss lady's company, so she's also laying on the guilt to see if Keek can be convinced."

Kamaka kicked back his chair, rose, stretched like a big old fat cat, headed out the door. "Good luck tomorrow, Chief. You're gonna need it."

Thanks, fella.

CHAPTER EIGHT

Tuesday morning

JUST OUTSIDE OF town, Keko braked to avoid a line of wild turkeys crossing the road. She yelled out the window at the birds. "This is nuts. Why am I letting him make me crazy? I'm an adult. I function just fine. I don't need a freakin' keeper. Just because he's fantastic in bed doesn't mean he gets to call the shots."

The turkeys didn't care, flipped her the feather, didn't hurry.

She reached MacBride's place. His personal vehicle, a beefy black-and-orange Hauk Jeep Rock Raider, took up the space in front of the left garage bay door. She parked the SUV behind the Jeep, ensuring no one could block her in. Since her dad died, not being trapped had developed into an obsession of hers.

In worn jeans, T-shirt, and stocking feet, MacBride came down off the porch to meet her. By the time they'd reached his front door, lunch had been forgotten. Once they reached the privacy of his living room, their clothing flew in all directions.

Keko wrapped her legs around MacBride's hips as he lifted her up. Her nails scratched his shoulders through the shirt fabric as their kisses grew hotter, more desperate.

He set her on top of the wide sofa back so she could unwrap her legs. Leaning forward to mouth her nipples, he let his fingers found their way into her pussy.

"God, you're so hot and wet for me," he murmured.

She threaded her fingers through his hair, pulled his mouth to hers. In between panting kisses, she warned him. "*Omigod,* baby, I'm so hot I'm gonna come right now. Your fingers, saints in heaven…"

"Are you that close, darlin'?"

"Oh yeah, you'd better believe it!" She writhed against his hand.

He stopped. She nearly screeched in frustration.

"Hold on, baby, if you're that hot…" He straightened up.

"No, don't stop, no-no-no-no!"

"Wait here, sweetheart."

"Oh yeah," she growled, in between panting, " like I'm going to sprint stark naked out the front door."

He returned in a moment, set something on the end table. He stood her on the floor, turned her to face the sofa. Placing her hands on the sofa back, he spread her legs. When she was stable, he caressed her skin, beginning with her shoulders.

As his hands moved down her body, he kissed her ears, the side of her throat. Her hair was up in a high ponytail, which gave him plenty of opportunity to kiss her neck—the go-to spot on her body—and his lips caressed the upper edges of her tattoo.

As his hands reached her hips, she opened her legs wider, thrust out her behind. Abandoning his position, he slid his hand between her legs. She reveled at how easily he brought out the warmth and wetness of her sex. He made a fist, rubbed just his knuckles firmly but gently against and between her labia— she liked it, from the very first time he'd introduced her to the sensation.

"I need you, MacBride, give me your cock." Her voice was hoarse with need.

Following her entreaty, she heard foil rip; he must have slipped on a condom. He guided his cock head to the opening of her pussy, slowly entered her—but she didn't want easy.

"Don't tease, dammit!"

"Whatever you say, sweetheart." He shoved, burying himself to the balls in her flesh.

"*Ooh*, yeah baby, just like that." She dropped her torso, rested her elbows on the sofa back, gave him a better target. "Do me hard."

Bending his knees, he nearly lifted her off the floor as he forced his shaft higher, deeper. Her hips were caught in his iron grasp as he worked his cock in and out.

He must have known she was ready to come, but he suddenly stopped thrusting.

"What the hell?"

"*Shh*, trust me."

MacBride remained buried, but seemed to lean to the side. He straightened; she felt lubricant trickle between her ass cheeks, then drip down to coat the lips of her pussy. She wriggled, her entire body jerking when he introduced a long, strong finger into her ass. She settled as he worked his finger in tandem with his pussy-gloved cock.

"Mmm, wow, that feels good," she purred, rocking back against him. "Oh, yeah, baby."

Her murmur of disappointment accompanied the removal of his finger. Before she could utter another sound, he spread the tight skin around her anus, pressed a cold, hard object into her flesh. She didn't think it was the dildo, but also didn't have time to inquire. With a firm push, he shoved what could only be a slippery butt plug into her.

Keko came back up on her hands, elbows locked. "Whoa, baby, what's up…?"

"Just relax, give it a moment." MacBride's voice was soft, low. "Just a moment, then I'll stop if you want me to."

She threw her head back. "Now you freakin' want me to relax?"

"Trust me, baby, I'll take care of you."

He slid out his cock to give the toy more room. Then he maneuvered the plug a bit, to give her muscles time to stretch. When it was time to enter her pussy again, she'd already begun moving to the rhythm MacBride set for the plug. The slow movement of his cock, as he pushed it deeper, made her crazy with need.

"MacBride, I'm *no* shit *not* kidding here. If I don't come, I'm going to go berserk, which means your sorry-assed life may be forfeit."

"Baby, not to worry, you're going to come."

With no more warning than that, he removed the butt plug, pulled out his shaft, then lined up his cock head with her lubed ass. Holding his shaft firmly, he penetrated her rosette slowly and steadily, until he was buried to the hilt.

From the first pressure of his cock's crown seeking entrance, Keko stayed quite still, apprehensive but not fearful. From all their sex play, she knew he wouldn't do anything she didn't want; he wouldn't hurt her.

Although she'd never engaged in such play with anyone before MacBride, everything he'd done to her and with her, had only added to her pleasure. Pleasure she'd never known with any partner in her past.

Pinned against the sofa back, she did her best to relax against the burn, to accept the size of his sex.

"Baby, do you want me to stop?" His hands caressed her hips, her buttocks. "Do you want me to pull out?"

She took a deep breath. "No, don't leave me."

He reached around, massaged her clit with his fingertips. Her pussy tightened immediately, causing the same reaction in the sheath around his cock.

Her head dropped; she tilted her hips to entice him to move.

Move he did. Slow and sure, he skewered her, hard and deep, while he fingered her clitoris. She spread even wider, pressed against his fingers.

"Keko, baby, I can't hold out much longer. You're so hot, so tight, my cock is so hard that I think the skin is going to split in two." He tweaked her clit, rolled her labia in his fingers, fucked her deeper.

"Don't talk! Hurry! Use your fingers. I'm right there."

As she demanded, he shoved two fingers into the opening of her pussy, slammed into her ass again.

The world exploded around her as every muscle in her body imitated the force of her orgasm. MacBride peaked a fraction of a second later; she felt every throb of his hot sex. *And damn, he does feel hot!*

As the pulsations eased off, MacBride still had her pinned to the sofa back. Finally, she felt his cock soften. After he pulled out, she felt very exposed as she continued to hang over the back of the sofa. She concentrated on catching her breath.

He walked away, then returned with a warm wash cloth and a towel to wipe her down. "Baby, are you all right?"

Her forehead was resting on her folded arms. "I'm not sure. My legs feel like rubber bands. I don't think they'll work so well."

"Not a problem." He lifted her, carried her into the master bedroom. He must have turned down the bedclothes after he washed up, because she found herself sandwiched between crisp, clean sheets. After he got her settled, he left again for a few moments. When he returned, he sat next to her, a mug in his hands.

"Hot chocolate, my own blend. I add vanilla and cinnamon. Careful, it's steaming."

"Too hot yet, I'll burn my mouth."

After a time, she blew across the foam; a cautious sip left her with a whipped cream mustache. Using her own finger, he wiped the mustache away with the tip, then slowly sucked the cream from her digit. Despite the incredible depth of the orgasm she'd just experienced, his finger-sucking mouth provoked a near ab-crunching reaction in her womb. She couldn't hold back the moan.

He licked along the length of her finger. "Mmm, you taste delicious."

He set the mug on the table next to the bed, pulled the blankets over her shoulder. "Can I get you anything?"

She was so sated, so completely relaxed, that even forming words took too much effort.

"Close my eyes, just for a moment..." Her voice faded.

Keko lay in his arms, in his bed, breathing smoothly, as out as the proverbial dead light bulb. Mac felt supremely comfortable. He considered that. No, the feeling was more than just comfortable—he felt complete. No other woman had ever been at his house who wasn't either a decorator or a housekeeper. Or, he grinned to himself, his mother. *Would this light Mom's fire?*

As Keko referred to it, his lair was his safe zone. He considered that, as well. In truth, both Sanctuary and his own home were his safety zones. He'd no sooner bring a date to Sanctuary than to his own place. Yet, here he was, with a woman in his bed, tangled in his arms. A wild woman who did her best to make him crazy, even if she didn't realize what she was doing.

It seemed that Keko had begun to trust him. In an unguarded moment, tucked against his body, she spoke of her father, about how much she admired him. How much she loved him. Mostly, how much she missed him. She'd even admitted she'd gotten the phoenix tattoo in his memory. The only other living person who knew the tale of the phoenix was Kamaka; she said Kamaka would never divulge her secret.

"What about your mom? You never talk about her."

He felt her body immediately tense up. "There's nothing to talk about. She's an artist, lives in Honolulu, sometimes Maui. End of discussion."

"Brothers? Sisters?"

"No. Just me. I guess I proved enough of a shock to her sensibilities that she didn't want to try it again."

He held her a bit closer, smoothed her hair with gentle fingers, kissed her face.

"No problem. I have two parents, three brothers. Well, two brothers to whom I speak. You can borrow as many as you wish."

She chuckled, and he felt her body relax again. "Kamaka always offers to share his family, too." She rubbed her cheeks against his chest hair. "Thanks, but I think you'll do. At least, for the moment."

He kissed her again. "Just for the moment? Cruel woman."

She snuggled closer to him. After a few moments, he felt her body grow heavy against him as she drifted back to sleep.

Keko's measured, even breathing soothed him. He gently nuzzled her honeysuckle-scented hair, careful not to wake her.

Mac had no idea how long they'd been napping when he was suddenly roused by a whirlwind trying to escape a tangle of bedclothes.

"Whoa, slow down baby, what's the rush?"

Keko looked panicky. "What's the rush? What's the rush? The rush is that I came here to have lunch and talk, and now it's damned near time for dinner. You bushwhacked me with loads of sex, not much talking."

He made a grab for a flailing limb, but she snaked out of his grasp before his fingers could close on his target.

He ignored the bushwhacking comment. "And loads of sex is a bad thing?"

Keko crawled on the floor to collect her clothes. She stood quickly, began to dress.

"Buddy, we have work to do, and we have people depending on us to do our jobs. You're the sheriff, for chrissakes—don't you have, like, sheriffing stuff to do? Y'know, official stuff?" She sat down to pull on her sneakers.

Mac leaned up on his elbow, the blankets barely covering his man parts. "My deputies have everything under control. Besides, I *am* doing sheriffing stuff. Don't you consider FBI business to be under the purview of the sheriff's department?

"I'm fairly sure that federal jurisdiction trumps local law enforcement, so I'm totally making myself available to the Fibbies while I'm guarding one of their freelance operatives. Doesn't that count?"

He sat up, hung his legs over the edge of the bed. He quickly ducked as one of his boots sailed across the room.

"Okay, okay, I'm moving, I'm moving. Don't you want to grab a shower first?"

"No time. I'll shower at the lodge." Keko redid her ponytail.

"Aren't you going back to Smitty's?"

"No. No time now. I promised I'd be back at Sanctuary before everyone left. Kamaka will have whatever data they collected sent to Lucian's comm center from Chandler's laptop."

"Everyone is leaving? That's unusual. Normally they let me know, so I can keep an eye on the place."

"Lorelei said she and the boys were going out for the evening, so Lucian planned an early supper."

He tucked his shirt into his uniform pants, fastened the web belt. "And Kamaka? Does he have a date, too?"

"Staying in, as far as I know. Comm center, then cabin."

"Fine. I'll check in at the office, then I'll see you at Sanctuary."

He pretended not to see the panicked look on her face.

⌖

At Sanctuary, Keko stared at her plate as everyone else hurried through a quick dinner, not much more than a snack. Lorelei, Lucian, and Adam headed out.

"Keek, we probably won't be home until tomorrow, so don't wait up," Lorelei said. Lucian helped her on with her coat.

Adam, Lucian, and Mac exchanged covert glances, giving Keko the feeling she'd missed a key detail regarding her hosts' planned activities. The guys were their usual handsome selves, but Special Agent Randall looked amazingly like a super-sexy Charlize Theron on her way to a red-carpet night out.

"Okie dokie. Marines are out for the night. SEAL is on the premises. This happy fella is off to my cabin." Kamaka headed out the back door with DVDs of *My Fair Lady*, the Audrey Hepburn version, *Priscilla, Queen of the Desert*, and *To Wong Foo, Thanks for Everything, Julie Newmar*.

Keko knew the bottle of white Zinfandel tucked under his arm would guarantee he slept like a *keiki* to the sound of "I Could Have Danced All Night." With MacBride in residence, Kamaka didn't need to worry about manning the gates.

Once the sun set and peaceful darkness prevailed, Keko and MacBride unabashedly shagged their way through the lodge from the great room to her bedroom, then to his bedroom.

No matter how many times she swore to herself that they'd go slow and easy, the plan never seemed to work that way. She was too hungry for him, too hungry for the fire he lit in her gut, in her entire nervous system. Left too hungry every time they'd been apart, no matter how short that time might be.

Now, as the first crash and burn banked down, as their overheated bodies cooled from hot to comfortably warm, she moved her hand over his chest with the light-fingered poise of a Ouija player guiding the planchette.

She was addicted to the feel of his skin against hers. His body hair wasn't as thick as his short, heavy mane indicated it might be, and she enjoyed the feel of the hair through her fingers, like playing with velour. Once, she dated a guy who told her quite proudly—during dinner—that he'd waxed his entire body. He emphasized *entire*. The news unsettled her in the extreme; that date was their first and last.

Caressing, fondling, and stroking MacBride occupied Keko for extended periods of time. His shaft kept nearly its full length when flaccid; her fingertips danced along his member, as the veins became engorged once again with his fast-heating blood. The skin covering his iron-hard rod felt so silky, so smooth. He stretched out on his back, then spread apart his heavy thighs, giving her all the room she wished to play.

She slid her cheek along his hard breast until her mouth reached his nipple. She flicked it with her tongue, excited to feel his balls tighten in her hand. Encouraged by the reaction of his testicles, she moved her hand up his shaft, first twirling her fingers in his heavier pubic curls.

With a groan, MacBride wrapped his arm more firmly around her shoulder, folded his other arm under his head.

She fingered his already inflexible pole, jacked him slowly, smoothly. As firm as he was, he became firmer yet. Her leg covered his, her sex pressed against his muscled thigh.

"Keek—"

"*Shh.*"

Her tongue laved his nipple again in broad strokes.

He groaned. "Baby, come to me."

"Not yet."

The groan repeated, louder, when she slid her hand up to the crown of his cock. Her fingertip rolled the pearl of pre-cum around the head, making it shiny and slippery.

With her cheek still pressed against his chest, she felt his heart rate kick up, felt his breathing quicken. She slid her hand to his testicles, fondled them, then began to drag her hand up and down the softer inner flesh of his legs.

Shifting her weight, she rose to her knees, straddled his thigh. Rubbing her sex against him, she stretched, locked her arms behind her neck, under her heavy hair. Her hard, tight nipples pushed forward, enticed him to cup her firm breasts in his hot hands.

"That's it, baby, hold me." She rubbed against his thigh once more, then pulled away from his hold on her breasts to kneel between his legs. Grasping his shaft in both hands, she bent forward, lowered her mouth to his cock head. Rimming the corona first, she took him in her mouth.

Suckling him, she met his gaze, then stopped what she was doing. "What would you like?"

"*Ooh*, baby, as good as that feels, ride me. I need to feel your tight pussy around my cock."

"Mmm, good choice."

Moving over him, she shifted so one knee was next to his hip, then raised her other leg so her foot was flat on the mattress, her pussy exposed. "Play with me, first."

She couldn't hold back her murmur of pleasure when his fingers caressed her labia, then sank into her moist opening. He pressed deeply as she pushed against him.

"Keek, baby, you're so ready. Cover me before I lose my mind."

"Your wish, MacBride." *My MacBride. My warrior.*

"Wait, baby. Condom."

He tried to move, but she pressed her hands against his chest.

"No need. Got it covered." If what Lorelei said was true, which came directly from Lucian, MacBride was always careful, always safe. Keko trusted them, but did wonder why Lucian knew so much about MacBride's sex habits.

She lifted, positioned her sex over his, settled above him.

"I want to feel every bit of you." Wired up, pressed against his heated flesh, she could barely get the words out.

"Baby, if you're sure you want me bareback—"

Responding to her nod, he carefully guided his long, thick shaft into her as she lowered herself.

"Jesus sweet freakin' Christ, sweetheart, you feel even more incredible around my naked cock."

As he slowly filled her, spreading her nearly to the tearing point, she could not put words to the feeling. The perfect feeling of flesh to bare flesh.

Trying not to hurry, she twisted her pussy downward, accepting his size. Her eyes closed, her head thrown back, she was in heaven.

Then, he moved.

In an instant, she was under him, his heavy arms braced on either side of her, his hips pinning hers to the bed.

"What the...?"

"Baby, ever since the very first time, I've wanted you without a condom. I need to empty my cum in you, so far into you that you're blinded by the pleasure. I need to feel every pulse as you take me, as you come on my cock."

With a quick thrust of his hips, he buried himself so deeply that she thought he'd finally cleaved her in two. She cried out, then wrapped her legs around his hips.

"MacBride, *yes-yes-yes*, I'm gonna come, gonna come now, right now, right now, right fucking *now*…"

With that warning, her glove-tight pussy grabbed him. Two, three, four hard thrusts later, he pursued her into paradise. She felt every twitch, every throb, as he filled her with his seed.

How can I live without this?

CHAPTER NINE

Wednesday morning

AFTER A QUICK breakfast followed by a peck on Keko's cheek, MacBride quit Sanctuary. He told her he needed to put in an appearance at the police station to set up work schedules for the week.

Lucian had phoned to say he, Lorelei, and Adam would probably return to Sanctuary around lunchtime.

That left Keko with Chandler and Kamaka at Smitty's place, in what they'd come to call the boom room. She and Kamaka gave a last look at every bomb component, then Kamaka foam-wrapped each piece before he handed it to an FBI agent for boxing and transport. Chandler's crew had already packed up the lab equipment.

Deputy Collins had discovered legal documents in Smitty's study before the Fibbies arrived, which gave authorities the name of Smith family members to contact in case anything happened to him. The FBI needed to completely vet the place, remove all evidence of Smitty's extracurricular activities, before they could release the premises to the heirs.

Keko needed time alone. Time to think. Time to think about the bomb. Time to think about MacBride. Time to think about her career, about her life. Whenever she was around the sheriff, the magnetism between them—even just the *thought* of volcanic sex in his arms—prevented her brain from processing anything clearly. *I wonder what the clinical definition of nymphomania is? Can it be directed at just one person?*

"If you boys are finished with me," she said, "I think I'll head back to Sanctuary via the scenic route."

Chandler laughed, then offered his hand. "Haven't you learned yet? Every road in Maine is a blasted scenic route. It's been great working with both of you. Too bad the circumstances weren't better."

Keko clasped his hand in return. "Maybe the next demolitions seminar, instead of a terrorist bomb plot."

"That sounds like a much better plan. Where are you off to now? Heading back to Boston? If you are, you can hitch a ride with us; that's where we're headed. We should be able to fit your gear into one of the vans."

"Thanks for the offer. That's very generous. We're not leaving quite yet, though—unless Kamaka wants to head back. Lorelei invited me, well, us, to dinner at a restaurant on the other side of town. The Woodlands. Do you know it?"

"A bit above my pay grade, but I've heard it's the place to go. The Hungry Bear Café is more the speed for us lowly government serfs."

Keko omitted the part about the dinner being a mini celebration of the FBI leaving town. She glanced at her watch. "It should be a fun night out. I need get to Sanctuary, shower and change."

She turned to Kamaka. "Makaha, if you're sure you don't want to go with us, I'll track down a cheddar bacon burger for you before I head back to the lodge. I'll leave it in the microwave."

"Kamaka," said Kamaka, correcting her automatically, tossing a bubble-wrapped piece from hand to hand. "Thanks, but not tonight. I feel like I almost have a grip on the problem here. Not ready to quit yet, until Chandler drags the last of the toys out of my hands. "

She picked up her shoulder bag. "Yeah, whatever, dude. Catch ya later."

He straightened up, gave her a wink. "Of course, unless you *really* want some company, Boss Lady? Maybe *really* want to talk things over? Just maybe?"

She knew exactly what sort of things he meant, but she couldn't face him before thinking over the situation on her own first.

"No, Boss Lady actually doesn't, but thanks for asking. If you're not coming to dinner with us, then one of the FBI guys can take you back." She glanced at Chandler for confirmation; he nodded. "Will, have a safe trip, wherever you're going."

She turned back to her partner. "Later, dude."

Kamaka had already turned back to the workbench. "Uh-huh."

Keko had the opportunity to consider her circumstances while she piloted the Explorer over the country roads, but she still wasn't ready to face her fears. She'd learned at a young age not to agonize over relationships. Her mother had broken her father's heart, and as far as Keko could tell, the wound had continued to bleed until the day he died. Father and daughter never discussed the situation. John refused to allow any open negativity directed toward her mother.

In the twenty-something years she'd lived with him, her dad had never gone on a date, never had a special woman in his life. Considering the possibilities for a moment, she amended that thought. *At least, none that I knew.* As much as she loved and adored her father, she grew up tough and independent. If he could live on his own terms, so could she.

She'd been fond of the women around her while she grew up, but they were her dad's employees. Her nanny, her tutors, Lilajane Kozak, John's super-efficient office manager who retired after John died.

Whatever tidbits Keko had gleaned about the world of relationships between men and women—but mostly about sex—she picked up from largely uncensored conversations with the powder monkeys employed by Larsson Demolitions. Living and working around the men, she concluded at an early age that their attitudes about love and romance were always colorful, always interesting in a train wreck sorta way, and always somewhat skewed.

Even as a child, she'd been one of the guys. Protected, but still one of the guys. Cherished in weirdness, but still one of the guys. If her father had known about the heart-to-heart birds-and-bees discussions his young daughter had with his men—especially the discussions prompted by Keko's habit of listening on the sly to Dr. Ruth's *Sexually Speaking* on the radio—he would have locked her in her room and grounded her forever.

A little smile skewed her mouth as she remembered how Eight-fingered Jack, her father's oldest friend and top crew chief, spewed a mouthful of beer across the room when she asked, with her missing-tooth lisp, what *fellatio* meant. After that reaction, even as young as she was, she had the good sense to stop before she tried to pronounce *cunnilingus* for Uncle Jack's benefit. After all, Dr. Ruth was an expert, right?

Actually, now that I think about it, Dad did try to ground me once or twice—then discovered how close the old oak tree limb was to my bedroom window. Upon its discovery, a chainsaw brought that escape route to an abrupt end.

All Keko's "uncles" had been slick during her post-puberty years. It had taken a while for Keko to realize the reason she didn't have *second* dates was intervention from her mentors after eager young men took her out on *first* dates. Furious with the constant interference, Keko finally hooked up on the down-low with a new hire of her father's—a handsome, buff, young Irishman from Oklahoma just a couple of years older than her. After the awkward first time, they continued to meet in secret—then shagged like bunnies for months.

On the day her paramour didn't show up for work, Keko found a small sealed envelope taped to her locker. The enclosed note read: *Keek, my mama phoned, needs me pronto in Tulsa. Don't know if or when I'll be back. Wish you well. Dustin.*

She couldn't prove her dad had anything to do with Dustin's abrupt departure, but confidence ran high that John had somehow found out about her liaison with the Tulsa boy—*thanks, uncles*—then solved the issue to his own satisfaction. That established the end of her short love life, such as it had been. *Everyone eventually leaves me. Maybe I'm just not lovable enough for the long haul. Maybe I have bad juju.*

To MacBride, a man full grown and knowledgeable, not an inexperienced youth to be easily frightened away, she *wasn't* one of the guys. To MacBride, she was a mature woman with strong sexual appetites. At least that's what the fine-looking sheriff murmured in her ear as their limbs tangled like a nest of daddy longlegs spiders. In return, he was like an addictive drug to her. She couldn't get enough. She needed more and more of him, wanted to ride the tidal wave crest of passion he created and never touch dry land. He was a powerful thirst that refused to be quenched.

Keko was at a loss, totally inexperienced in this new arena of having a man who was her sexual equal. Didn't know what to do about it. *And what if this relationship affects my professional judgment? Affects my job?*

Relationship? They didn't have a relationship. She hated the phrase when the guys used it, but she admitted to herself that she and MacBride were stuck at the level of being, well, fuck buddies. At the very least. What was the other phrase she disliked nearly as much? Oh, yeah, friends with benefits.

What exactly did that mean in the real world, friends with benefits? Did that mean they could each go their own way, see other people, have other playmates? She didn't want that. As far as she was able to tell, she seemed to be a one-man sort of woman. Or, at least, one man at a time.

MacBride was clear—he wanted her to leave Sanctuary, bunk at his house. Despite what he said, she knew he did *not* intend her to sleep in the guest room. If she stayed at his place, she'd never be able to keep her hands off him. Knowing how he affected her whenever he was within sight, she guessed MacBride would need to escape to the cop shop to catch naps and rest up between bouts of lava-hot sex play.

Sanctuary, on the other hand, definitely lived up to its name. It was her refuge, her haven. Her shelter. She knew she could hide out there for as long as she desired.

Is that what I want to do, hide out? I've never been a coward in my entire life. I took the world on when I was five years old. Do I really want to escape from him?

It appeared that everyone in town had grown hungry at the same time. That meant Keko was forced to park along the far side of the town square, then walk to the Hungry Bear Café. She'd promised to pick up a cheddar bacon burger and deep-fried mushrooms for Kamaka, bring them back to Sanctuary.

Just as she stepped to the sidewalk, a tall, lanky man with slicked-back hair approached her. Loose jointed, his head and shoulders bobbed like Big Bird's.

"Miss, uh, miss." He pushed his thick, brown-rimmed Clark Kent glasses back up his long nose. His upper teeth protruded a bit. He'd dressed in total tourist garb, right down to the white embroidered shirt that was too long, red plaid golfing slacks that were too short, white socks, tennis shoes. "Do you live around here?"

Oh goody, someone more displaced than I am. "No, I don't. But maybe I can help. Where are you trying to go?"

The man took a colorful local street map from his back pocket. "I'm attempting to locate an establishment called the CataLodge. I arrived with my history professors' tour group, but my contemporaries appear to have left me behind. We are domiciled at the Lodge."

He was well-spoken, but his voice sounded wimpy, nasally. His speech was correct, but the tone whiny.

Not a good trait for someone who must command his students with authority.

Keko wasn't familiar with much of the town, but she knew the CataLodge because some of the Fibbies had been bunking there. "No problem. You probably missed the corner. The Lodge is on the other side of the Hungry Bear. You came too far."

She pointed in the correct direction.

He grabbed her outstretched hand, which surprised her, then shook it vigorously. "Thank you so much, you are very kind. I am Professor Simms. One would think you are a native. Where is home, exactly?" He looked at her expectantly, did not release her fingers from his grasp.

Trained more carefully than that, Keko did not reveal her name or her hometown, but did reclaim her hand. "It was nice to meet you, professor. I hope you find your tour group. Enjoy your holiday."

"Oh, I'm sure we shall. It's sort of a busman's holiday—such a historic region."

"Is it really? I didn't know. The beautiful scenery does it for me."

He adjusted his glasses, again. "Forgive me for being forward, but you could even join us, if you wished. I'm sure the others wouldn't mind. Having a young person in our midst would be refreshing. Offer a different point of view."

Jeez, fella, go the fuck away already. She pointedly looked at her watch. "That's very generous, but no. I do have an appointment, and I'm already pressed for time."

She watched the odd professor amble away like a disjointed scarecrow, then she took a moment to scan her surroundings.

Standing on the cobbled walk in front of the Hungry Bear, its stones as precisely fitted as those of the pyramids, and, hopefully, as long-lasting, she watched families scurry like picnic ants around and through the town square.

Larger-than-life bronze statues of those whom she assumed were historical heroes, mounted on fiery steeds, sat on large concrete bases in the park. Children laughed and teased each other into healthy games of catch-me-if-you-can and tag-you're-it. She wondered what small-town life had to offer its residents after the tourists went home, versus living on the outskirts of Boston, where the action never stopped. She wondered what it might offer to her.

"I can assure you that he's not going to leave here."

Surprised, Keko spun around. "I beg your pardon?"

Well, hello again, Miss Dock Bumpers U.S.A. The bimbo from the airport—the platinum blonde of the poofy hairstyle— encroached on Keko's personal space. Except the over-teased hair had been pulled back smoothly, fastened with a wide, brown, grosgrain bow. Still well-tailored, the busty blonde wore a crisp white shirt, pleated beige slacks, cream angora sweater with the arms tied across her chest, rust-colored loafers. A large designer handbag hung from her shoulder.

Keko backed up as she raised an eyebrow. "Are you speaking to me?"

"Sheriff Mac. He won't leave. He's made a home and a life here, so you can just forget about enticing him away."

Sheriff Mac? Give me a break. "Ma'am, I have no idea who you are, and my private life is none of your concern." Keko turned toward the diner doors. *Damn, she has a giant set of cojones.*

"Don't play coy with me, missy. We met at the airport, even though we weren't properly introduced. Men aren't very good at that sort of thing. Pepper Hunsacker, of *the* Hunsackers, and it's Miss, not Ms. or ma'am. And don't you even think about walking away from me." The woman grabbed Keko by the wrist with polished talons.

Before Pepper of *the* Hunsackers could draw another breath, her arm was twisted behind her back.

Being somewhat shorter, Keko growled close to her nemesis's ear. "What the hell is your problem? Have you lost your freakin' mind? Don't you ever, *ever*, touch me again, or I'll tear your arm off at the elbow then beat you to bloody death with it."

To avoid making a scene, Keko released the woman's arm. She hoped no one noticed the altercation. "Didn't your mama ever teach you to keep your freakin' hands to yourself? Go shop for yarn or something. Leave me alone."

Pepper rubbed her arm where Keko had gripped her, but she didn't disappear. "He's not going to leave. Men are always interested in things that are different, and you're just the shiny new toy. Sparkly. When the sparkle wears off, Mac will see you for what you are. A stranger, an interloper. Not made for durability, not for the long run. This isn't your town, you don't have any history here. You don't belong."

She folded her arms under her sizeable bosom. "My family has been here for generations. You won't last. You should leave here while you still have some measure of dignity."

Oh dear saints in heaven, is this broad for real? Keko leveled a hard look at the Pepper person. "Are you still here? I see your lips moving, but all they seem to be spewing forth is meaningless bullshit. I don't know why you decided to fuck up my day, but if you have a personal issue with Sheriff MacBride, I strongly suggest you take it up with him."

"You shouldn't use such bad language in public. It's not polite, not very ladylike. The use of profanity is nothing more than strong words delivered by a weak mind."

Keko muttered as she turned away, walked toward the diner. "That's good to know. I'll try to remember not to spew goddamned profanity the next time I'm accosted on the freakin' street by a raving fucking lunatic."

"But I'm not finished speaking—"

Keko continued to walk, spoke over her shoulder. "Lady, you may not be finished speaking, but I'm *so* finished listening."

"Problem, ladies?"

Joe Collins, MacBride's right-hand man, casually placed himself between Keko and the source of her irritation. With his long, lean, lifeguard look, the blond-haired, blue-eyed deputy managed to look downright sexy in his tailored police uniform. Sexy enough to change the focus of the discussion.

Pepper-of-*the*-Hunsackers' demeanor changed as quickly as a chameleon changes colors. She practically salivated as she slid her arm in his. "Deputy Joe, how *nice* to see you. No problem at all. Just a bit of silly girl talk, nothing that would interest you, a man of the law."

More like trash talk, you evil conniving bitch. A brief glance from Joe told Keko he knew exactly what had been going on. She gave the slightest nod by way of thanks.

"Miss Hunsacker," Joe smiled as he spoke, "my shift begins shortly, and I thought I'd hit up the ice cream parlor for a root beer float. Will you join me? No one in town makes them better than Shenanigan's. Don't you agree?" With a wink to Keko, he led the over-aged debutante across the street, toward the far side of the square.

Keko could no longer hear the conversation, but it appeared that Pepper Hunsacker's chatter was incapable of slowing down. *Joe, I owe you one, buddy. You prevented me from being arrested on a charge of justifiable homicide.*

As she waited at the Hungry Bear's take-out counter for Kamaka's order, Keko tried subtle deep-breathing exercises to pull herself under some sort of control. *How dare that bitch waylay me on the street, right out in public?*

Keko made it back to the Explorer with no further interruptions, cardboard box in hand. Still seething, but at a somewhat reduced level, she circled the town square. It being her first solo trip from Scotty's to town, then on to Sanctuary, she followed the arrows on the graphite-smudged map that Chandler had drawn for her.

Sheriff Mac and Pepper of the *Hunsackers? No way in hell.*

CHAPTER TEN

Wednesday early evening

WITH THE SETTING of the deep orange sun, the shadows were growing long by the time she reached the now familiar lodge driveway. She used her key card to get through the gate, then sat in the parking area for a few minutes, taking in the view.

Funny, it already feels like home. But I have a home—in Boston. And the high and mighty locals in Catafuckingmount Lake, Maine did not see fit to roll out the red carpet for me.

"Keek, you're late." Lorelei was in the great room, clad in a slinky knee-length emerald-green sheath with a matching shorty jacket. She fussed with silver hoop earrings as she hopped on one foot, searching for her other shoe. "You barely have time to dress for dinner if we're going to make our reservation."

"You'll never guess…" Keko choked back the rest of the words before she blurted out what happened in town.

"I'll never guess what?"

Keko laid her shoulder bag on a coffee table. *Deep breath, try a more casual approach.* "Um, you'll never guess how much I'm looking forward to dinner. Y'know, see more of the town. By the way, I think I recognized a woman from when we arrived at the airport. Platinum blonde hair. Junior League bullshit."

Lucian responded without hesitation.

"Pepper Hunsacker. Of *the* Hunsackers. Named Penelope after some great-great-grand-someone. Hates the name, insists on keeping her sorority moniker." He grinned. "The Hunsackers are one of the founding families of Catamount Lake, as she'd be glad to tell you. She's had a thing for Mac since he moved into town, but he's been too smart to bait that hook."

"Lucian, that's enough. Keko doesn't need the gossip. Keek, you won't see much of anything if you don't get your butt in gear."

Damn. I wish Lorelei hadn't interrupted him. I do so need the gossip! Hmm, the evil Pepper person has a thing for MacBride? "Trust me, I won't take long."

Keko practically leapt up the stairs to her gallery bedroom.

After a lightning-quick shower, she pulled a short leather skirt from her closet that she knew made her look totally hot, then chose a pair of skinny leather pants with leather lacing up the sides. Posing in front of the mirror in her red satin boy-cut panties and red sequined, sleeveless tank top, she alternated holding the garments in front of her.

"Skirt. Pants. Skirt. Pants. Skirt might look too flirty, which is like totally inappropriate in front of Lucian and Adam. As well as inconsiderate to Lorelei. I guess it's pants for the evening. Plus, no pantyhose to worry about." Try as she might, Keko usually managed to ruin at least one pair of hose every time she dressed to go out. Her best all-time record was four pairs in as many minutes.

She shimmied into the low-riding leather, which barely covered her hipbones, added her thin silver chain belt. She loosed her long hair from the shower cap, brushed it, twisted it on top of her head, then pinned the coil with the dolphin barrette. She selected tendrils to drape artistically over her shoulders and back. Then she posed while standing on her toes.

"Okay, people, that's as good as it gets." She made a few quick swipes with eyeliner and makeup brushes, added an application of her favorite ruby-red lipstick. She grabbed her choice of footwear, then flew down the stairs in bare feet.

The wall clock showed a scant nineteen minutes had passed when Keko descended into the great room.

Lucian whistled. "A woman who's actually on time. Imagine the concept. And wow, that's some transformation!"

Even Adam stared for a long moment. He nodded, just once.

Keko had topped off the black leather pants and sparkly red top with a vintage leather bomber jacket—she'd learned that, although the September days could still reach the upper 60s, even the low 70s, the nights could be surprisingly chilly in Sanctuary's neck of the woods.

Her favorite stiletto-heeled, black suede half-boots finished the ensemble, which perfectly set off the wide, flat, red-enameled necklace and matching earrings.

Lorelei finally found her high heel under the bottom edge of a chair, straightened, slipped on the shoe, then straightened up. She gave Keko a serious once-over. "Keek, next to that outfit, I look like a sack of wet laundry. Just think I've been outdone by a demolitions expert. Good job!"

Keko felt the blush reach her cheeks. "Then I pass muster?"

Lucian grabbed her around the waist, lifted her without effort, swung her in a circle. "Oh yeah, you definitely pass muster. You clean up good, darlin'."

Lorelei sent an indulgent smile Lucian's way.

Adam walked up, wrapped his arm around Lorelei shoulders, then just shook his head. "Damn kids."

Lorelei clapped her hands to get everyone's attention. "Come on, children, time's a-wasting, and this mother-to-be is starved. I'm sure I could eat half a steer, grilled to medium-rare perfection."

Lucian planted a kiss on her cheek in passing. "Aww, how sweet. Our own little carnivore."

Adam led Lorelei to the exit next to the foyer that opened into the garage, then held the door for the ladies. Out of their choices, Adam decided they should take Lorelei's Volcano Red Metallic Audi Q5, which hadn't gotten much use since it had been trailered up from DC.

Keko totally enjoyed the drive back to town. Lucian regaled her with tales of their recent visit with his madcap family, amid her howls of laughter.

Her face hurt from grinning when she finally caught her breath. "You're making up fairy tales—that can't all be true."

From behind the steering wheel, Adam grunted. "Believe him. It is true. Every blasted word."

Although The Woodlands' exterior oozed rustic north country charm in tune with the town, the interior dazzled. The crystal and silver, the crisp powder-blue linens, the well-chosen Art Deco accoutrements gave the establishment definite upscale appeal. None of the well-tailored wait staff could be mistaken for the servers at Hooters.

Keko looked around, nodded in appreciation. "Totally awesome. Is the food as good as this place looks?"

"Keek" – Lorelei grinned— "do you really think the boys would bring us here to dine if they could do better back at the lodge?"

"Okay, good point."

The restaurant was still relatively empty; the *maître d'hôtel* approached without delay. "Ladies, gentlemen, your guest is already seated. If you will please follow me."

"Guest?" Keko looked around, but no one offered an explanation.

As they approached a round table set in a corner between two stained glass windows done up in blue and white, Sheriff MacBride rose from his seat. He stood, momentarily looking as spellbound as a teenage boy seeing his prom date all dressed up for the first time. Stared at Keko like he'd never seen her before.

Lucian grinned. "Sure cleans up great, doesn't she?"

"Oh, yeah. Yes, she certainly does." MacBride shook himself free of the spell he seemed to be under, pulled out a chair for her.

She didn't want to be rude and stand there like an idiot to stare at him, so she allowed him to seat her.

Lucian seated Lorelei. Adam shook his head at the other two men, then seated himself.

Keko arrowed a sharp glare at Lorelei. "I guess he just happened to be in the neighborhood?"

Lorelei feigned innocence. "Did I neglect to mention inviting Mac? With so much happening these days, I've become absolutely absentminded. So sorry. Must be all the baby hormones."

"I'm sure," Keko muttered. "That must be it. Baby hormones."

As annoyed as she was with the too-obvious efforts at matchmaking, she had to admit that MacBride looked luscious. A snug, black Henley with the long sleeves pushed up made the most of his wide chest and shoulders, his long, lean torso. Tailored gray slacks and black shoes finished the picture. He wore a simple gold watch, and a large gold ring with some sort of insignia that she couldn't quite make out. It could have been a trident.

Keko played the game. "Wow, great look!" And he honestly did look fantastic. Totally awesome, actually. He'd been in jeans, polo shirt, and sports coat at the lounge in L.A., which had suited him well enough. Otherwise, she'd seen him only in uniform—or out of it. The Henley did nothing to hide his muscular upper body and taut abs. The slacks looked custom fitted.

Her nipples perked in response to his proximity; her intimate parts became all tingly. She shifted in her seat, attempted to cover her body's reactions. "And you know how to dress yourself. Impressive."

Before MacBride could reply to her sarcastic comment, a neatly appointed blonde girl presented herself. "Good evening, I'm Ashley. I'll be your server. May I start you out with drinks?"

MacBride glanced at Keko, one eyebrow raised in question. "Long Island Iced Tea?"

She couldn't tell if he was serious, or retaliating for her smartass comments about dressing himself. "Not ever again, not in this lifetime."

She made eye contact with the waitress, smiled. "A Shirley Temple, please."

Lucian sat back, grinned widely, arched an eyebrow. "I'd love to hear the rest of *that* story."

Keko directed a tight smile back at him. "No."

"No problem, honey lamb. I bet Kamaka will tell me." He reached for his phone, but Lorelei was faster. She snatched it out of his hands.

"You can have it back after we get home. I intend to enjoy our evening out."

Lucian played at being crestfallen, but Keko knew it was an act. He sighed, dramatically. "You're no fun."

Lorelei arched an eyebrow. "Watch it, buster, or I really won't be."

"Aww, Lorelei, baby," Lucian blew her a kiss. "You know you love me."

Keko glanced at Adam, who stoically observed his partners. "Are they always like this?"

"Unfortunately, yes."

MacBride reached for Keko's hand. "If these yay-hoos get to be too much, remember that my house is always at your disposal."

All movement ceased as the group awaited Keko's response.

She suddenly felt like she was on trial, or waiting outside the principal's office.

"I beg your pardon?"

He shrugged, rubbed the top of her hand with his thumb. "I'm just saying, I have a perfectly good guest room at my place, which is well situated in town and convenient to just about everywhere."

Yeah, with the chairwoman of your friendly neighborhood welcoming committee ready to scoop out my beating heart with a dull spoon at the first opportunity.

Mac appeared relaxed and casual, but his posture was watchful, almost possessive. His repeated offer hit her in the gut. *Why is he pushing me—again?*

Keko retrieved her hand, took a deep swallow of her ice water, waited a moment to get her feelings under control. She battled silently between fear and anger. Fear that he was trying to rope her in, anger that he cornered her in public. He probably banked on the fact that she wouldn't create a scene. *Keep it up, buddy, and see how poorly that logic works for you.*

The longer she considered his behavior, the more MacBride's possessive alpha attitude annoyed her. She perceived his posturing as a threat to her personal space—and she didn't handle threats very well. Threats, real or perceived, immediately brought out her strongest defense mechanisms.

"Thank you, that's very kind. I couldn't think of putting you out." The snarkiness slid out before she could stop it. She could feel her teeth grate at the effort to smile, to be pleasant. *Damn, my jaw is gonna be killing me later.*

He pressed on, now getting questioning glances from Lucian, as well as Lorelei. "You wouldn't be putting me out—I'm not at the house all that often. Someone should take advantage of it."

Keko sighed, fingertips to forehead. *Yeah, and that's the problem. I'd like to take advantage of you, for hours and hours at a time, days, even. But not as your live-in girlfriend. At least not yet.* A scene from the movie *Pretty Woman* popped into her head: Julia Roberts' character cooing to Richard Gere, *"I'd love to be your beck-and-call-girl, but…"*

Keko shook herself loose from those thoughts as her nipples perked up again, oddly out-of-step with her anger. *Okay, girls, on some level, you're beginning to worry me.*

It appeared that Lucian was about to speak, but Keko saw Lorelei shoot him a look. He apparently decided to quit while he was ahead.

Conversation remained on hold as young Ashley arrived in the nick of time with their drinks.

Ashley took their orders, then scurried away like one of Cinderella's mice. Keko stood, looked around to get her bearings. "If you'll excuse me."

MacBride immediately rose as she did.

Oh dear god, what the bloody hell does this man want from me? Is he being polite like his mama taught him, or pushing more of my buttons?

Lorelei motioned. "Go behind that wall, down the hall toward the kitchen. The rest rooms are on the right. Can't see from here. Very posh."

"Thanks." Keko turned to leave. *Please, don't let me trip.*

The ladies' room was indeed well-appointed, and thankfully empty of customers. Keko splashed water on her face, patted it dry. She reached for her makeup case, realized her purse still hung from her chair at the table. *Shit.* MacBride's unexpected presence screwed her up more than she'd realized. *Shit-shit-shit.*

Plush blue velvet benches were placed artistically along the wall, opposite the long white- and silver-flecked granite vanity. Keko sat and fumed. *How dare he put me in such a position? In front of everyone, for chrissakes.* Her new Sanctuary acquaintances had indeed become friends, and therefore important to her.

She returned to the mirrored vanity, finger-combed her mane, rearranged the hair clip, then smudged her eye makeup with a fingertip until it was even again.

"Sonofabitch, he can't do this to me." She growled at her reflection in the mirror. "I won't be pushed, or shoved, or molded like warm putty."

Keko jumped when she realized a large woman in a floral pantsuit had come into the room.

"That's right, girlfriend, you tell him. Do it. Go for it. Give him hell. You go, girl." The woman used the facilities, then returned to the sink to wash her hands. She fluffed her already fluffed bright orange hairdo. "Although, if your man is one of those fine lookin' gents seated at the corner table, you might consider giving him the opportunity to apologize. Then, hold out for make-up sex."

The woman reapplied her lipstick, orangey-red to match her hair.

"Oh, yeah, that's what I'd do. Hold out for make-up sex with one of those fine men. *Mmm—mmm.* Those boys are tasty morsels." After offering that pearl of wisdom, the woman departed in a cloud of floral perfume.

Keko knew she couldn't hide in the bathroom forever, but MacBride really had her off center. When he was near, she wanted to tear their clothes off, fuck like minks until there were no orgasms left in their bodies, then swoon from exhaustion.

Out of bed, in polite social situations, she couldn't seem to deal with him. *What the hell is wrong with me? I know how to act civilized in public.* Then again, that hadn't worked out so well at the hotel lounge in LA. *Fuck it.*

Figuratively girding her loins, Keko took a couple of deep breaths to calm herself. She headed down the hallway toward the dining area and their table.

Keko heard MacBride's voice, but couldn't quite make out the words. She stopped before the wall ended and she lost her cover.

He pressed his point to someone. "What's wrong with wanting her to live with me?"

Live with him? What the hell is he talking about?

"Have you discussed such a possible arrangement with her?" That was Lorelei.

Lucian's voice. "So, did you buy a ring yet?"

Lorelei again. "Lucian, you're not helping. Will you hush?"

Silence.

"Well, I might have looked around a bit," MacBride said. "Just in case."

Lorelei responded. "Just in case? Just in case, what? The girl's only been here a few days, and she lives in Boston—have you spoken about any of this with her?"

More silence.

"I sorta broached the subject about staying at my place." MacBride again. "She didn't exactly jump at the opportunity, but she was probably still suffering from jet lag."

The rude comment that followed was surely Adam.

"Oh boy, Mac," Lorelei continued, "this course of action has doom written all over it. It's too soon. She just lost her father, for heaven's sake, under really nasty circumstances."

Go, Lorelei, that's it, tell him. Tell him! Convince him that I'm not ready for cohabitation and engagement rings. Jeez, engagement rings?

"Yeah," Lucian chimed in. "We're talking about a woman who deals with high explosives on a daily basis, who stomps all over those big ol' powder monkeys to keep them in line. I'd damned well think twice, maybe three times, before pushing the wrong buttons. You might want to be *really* careful handling that fiery package of attitude."

Keko pulled back, pressed against the wall, missed Lorelei's response. *Motherfuckin' cocksucker.* She'd been sure MacBride understood her need for space. They'd discussed it. *I just need time—time to deal with Dad's murder, time to get my bearings in the business. I need some fucking time. He needs to stop pushing me.*

Just as she was about to clear the wall, she heard MacBride respond.

"Okay, so maybe I bought her a little gift."

Lorelei again. "Mac, I love ya like a brother, but you're pushing her too hard, too fast."

He must have produced a jewelry box. "See, it's not a ring. It's more like a collar. Silver and garnet. She seems to prefer that style, and she looks great in red."

He bought a collar for me? He thinks he's going to collar me? Me? When did our quasi-relationship warp into BDSM territory?

"Damn, chief." Lucian sounded either impressed—or apprehensive.

Adam uttered two words. "Too soon."

There ya go, buddy. Adam has the right of it. Too soon. Well, enough is goddamned well enough. Keko stepped quietly back down the hall toward the kitchen. The busy staff barely noticed as she tried to grab someone's attention.

The server, Ashley, looked surprised when she realized her customer had wandered belowstairs, in a manner of speaking. "Ma'am, is there something I can get for you?"

Keko pulled her jacket tighter. "Yeah, you can tell me where the back door is—then forget you saw me. Please."

Ashley barely hesitated, then nodded, pointed. "Between the walk-in freezers."

"Thanks. I owe ya."

The young woman shrugged. "Been there, done that, have the T-shirt. Too bad, he's a total fox. Always thought he was one of the good guys in town."

"No, you're right, he *is* one of the good guys," Keko said, heading for the rear exit. "He really is." *Just not for me, and not now.*

Once down the steps and onto the gravel, it became abundantly clear that any footwear incorporating the use of stiletto heels was not suitable for marching across the pea stone gravel parking lot designated for the employees. The footing was so tricky, she found it impossible to storm off with any sort of dignity. *At least I'm not wearing a skirt.*

With the sun down and the night at full dark, Keko felt the coolness of the autumn breeze against her cheeks, snuggled into her jacket. She reached into her pocket for her phone to call Kamaka to come to her rescue. Beg him, if necessary.

Damn it, the phone is in my purse, and my purse is hanging on the chair in the restaurant. Damn it, damn it, damn it. She had no intention of sneaking back inside, slinking to the table as if nothing had happened. *Lord knows, I'll miss Sanctuary, but I think I've overstayed my welcome.*

She hoped there was a pay phone in town, preferably within stiletto-heel walking distance, one from which she could make a collect call. Surely at the diner.

Kamaka can bring my luggage. I'll sleep on the sofa at Smitty's. Or, maybe there's a room at the CataLodge. That would be even better. Then catch the first fuckin' flight back to Boston. If no flights, I'll find someplace to rent a fuckin' car...

Keko tripped again, wondered how she'd gotten entangled in this predicament. *What the hell am I doing out here? Why am I letting him do this to me? I know better. I shouldn't allow him to run me off. Since when did I become such a freakin' coward?*

She stopped in her tracks. Why in blue blazes *was* she trying to get away? *Do what John taught you to do. Stop running. Take a deep breath. Exhale. Think it through.*

Had MacBride really done anything so terrible? In addition to the Olympic-quality sex, MacBride offered her companionship. A place to rest her head. He worried about her safety.

In the restaurant, he treated her like a lady, treated her with old-fashioned respect. It sounded like he bought her a gift because he thought she'd like it, not to propel her into matrimony—not to push her into a Master/slave, Dom/sub relationship.

Lorelei had reminded Keko that she was a strong woman in a man's world. So why was she frightened by a man who showed her affection and kindness? *Oh, hell, I am so stupid.*

A sudden chill of foreboding ran along her spine; she spun around, turning a full three-sixty, made more difficult by her heels. Nothing to see, but the little hairs on the back of her neck persisted in standing up. *Danger, Will Robinson, danger!* Not frightened of the dark, not frightened to be on her own—she had plenty of experience being alone—she couldn't shake the uncomfortable feeling that she was being watched.

Keko headed back toward the restaurant. *Okay, maybe I can sneak in before they realize I left.*

She paid less attention to her footing than she should have, causing the heel of one shoe to turn under. She wobbled unsteadily as she tried to regain her balance. *Damned stones. They're gonna wreck my shoes, then I'll be even more pissed off at my own stupidity.*

"Hold on there, miss."

What the hell? Startled, she tripped. No one had been nearby just a moment ago.

A tall man with strong hands grabbed her by the upper arms, steadied her.

"Thanks. I'm fine now."

"You should really wear more appropriate shoes for walking." His grip solid, he seemed hesitant to release her.

"Yeah, thanks, I already figured out that part." After she said it, she felt bad for snarking at a Good Samaritan.

"Of course you did, silly of me to mention it."

The man's voice sounded familiar. She turned to glimpse his face, his features outlined in the glow of the streetlight at the edge of the parking lot.

"Professor Simms. Fancy bumping into you again." *Hmm, old nerd guy is stronger than he looks.*

"I had supper at the diner—quaint, isn't it?—but I think I've gone astray once more. I seem to have lost the CataLodge again. One doesn't usually misplace an entire building." He pushed his Clark Kent glasses back up his nose.

Semi-ashamed at the harshness of her previous words, she tried a lighter tone. "Professor, with your sense of direction, or lack thereof, you should probably stay with your tour group. You turned right again instead of left. Okay, so go back to the Hungry Bear, then another couple of blocks over…" One arm still in his clutches, she tried to pull away from him to point. He didn't let go.

"Young lady, are you alone?"

"Looks like it, doesn't it?" *Uh-oh, not something to admit, ever. Damn, MacBride really does have me off balance.*

An odd noise alerted her. She turned in time to catch the weird expression on the face of the bespectacled professor. He released her arm, then quickly grabbed her by the back of the neck. A damp cloth was forced over her nose and mouth.

With her face covered tightly and a strong arm around her neck, she couldn't scream or bite or do anything to escape. But she did have time to rip off her necklace and throw it to the ground—a fraction of a second before her world spiraled down the rabbit hole.

How long do women take in the damned restroom?

Mac was edgy. Their meals had been served, but Keko's braised medallions of duck with orange reduction sauce had gone cold, as had the basket of once-warm rosemary artisan bread in front of her place setting. He knew she liked her food.

"Lorelei…"

She nodded and rose before he completed the sentence. She laid her napkin on the table, pushed her chair back. "I know. Keek's been gone too long."

Adam and Lucian cranked up to alert status the moment Lorelei stood, which added to Mac's feeling that something wasn't right.

It took only a moment for Lorelei to check out the situation, then return to the table. "Houston, we have a problem. No sign of Keko. No sign of a struggle. Nothing out of place."

Mac stood, immediately.

At that moment, the server returned to check on the status of everyone's drinks. Lorelei morphed into Special NCS Agent Lorelei Anne Randall right before their eyes, got in the young gal's face. "Ashley, we don't have time to screw around, so out with it. The woman who was sitting with us—when did she leave?"

The waitress scanned the expressions on everyone's faces, didn't hesitate. "Ma'am, she seemed upset, asked me not to say anything. She went out the back door just a few minutes after I put your dinner orders in."

Lorelei glance at her watch, looked around. "Keek didn't take her purse. Mac, you're the cop. Check the contents."

He rummaged through her leather shoulder bag. "Shit. ID, money, cards—and her cell phone. All here."

Lorelei punched numbers into her own phone.

"Kamaka, is Keko with you?" She listened. "Yes, I know where she's supposed to be. No, stay put. We'll get back to you."

She disconnected.

Mac took the lead. "Kamaka hasn't heard anything yet, but there's a pay phone at the Hungry Bear. Luce, head up to the diner, see if anyone remembers seeing her, but keep it on the down low. Adam, you're with me. You head out the front door, I'll go through the kitchen, meet you in back. Lorelei, bring your vehicle around to the rear so we can use the headlights. Stay inside the truck, lock the doors. Lucian, also contact Garrett—put him on alert, we may need his surveillance skills."

No one wasted precious time arguing.

They didn't take long to scan the area. Mac's gut churned, and his heart dropped to his feet.

Keko had disappeared.

CHAPTER ELEVEN

Wednesday night, into early Thursday morning

AFTER A CALL to Kamaka to meet them, after traversing the immediate neighborhood, they gathered in the conference room at the police department. Mac tossed Keko's broken necklace up and down in his hand.

"This is all we found. Keko's necklace in the middle of the employees' parking lot. One of the kitchen assistants had been standing outside by the hedge, taking a smoke break. He said he saw a black-haired female heading out of the parking lot on foot. He said she stopped, seemed to change her mind, turned around, then headed back to the restaurant.

"A tall man intercepted her, they spoke for a moment, then he 'helped' her into a big black SUV that had been parked along the street. The kid assumed the woman had too much to drink— he said she seemed 'sorta limp,' in his words. He knew his trucks, thought the vehicle looked like a Cadillac Escalade. Something heavy like that. There was enough streetlight illumination for him to get a decent look at the tags when the vehicle reversed into the parking lot, then headed in the other direction. Out-of-area license plates. He came in, scrolled through our license plate ID book, thought the tags might be from D.C. He wasn't sure of the age of the female, only that she was, in his words, just a little bit of a thing."

"Anyone check Pepper Hunsacker's back seat?" Lucian asked.

Mac shot him a look. "Not amusing, Luce."

"Wasn't meant to be, chief. Seems there was an altercation in town today in front of the Hungry Bear. Pepper threatened Keko, told her in no uncertain terms to get outta town." Lucian indicated Deputy Collins. "Joe interfered before there was bloodshed. And we know whose blood it would have been."

Joe gave a quick nod. "Yeah, that was pretty much it in a nutshell. I sidetracked Pepper, led her to Shenanigan's. Keko went into the diner."

Mac shook his head, placed hands on hips. "Fuck."

"However, Pepper doesn't have a black Escalade, and I think the witness would have noticed if a woman was helping a woman into an SUV," Joe said. "The kid was surprisingly observant. Sounds like it was definitely a man, on the tallish side, which lets Pepper off the hook."

Kamaka-the-clown had vanished, replaced by Kamaka-the-professional. He sat forward on the seat of his chair, hands on knees, his long black hair hanging loose, his expression hard. "Why didn't Miss Keko take her purse or her phone? We're always on call, so she never leaves her phone behind."

Lorelei reached over, placed her hand on his arm. "We don't know why she left, so those questions can't be answered."

By the hard look Kamaka gave him, Mac knew Keko's wingman had already decided where to lay the blame. *And I'm sure he's right. Somehow, this is my fucking fault.*

Kamaka took the lead. "I don't know your Pepper woman, but unless she's a Sumo wrestler, let's assume she's not strong enough to lift or carry Miss Keko, even as small as Boss Lady is. We checked the main roads; Keko's not walking. If she hitched a ride, which I doubt she would do, she'd be back at Sanctuary already. She'd call me from the first pay phone she found. I know there's one inside at the Hungry Bear. I assume you check that out."

Nods all the way around.

"So, what are you saying?" Lorelei asked.

"Let's make a leap, here. As far as we were able to establish through our research, Keko is the only person beside Smitty who actually had hands-on experience with the fail-safe device. So, let's assume a third party, an unfriendly party, has the same intel. Let's further assume we have a snatch and grab.

"What no one knows is that John talked Keko through the disarm—she did the deed because John had injured his wrist playing with his motorcycle, couldn't handle the tools. She just followed directions."

Mac's gaze grew flinty. "Then why the hell didn't he excuse himself from the mission?"

"That's where it gets tricky—it wasn't a mission. At the time, the circumstances appeared totally serendipitous."

Kamaka ticked off each item on his fingers. "John *happened* to be at the post office to pick up a special delivery package. He'd received a phone call from a woman who identified herself as a postal employee, said a package addressed to him was too large to fit in the mailbox, *and* it was marked urgent. When he *happened* to be next in line at the counter, the postmaster *happened* to receive a call saying that a box with a bomb had been placed in his facility.

"The caller demanded ten million dollars, or else, instructions to follow—no police, no FBI, standard bomb-threat bullshit. The postmaster knew John Larsson, signaled for help. Not knowing what was going down inside the building, Keko and I were waiting in the SUV for John. The three of us had planned to grab lunch after the post office stop. John phoned Keko to bring the tool kit into the building."

"You didn't go in with her?" Mac knew he sounded critical, but he couldn't help himself.

"No. My assignment, per John's instruction, was to make the necessary calls to the local authorities to evacuate the area, then see the evacuation was carried out. Beautiful sunny morning, civilians all over the place. We're trained to do our jobs, not ad lib, when the boss gives us explicit instructions."

Mac nodded. "Understood. Then what?"

"Keek completed the disarm, the clock stopped. She wrote the time on the back of her hand—that's what she always does, writes the time on her hand. John sent her out. He stayed behind to secure the device, examine it, babysit the thing until the bomb squad arrived with their explosives containment vessel. I met her outside as she exited the building. Then hell on earth happened."

Adam growled. "Someone set up Larsson. Took him out. He was in the way."

Kamaka nodded. "After the facts were in, that's what Keko and I concluded. Too many coincidences leading up to the explosion. The real substitute postal clerk denied making any phone calls; forensics bore her out. Impossible to know if there ever was a parcel addressed to John; everything made of paper or cardboard within the zone was blasted into confetti."

Everyone was silent—they all knew John's body would have been shredded the same way. He had no chance of surviving.

"No such thing as coincidence," Lucian said. "Someone went through a great deal of trouble to make sure Larsson was in the right place at the right time."

"Exactly. With the device disarmed, John sent Keko out to me. I met her at the front door. Of course, the moment the news broke about the evacuation of the post office building, everyone was taking photos, video recording, texting. That's how we learned that exactly seven minutes after Keko disarmed the bomb—or thought she did—the device rearmed and exploded."

Lorelei shook her head. "Bastards. Lucky you both made it to the SUV."

"We didn't."

Mac jerked upright. "What?"

"Scoff if you will," Kamaka said, "but I sense explosions a microsecond before they happen. It's a gift—of sorts. John saw it in action more than once. It's one of the reasons he recruited me. I'm like a canary in the coal mines."

Four sets of eyes zoomed in on Kamaka, mirrored varying levels of disbelief.

He sighed. "Man, I really hate this part."

He rose, turned away from his audience. The big man unbuttoned his colorful Hawaiian shirt, exposed his broad back.

Lucian hopped to his feet. "Jeezus jumped up holy kee-rist and all the saints in heaven."

From the waist up, the flesh of Kamaka's back, shoulders, and the backs of his arms was pockmarked with scars of all shapes, sizes, and colors. "I'd show you my sexy ass, but you already have the idea. A square trash receptacle flew into us, which protected my legs, probably saved me from being hamstrung, or having arteries ripped open. Or even worse."

Everyone looked solemn. They all knew what an explosive device in such a situation was capable of doing.

"Hold on, let me give you a hand." Lorelei helped Kamaka get his shirt back on, turned him around, secured the buttons. "There you are, all prettied up again. What happened to Keko? More scars?"

Mac, about to jump in to say he hadn't seen any evidence of old wounds, held his tongue. *Maybe the tattoo hides the damage?*

"No," Kamaka said. "Just scrapes from the sidewalk and bruises from me. I felt the bomb when it went up, had a millisecond to throw myself over her. Pretty much squashed poor Boss Lady. Then the trash receptacle hit us. A fancy trash receptacle. Four-sided and sturdy, imbedded with round beach pebbles. Prevented worse damage."

Mac felt a chill sprint through his body at what could have been, had Kamaka not acted so quickly to protect Keko. *Regardless of what you think of me at the moment, you're a good man, Charlie Brown.*

Adam shook his head. "Damn."

"Yeah." Kamaka sat again. "You might say that. Bits of shrapnel from the brick walls and metal window frames, plus lots of glass slivers, still work their way out of my hide. Plastic surgeon dudes said it would continue for the rest of my life. But at least I *have* a life. So does Keko. We would have been stir fry if we'd been inside. Collateral damage. We don't believe we were included in the original plan. John had to be the intended target. No one waited for ransom to be paid, that's for sure."

"None of those details showed up in the news reports." Mac tapped his pen against the pad on the conference table.

The Hawaiian nodded. "Lots of pull ensured the important stuff didn't reach the media. The officials leaked the version they wanted, so that's what was reported. Keko and I checked as many news stories as we could find—the same reports, nearly word for word, skirting around the truth as we knew it. The bitch of it was that no one took credit for it, none of the bad dudes. That proved the most worrisome."

Mac tried to get a grip on the situation. "So, upper echelon didn't want the bad guys to know that the good guys figured out what really happened."

"Best guess, yeah. NSA, Homeland Security, that crew. We were debriefed until our eyes crossed and our voices gave out, especially Miss Keko. After that, she and I tore the scenario down from every possible angle. The only conclusion that made sense pointed to the device being a prototype."

"Prototype? For what?" Lucian asked.

"Okay, this is how we scoped it. Consider a hypothetical situation. Let's say a bomb threat is made during a very public occasion, maybe during a big-deal fundraiser, or a speech of some political significance. Loads of politicians or military officers or upper-level government types, whoever. Doesn't matter, as long as they're newsworthy. Pick the best target to create fear and chaos, or to take out key leaders. Then, call in the bomb threat. The bomb is found—too easily—and dismantled."

Kamaka shifted in his seat. "Everyone is pumped up with the success, congratulations are in order, cigars handed out. Assured that the threat is nullified and the white hats triumphed one more time, the party proceeds as planned.

"The device is surrounded by experts to examine while they wait for a containment unit to arrive. Seven minutes later, *kaboom*! The experts are taken out, and so is everyone else in the immediate vicinity. Bad guys win, deal our side a serious hurt. Depending on the size of the device, hundreds, even thousands, could be killed or injured. Another 9/11."

Lucian raised his hand. "Why seven minutes?"

"Again, best guess? No significance at all. Think of the blast that took John out as a test that just happened to be seven minutes long. As long as the device worked as planned, it could be set for any length of time. Someone would have studied our protocols, gotten a good enough grip to guesstimate how long it would take for our people to carry out various procedures. Brilliant, in a sick and demented way."

Lorelei nodded. "That scenario has merit. Bomb defused. Crisis averted. Everyone feels safe. Politicians short-stroke it, everyone does a Snoopy Dance of Happiness. Guests do their best to ignore it and continue to party on, show they aren't afraid of a harmless explosive device in their midst. Instead of taking a bigger risk by planting a second device, one bomb could do the job."

Lucian nodded, picked up the thread. "Figure in the logistics. The bad guys estimate it will take the vehicle with the containment device, say, fifteen minutes to arrive, since the bad guys probably have everything timed to the second—distances, traffic, as many variables as possible. They set the delay for eighteen minutes. The experts and the curious will check out the device while they wait. Maybe a SWAT team is hanging around. *Boom!* Major death and destruction to strategic personnel. Major damage to national morale."

"All right." Mac abandoned his notepad, tapped against the top of the table with his pen. "They know the device works." *Tap tap tap.* "We know our enemies have their own explosives experts. Why grab Keko?" *Tap tap tap.*

Lucian picked up the ball again. "Right. Follow me on this one. It's safer to construct the devices here, rather than try to sneak them into the country. Okay, then. Smitty cops to the game, discovers he's not working for our own red, white, and blue. He refuses to assemble the new device. The bad guys cut their losses, he's toast. They set him up as the fall guy, a traitor to his country, if and when the killing is discovered before they sterilize the area. They get sloppy; our police force finds the devices too soon.

"Someone hangs around to observe the direction of the investigation, or maybe they intend to retrieve the components, which cost a pretty penny. Probably leaves the tracks Black Crow found.

"Lo and behold, another specialist arrives at Smitty's place—the same little gal who managed to be photographed at the post office by tens, maybe hundreds, of cell phones and cameras. Surveillance must have been trained on John, to assure they pulled off the assassination, which made Keko visible. Everyone exited the building, except her—she hurried *into* the building. With their video running, the bad guys would not have missed her and Kamaka in the aftermath."

"So that's good news," Mac said. "They'll keep her alive for as long as she can stall."

When his pen resumed its maddening tapping, Lorelei snatched it out of his fingers. "And you think she'll be able to stall."

Mac and Kamaka replied instantly. "Absolutely."

"Luce," Adam said, "find Black Crow. If you can't locate him, track down Abigail, send her after him. We're going to need them both."

Lucian snapped to attention. "What are you thinking, hoss?"

Adam kicked back from the table. "I'm thinking our kidnappers didn't go too far."

"And I'm thinking our kidnappers needed a backup plan," Lucian said. "If Keko fails to complete the device, or she majorly pisses them off, who's next in line if they take her out?"

He stopped Mac with a palm-up hand gesture. "Don't panic yet. I'm just sayin', follow the logic."

Lucian tossed the broken necklace onto the table, turned to Kamaka.

"If what you say is true, the bad guys won't have fled the area. You're their fail-safe, big guy. They didn't go far."

Keko opened her eyes, but the world still looked black. She took stock. *Hands bound behind me. Blanket is fucking scratchy enough to sand off my skin.* She rolled onto her side, but waves of dizziness and nausea resulted. *Okay, maybe not such a good idea.*

While she waited for the effects to pass, she rubbed her face against her shoulder. Not blind, only blindfolded. *Feels like a hood. I can deal with that.*

A thin but lumpy mattress barely cushioned her from whatever hard surface on which she'd been dumped. She wriggled a bit, discovered the mattress edge was shoved against a wall. When she felt along the wall with her chin, she identified it as wood paneling, but rough. Maneuvering until she could sit upright, the feeling of disorientation and the hangover headache began easing off.

Most of her clothing appeared to be in order, which was promising, but her jacket was missing. *Damn, that bomber jacket is authentic.* When the blanket slid off, she felt a definite chill on her shoulders. Her feet were naked. *Okay, enough is enough. Who the hell snatched my Christian Louboutin's?*

"What the fuck." Her voice didn't echo, so the room wasn't too large or high-ceilinged.

"What the fuck, indeed. How colloquial, Ms. Kailani Holokai of Larsson Demolitions. Nice to see you awake."

She faced the direction of the voice. *Male. Cultured. Possibly British, but more likely American with an affectation.* She needed more to determine nationality for sure. "And you are?"

"Your captor at the moment, my dear."

Definitely American. Urbane. Cocky. Hmm, also sounds familiar.

"At the moment. I see. Does that imply the relationship may change?"

"Possibly."

"From what to what?"

"From captor to executioner."

"Forget I asked."

"As the lady wishes."

"Uh-huh. I don't suppose I could bum a drink of water. Whatever inhalant you used leaves a nasty taste and burns one's mouth."

"Clever girl. Of course."

The floor creaked under him. *Wood planks? Old house?* He twisted the top on a plastic bottle—she heard the plastic snap as he broke the seal. *New bottle, probably safe to drink, not drugged.* He moved closer, touched the opening of the bottle to her lips.

"It would be easier to drink if the blindfold was off and my hands weren't tied."

"No doubt. But then you might feel honor bound to try to escape, and I would be equally honor bound to kill you."

"Good point." She sighed.

He put the bottle to her mouth again. This time she drank. *No sense pissing him off. Yet.* "Thanks."

She sniffed the air without moving her head, tried to get her bearings. *Musty. Damp.* "So, is there a point to all this, or are you simply terribly attracted to me, but too shy to ask for a date? I'm really not that unapproachable, y'know."

"Not that an evening with you is an unpleasant thought, considering your attire, but we do have business that requires our attention."

Aha. Finally. "And what business might that be?"

"The one thing we have in common, my dear."

"The desire for a really good medium-rare rib-eye cooked over flaming coals?"

"Bombs." He sounded piqued.

"I beg your pardon?"

"You know, bombs. Explosives. Devices of destruction. Bombs."

She wiggled around until her legs were in front of her. "Sorry, can't help. I seem to be fresh out of bombs at the moment. However, I'm willing to hold out for a well-grilled open-faced Reuben with very tender corned beef, light on the sauerkraut, lots of melty Swiss cheese, loads of Russian dressing. Rye bread, no seeds. Seeds get stuck in one's teeth. Very unattractive on a date."

"For such a small person, you seem surprisingly food motivated. As enjoyable as this badinage is after dealing with fanatics and mindless drones for far too long, I have a deadline, and you are wasting my time."

"I see." *Sanctimonious asshole.* She tested her bonds. *Shit. Duct tape.* Wrestling with duct tape would be a lesson in futility.

The floor creaked again, followed by a metallic sound, something being dragged. *Maybe a chain?*

"I do apologize, but I simply cannot allow you the opportunity to escape." He snapped a cuff around her left ankle, the harsh metal rough against her skin.

Shit, not even fake fur lining, the barbarian.

"I will release your hands, but I must warn you that I'm armed. Please don't try anything heroic. When I give you permission, you may remove your blindfold. You cannot work if you cannot see."

Work? Work at what?

He cut through the tape that bound her hands, then the creaking floor indicated he'd moved away. "You may remove your blindfold."

Oh well, thanks a fucking lot, fella. Self-righteous prig. Once she pulled the scratchy fabric away, her eyes smarted and burned. It took several minutes until they became accustomed to the light, then able to focus.

A fairly long section of what appeared to be a shiny, lightweight tow chain tethered her to a metal ring newly bolted to the old wooden floor. Her prison looked like a small garage, or large workshop. Black roofing paper covered all the windows. The overhead door looked wide enough for a vehicle to fit through.

Probably a smallish vehicle, nothing as large as a hefty truck or SUV, definitely not a tractor-trailer.

Recently built from new lumber—the fresh-cut pine smell was still pungent—a long, sturdy-looking workbench ran along the opposite wall. Recently installed banks of fluorescent lights hung overhead, extension cords hanging to floor outlets.

Two sets of bomb components were laid out on what looked like parchment paper, in the identical pattern as the unassembled device had been in Smitty's workshop before the FBI messed with it. Before she and Kamaka messed with it. *Aww, for fuck's sake. I can't get away from these freakin' things.*

"I see you've deduced the state of affairs. Two sets of components, two bombs. Your job is to assemble them, and assemble them correctly. If you find that impossible to do, your use to me comes to an end. Unfortunate, but that's the way it is."

After scoping out her surroundings, Keko finally turned to her kidnapper. The man made no effort to hide his features. *Which means I'll survive about thirty seconds longer than it takes me to complete the devices.*

"Well, well, well. If it's not Professor Simms, the tourist with the bad sense of direction and poor fashion taste."

He inclined his head.

"Nice disguise. Well done."

"Simple, really. False teeth, wash-out hair coloring, glasses, a bit of makeup, appropriate wardrobe. People see what they expect to see." He nearly preened with the thought of his own cleverness.

"How did you ID me, just for the sake of curiosity? It's not like I'm on Facebook, nor do I tweet or blog."

Moving closer, but staying outside the reach of her tether, he pulled a smartphone device from his front pocket, turned it toward her so she could see the screen. He scrolled through digital photo after photo. She and Kamaka exiting the post office building. Segments of the actual explosion. People running, bleeding from the shrapnel. Parents dragging children away from the devastation.

In the aftermath, zoomed-in close-up shots of a bloody Kamaka, belly down, secured to a gurney, then being loaded into an ambulance. A full body shot of Keko from the back, her clothing ripped, her long ponytail very visible. Then she turned, and a full, clear face shot stared back at her, her green eyes wide with shock and disbelief.

"Just to make sure, we backed it up with facial recognition software. I must say, you weren't easy to find."

"Maybe not, but it appears someone was very thorough."

He gave a half bow. "We do try."

In spotless, sharply-creased sand cammies, without the touristy guise, the man was tall, tanned, fit, football-quarterback handsome in the blue-eyed, square-jawed manner of the confident and well-bred. His hair must have been jet black in his youth, now sprinkled with silver in all the right places, cut military short.

She would take bets that Joe Jock never saw one iota of front-line action. *Faker. Wannabe. Poser.* She immediately hung a nickname on him: Captain Perfect.

"And if I don't?"

"Ms. Holokai, let's not play games and waste even more time. If you don't cooperate, I'll be forced to kill you now, then bring in the B team. Your Hawaiian co-worker is our...my...second choice. He's good enough for the FBI to bring in, he's conveniently close, and time is an issue."

Oh fuck. Again.

"He's just a friend, came along for the ride to keep me company."

"Ms. Holokai, you saw the photos. Let's not get off on the wrong foot by insulting my intelligence."

"I'm just sayin'…"

"My dear, the decision is yours—but you have less than a minute to decide." He checked his expensive-looking watch. "Forty seconds."

"*Fine*, whatever. Exactly what am I supposed to do?" Keko sat on the edge of the mattress and wiggled her shackled foot.

"We already covered that. Let's not pretend."

She dragged the chain over to the bench. "This is no time to be guessing. I need to be sure. You do realize my co-worker, as you call him, never saw the device. And you do realize there are flaws in these materials, right?"

"I warned you…" He took a semi-automatic pistol from the top of the old Formica kitchen table, next to which he'd been sitting.

She held up both hands in a defensive posture.

"*Whoa* now, Sparky, let's not be hasty! Pay attention, fella. This isn't a stalling tactic, this is a potential technical difficulty. I noticed it at Smitty's. My Hawaiian, as you call him, noticed it as well. I don't particularly wish to get blown to smithereens working with this shit."

The gun went back onto the table, within sight, but out of her reach. "All right, I'll concede your expertise. What sort of flaws?"

"I'm not sure. The gauge and covering of the wires aren't consistent, and the C-4 is either contaminated or from a totally unfamiliar vendor. I never saw C-4 that color. Plus, it smells weird."

"Can you substitute Semtex instead?"

And what are you going to do, asshole? Pop down to the local market and grab a block of plastique off the shelf? "Are you a demolitions expert?"

"No, it's not my forte. That's why we…I… have you."

"Well, then, trust me on this—explosive material is not interchangeable for this very specific application." Dragging her leg chain, she pulled over the other kitchen chair, then parked it next to the workbench, backward. She swung her free leg over, rested her folded arms on the back of the chair. "I wonder if Smitty had the same questions—which would account for the way the components were arranged on his workbench."

"What do you mean, how they were arranged?"

Keko hadn't been sure before, but now she reconsidered, reached a conclusion. She stared at the items on the bench. "Hmm, maybe he *wasn't* assembling. The pieces were spread out like he was examining, not assembling." She nodded, more to herself. "Did you find notes, workbooks, a laptop, maybe scraps of paper? Anything?"

"Not that I am aware. He said he kept the schematics in his head. I assumed he was bragging."

"Well, you killed him too soon."

She followed the direction her thought associations took her, ignoring the man with the gun.

"For the sake of security, I'm guessing Smitty wouldn't do anything to attract attention to himself. So, he wouldn't have ordered materials directly. He probably wrote out a grocery list, then his handler or contact procured the components. However, as it turns out, he assumed that the supply trail was legitimate, from United States government sources. Maybe it was, at least at first."

She turned toward her captor. "So, where did these materials come from? Who supplied the works? Can you backtrack to the supplier, put me in touch? If I could speak directly to whoever has intimate knowledge of the components—"

"Not going to happen." Captain Perfect's cool slipped. "I don't know, nor do I care, who supplied the works, as you call them. You're wasting precious time. Smith's untimely death already cost us. Then the local police found the shop too soon, brought in the FBI."

"Yeah, I'm sure Smitty felt real bad about that, screwing up your timetable."

I wonder if this asshole was the bozo hanging around Smitty's, the tracks that Black Crow found. Turning her glance toward him, she decided not. *And get his fingernails dirty? His clothes mussed?* There must have been someone else hanging around. Or, more than one someone. She returned her attention to the items on the workbench. "Something just feels wrong about this stuff."

The man stood, straightened the creases in his slacks, picked up his gun again. "Sadly, you've become tiresome. I hope your Hawaiian is more cooperative."

He leveled the muzzle at her lower torso, which indicated to her that he wasn't familiar with shooting people. At least, not efficiently. She wondered if he shot her in a non-lethal part of her body, she could survive long enough to scratch his eyes out, or stab him with a screwdriver, before she bled out.

"A shame, really. You're very pretty. I enjoy exotic women."

Yeah, but do they enjoy you, numb nuts?

"Hang on a damn minute, Quick Draw. I didn't say I *wouldn't* do it, I'm just saying there might be problems with the stability of the devices. *Sheesh*, Mr. Crabby Pants. Take a chill pill. And forget any possible mutual attraction. I'm only half Hawaiian, so half exotic."

Make one grab for me, you sonofabitch, come close enough, and I swear to all that's holy that I'll castrate you with my fingernails, then gut you and leave your steaming entrails on the fucking floor.

Keko stepped to the platform that had served as her bed, grabbed the thin blanket, turned the chair around, covered it with the blanket before sitting again. She left enough to cover the floor near the workbench.

"What are you doing?"

"Number one, it's freakin' cold in here and my feet are frozen. Number two, I don't want any metal exposed that could provide an accidental spark or connection. Number three, I'm not wearing rubber-soled shoes to ground me."

"Oh. Well, proceed."

"I hate to bring this up, but I really need to pee. I don't suppose there's a ladies' room available?"

He looked around. "Use the bucket in the corner."

"Oh, yuck. That's not gonna happen." Scoping out the opposite corner, she caught a glimpse of her jacket and shoes on the floor. "Look, I'm chained up, right? I don't suppose you'd consider opening the door to let me squat outside? Just promise not to peek."

To her surprise, he agreed. *Okay, so he's not afraid I'll be seen. We must be really isolated.*

When she stepped outside into the damp chill of the early morning, she verified her assumption.

The building, constructed of rough-cut lumber weathered to silvery gray, sat in the middle of a small clearing surrounded by heavy tree cover. The leaves were turning colors, but not yet fluttering to the ground, which left the overhead canopy heavy and lush. *Probably impossible to see from the air.*

A black Cadillac Escalade sporting D.C. tags loomed nearby, but a rental agency's name framed the license plate. *Not much dust, no mud—he couldn't have driven too far into the woods.* Next to the SUV sat an older Jeep with Maine tags; dried mud caked the bottom half. *Probably Smitty's.* It verified her theory that at least one more man had been around to assist moving vehicles.

The chain wasn't long enough for her to see around the building.

She took care of her immediate business before her jailer got edgy, then returned inside to the workbench.

With great caution, Keko began assembling the devices, mimicking each step she took on the first bomb with the second.

Smitty, old man, what the hell worried you? What am I missing? What am I not seeing?

"Why are you doing that? Can't you complete the first bomb, then the second?"

"Look, buddy. I don't have a schematic to work with, not even a scribbled note with stick figures. I'm assembling these things based on what I remember of the device that killed John, using customary protocols, plus a few tricks I know. So, unless you'd rather take over, leave me the fuck in peace."

"You're lying, We know that you're familiar with the bomb."

"No, Mr. Wizard, your intel sucked. I didn't build the damned thing. I didn't even work on it. I disarmed the device under the direction of my boss. John pointed—I did what he told me to do, no more, no less. Big difference, Sparky. Then the device exploded anyway, and he was blown into a billion tiny pieces. Now go away."

Keko kicked into professional mode; the world around her disappeared. Her total focus became the device. As her little gray cells screamed into linear overdrive, her subconscious took an alternate route. She began to process minute data in lateral progression, which her conscious brain was too busy to decipher.

The floor is wooden planks, not concrete. The site is either too far away, or the road too rough, to bring in a concrete mixer to lay a foundation. So, we're in the woods somewhere, probably off a seasonal road, but his vehicle isn't encrusted with dirt or mud. The building smells musty, damp, unused.

It was late dinnertime when I was grabbed, and it's still early morning. I've been missing maybe nine, ten hours. Probably kept me unconscious while he—or they—moved me and brought in the components. Maybe used small whiffs of a sedative inhalant to keep me under. Couldn't risk an overdose.

Keko's hands kept moving, doing the work they were trained to do. Her mind segued between the two primary problems. First, get out alive. Second, call in the troops. *Smitty was a specialist. What bothered him about the device components? Okay, the bomb was his design. But, the materials weren't. What if he discovered the components were substandard? What if he questioned the supply trail? What if the components were not to spec…? What if, what if… Holy deep-fried monkey nuts! What if he knew? What if Smitty knew!*

Think this through, Larsson. What would Dad do? Okay. What if Smitty finally realized the game plan was bogus, discovered that he'd been played? Discovered he was assembling state-of-the-art weapons for the wrong side. *Think.* Trapped in his backwoods shop with no way to summon help, what if Smith intended the device to go off while it was in the possession of the bad guys? But the faulty components fucked it up. *Then John's death was an accident! Smitty didn't build in a trick timing device—the components failed!*

MacBride, if you can hear me, I need you in SEAL mode, baby. I need you in SEAL mode, and I need you to find me quickly, or it's all over but my eulogy

Keko's captor had been gone for a while. By the time he returned, the devices had begun to resemble something more than piles of electronic scrap.

"Yo, buddy, I don't suppose you can round up something to eat. It must be at least twelve hours since you snatched me off the street, and I haven't eaten since lunch yesterday. You really fucked up dinner for me. Braised medallions of duck with an orange reduction glaze, served over a bed of a wild rice medley. Such a waste." She sighed.

The man settled himself, stretched out in the chair, unfolded his legs to avoid wrinkling his trousers. "Sorry, but you're quite at fault in that capacity. You left the restaurant and fell right into my arms, literally, without an escort of any sort. By the way, I neglected to tell you how much I appreciated your assistance in that endeavor. So, the quicker you finish the job, the quicker you get to eat. Deal with it."

Oh yeah, like he plans to drop a Happy Meal in my lap after he has the devices in his hot little hands, then release me so I can hitchhike back to Sanctuary. "Sure, fine, okay, whatever you decide, Sparky. I'm just saying, hypoglycemia is setting in and my hands are getting a bit shaky."

She selected a wire, stripped the plastic coating from both ends, held it up as an example of her shaking fingers. "Considering that you're as close to the explosives as I am, I thought I should bring the problem to your attention."

His posh attitude dropped. "Woman, you're a real ballbuster. Has anyone told you that?"

"It's been mentioned a time or two. Probably bad breeding, or at least bad upbringing. I was a deprived child. And that's deprived, not depraved."

He swallowed whatever else he was going to say, then slammed out of the building.

"Ooh, testy sort, isn't he?"

The man returned in a few minutes with a paper sack and a pint-size cardboard carton with a pour spout. He handed them to her.

"Thanks. I don't suppose you have a pair of ladies' tennis shoes tucked away somewhere, size six? If not, maybe a pair of socks. No shit, my feet are really freezing on this floor."

From the apoplectic look on his face, Keko suspected she'd finally overstepped the boundary of Captain Perfect's patience. Instead, he left again, returning with a new pair of men's heavy boot socks, still in the packaging.

He threw the socks at her. "Here. This had better be the last fucking delay. I'm out of fucking patience, which means you're out of fucking time."

Ooh, bad language, which probably means whoever's pulling your strings is out of patience, dirtbag.

She dragged her chain over to her chair, pulled on the socks. She nearly sighed with relief, but didn't want to give the bad guy any recognition for performing what could be construed as a charitable act. She tried to tuck the top of the sock under the ankle cuff, but there wasn't enough play between her skin and the cuff. She pulled the sock as far over the steel as she could. The food came next—no lie, she was really hungry. The foil wrapper identified the cheesesteak sandwich as a Hungry Bear item. It retained barely a smidgen of warmth; the once-melted cheese resembled wall spackle. The carton held lukewarm chocolate milk, probably from sitting next to the once-hot sandwich in Captain Perfect's vehicle.

Sonofabitch, we can't be that far from town. Okay, guys in white hats, you can rescue me now, any time, without further ado. Please. And hurry!

CHAPTER TWELVE

Thursday, mid-morning

MAC CALLED IN anyone he thought could be useful, as well as circumspect. Adam and Lucian arrived. They stayed in touch with surveillance expert Glennon Garrett by satcom link; he had his spider web of international electronic feelers out.

Although Lucian argued with her—and Adam backed him up—Lorelei refused to remain at the lodge just because she was pregnant. Kamaka stayed by her side, not so much to protect her as to prevent the hormonal agent from causing mayhem while they waited.

Abigail managed to track down Bobby Black Crow. Deputy Collins quietly called trusted individuals from the roster of the Catamount Lake police force, first-aiders, rescuers, and firefighters.

Over a dozen people met behind the police department in the cavernous garage, which had been emptied of all vehicles for the purpose of their clandestine meeting.

Mac faced the gathering. "All right people, this is the situation. We have a missing person, an expert in demolitions and explosives. I am not at liberty to discuss the details, other than to say that we strongly suspect she's been kidnapped by an unfriendly faction. She went missing at about nine o'clock last night from the employees' parking lot behind The Woodlands. Lucky for us, one of the kitchen staff happened to be taking a cigarette break, observed Ms. Holokai being put into a black Cadillac Escalade with Washington D.C. tags. We determined that lead to be solid."

He pulled papers out of his briefcase.

"A few of us searched all night, with no results. No GPS to track the Escalade, either—at least none our sources found so far. So, let's try a different approach. Here's a list of every establishment in town. They should all be opened for business by now. Each of you, pick a section of the list. Check every business, kiosk, storefront—I want them all covered. Quietly. No fuss. Don't get anyone agitated.

"It's a long shot, but someone might remember something that stuck in his or her mind that may have seemed slightly off at the time. Try to hit the known busybodies first."

He handed the stack of lists to a firefighter, who took one, then passed them on. "Your cover story can be that we're doing an informal survey to see how to improve our tourist business. Take a clipboard, act at least semi-official. Tell them anything that sounds plausible. Just don't give away the mission."

A second stack followed, copies of a color photo of Keko with all her stats, and her tattoo. "These are for your eyes only. We don't want questions, nor do we need folks to jump to any sort of conclusions. We don't want to tip our hand to the bad guys, just in case."

One of his deputies raised his hand. MacBride shook his head in response, before the question could be voiced. "I know, Lou, I know. It's tourist season. Lots of weird stuff goes on. The problem is that we're running out of time. Keko—Ms. Holokai—has already been missing for about twelve hours. We have reason to believe the kidnappers have not left the area, and our window of opportunity is dwindling by the second."

Mac checked his watch. "We'll meet back here no later than one hour from now. If we don't have something by then, we probably won't have anything at all. Then we'll need to come up with a different plan of attack. Please be thinking of an alternative while you're out there."

He turned to leave, then remembered something. "I don't need to remind everyone not to take action on your own—if you turn up anything at all, contact me immediately. Assume we're dealing with an individual or a group who will be armed and dangerous. Don't attempt any heroics."

He responded to Adam's hard look. "Not that there's any doubt that you wouldn't be able to handle any hostiles, but we need intel. It's tough to question a corpse."

Lucian grinned at Adam's disgruntled expression. "Hoss, he has you pegged."

One hour and five minutes later, Joe Collins directed everyone's attention to the large township map permanently affixed to the garage wall. He tapped the map with a long, rubber-tipped, wooden pointer. "Buggy Adderson's place. It's the only site that fits."

Lucian looked over the entire section of Catamount Lake proper, then the site Joe indicated. "That's not far from town at all. Are you sure?"

"Best guess, with the intel we gathered." Joe held up the sheets everyone turned in, before the others left for their sleep shifts or day jobs.

"Adderson's old fishing camp. Buggy is currently chasing elderly ladies around the Pine Knoll Rest Home in his motorized wheelchair. He still owns the camp property, which is handled by a local realtor. Two weeks ago, the realtor had a single inquiry about renting the place, offered to pay a sizeable bonus if the realtor could get him situated quickly. Fits our time frame.

"The camp is so far off the beaten path, you'd never find it without a map. The access road is nearly grown over, not much more than a game trail now. Buggy hasn't used it for at least a decade, just rents it out once or twice a season. Word is that he hasn't done much in the way of upkeep on the buildings, but they're still standing."

Adam stood. "Two questions. One, could the kidnappers get vehicles back there? Two, can we get behind the camp to flank them?"

Game Warden Abigail O'Connell took Deputy Joe's pointer, traced a path from the nearest main road to the site. "Yes, and yes. The access road is overgrown, but with brush, not trees. If you don't mind scratching some paint, vehicles can make it without too much of a problem. In its heyday, the dirt access road was actually filled in with highway stone and gravel, so it isn't totally deteriorated. Passenger vehicles should be able to handle it, trucks definitely. Last time I was through there, the cabins and outbuildings were moldy and in danger of disintegrating, but they were actually still standing."

"All right, so Adderson's place is our strongest possibility." Mac turned. "Bobby, can we flank them without being seen?"

Bobby Black Crow traded places with Abigail, took up the pointer. "Yep. There are game trails here, here, and here. Boulders and thick scrub brush for cover here and here, plus heavy stands of trees. Can't get close with any sort of full-sized vehicle, though, trees are too tight. ATVs make too much noise. Horses could get through, but I'd be worried about snorts and neighs—plus, it'll take too long to trailer them in. Whoever goes in will be on foot for about, say, a half mile, maybe three-quarters, depending."

Lucian hopped off the table he'd been using as a seat, snapped a smartass salute to the sheriff. "Sir, Marine sniper and spotter team at your service, sir. We already grabbed our gear."

Mac nodded. "All right. Adam and Lucian with me. Bobby, bring us in from the nearest secondary road, then pull back and stand ready in case we need to relocate in a hurry. Joe and Abigail, station yourselves in the woods near the head of Adderson's trail, close to the road. Do *not* take any action. Observe and advise only. Lorelei, will you and Kamaka return to Sanctuary, staff the comm links and relay whatever Glennon Garrett sends? Good. Everyone: earwigs only." He handed out the tiny devices.

"We'll be connected by GMG satellite feed. We don't need any comm equipment crackling or voices being overheard. You know how sounds can travel in the woods."

He massaged his temple, knowing that a massive headache was barely holding off. "New intel. I checked in with the M.E. According to Blake, he's ruled Smitty's death a homicide. Neck broken, dead before he went off the cliff. Traces of blistering around the mouth and lips from a sedative inhalant that has yet to be identified, would also explain how Ms. Holokai disappeared so quickly and quietly. Especially the *quietly* part.

"People, I don't need to remind you that this mission is unsanctioned and totally unauthorized. Volunteers only. If anyone wants to bail out, now is the time. Believe me, I will understand. We'll all understand. The Fibbies are gone. According to Garrett, they're already back in Boston, working their next case.

"If we wait to go through channels, Keko may not survive. Make no mistake. The FBI and the NSA are not going to be pleased if and when they hear about us working on gut instinct, but we're the best—the only—chance she has. If this goes tits up, we may lose Keko *and* our asses are gonna fry."

Lucian grinned. "Even if this does go right, we'll save Keko and our asses are *still* gonna fry."

Keko kept her hands moving, but not necessarily productive, dragging out the moments. *Guys—please be fantastic at your jobs. Make me proud. MacBride, I'll move in with you, wash your dishes, do your laundry, have your babies—ten of them—I pinky promise. Just get me out of here!*

She attempted to engage her captor in conversation, with the hope of distracting him, using up as much time as possible.

"Doesn't it bother you at all to be a traitor, to betray your country? To help terrorists destroy democracy and murder innocent people? I don't understand."

Captain Perfect gave her a supercilious look. "Terrorists? Stupid woman. You have no idea what goes on in the real world, do you? Democracy only works for those with money. Lots of money. Then it works like a dream."

She didn't have sleeves on her once sparkly tank top, so she used a rag to wipe her brow. "Okay, since we're stuck here together, educate stupid little ol' me. What's the real scoop, if you're not embroiled in an almighty *jihad*? If I remember my history, democracy and *jihad* don't exactly mix well."

She must have pricked his ego.

He pulled himself upright, postured like a rooster. "You build bombs, yet you have the unadulterated gall to castigate me?"

"Look, fella, we usually blast tunnels and road beds and deep wells, or bring down buildings without damaging anything around them. What we do is just a tad different from blowing up people on purpose just to make a point. Or to grab their sand to add to your sandbox."

"Don't get all righteous, Ms. Holokai, demolitions expert. Your people are all ex-military, and there are buckets of blood on their hands. Our work is the same—the difference is that *we* get paid for it, you don't. *You* are poor patriots, *we* are wealthy businessmen. Meaningless labels for different results."

Ooh, a lead. "What the hell are you talking about? We're well paid for the jobs we do."

"Seriously?" He needed to stop laughing before he continued. "You're paid a pittance, compared to the money available for people with your talent. Do you have any idea how much your job skills are worth out there, on the open market? Millions. *Millions*." He swung his arm toward the nebulous *out there*. "You still don't get it, do you? We don't give a damn who wins battles, who wins wars—as long as the fighting continues."

"Huh? Okay, let's try this again. What the hell are you talking about?" *This guy is beginning to freak me out. His mind has gone 'round the friggin' pipe.*

"Conflict, you foolish bitch. Conflict. Wars generate money—huge amounts of money. Billions. Can you understand the concept? Billions! Billions for firearms, weapons, troop and security training. We're not rebels or revolutionaries or jihadists. We don't give a flying rat's ass about your so-called righteous causes. Why should we fry in the heat or eat sand every day?

"We are a consortium of businessmen. The ventures are a straightforward case of economics. Peace brings an end to our income. The right push at the right moment, the right leaders assassinated, the right people moved up the political ladder…we can juggle wars forever." He straightened his legs, then crossed them again, fussed with his fucking seams one more time.

"Too bad about bin Laden—he was losing his edge, but the fear of having him on the loose made us a bloody damned fortune. No so much with Gaddafi. No matter. We'll find fanatical tyrants to take their places soon enough. It *is* purely business, after all." He smirked.

His coldhearted declaration sent chills racing over Keko's skin, and not the good kind. At first, she couldn't even find the words. Then they tumbled out of her mouth without restraint.

"You're fucking insane! Psychotic! You incite riots, conflict, wars, kill innocents by the thousands, by the tens of thousands? For the money? For the fucking *money*? That's too horrific to even contemplate. You hide under the vanilla labels of finance and profit, of consortiums? You're not businessmen, you're all a bunch of bloodthirsty fucking psychopaths! Sociopaths. Murderers. Assassins. And there you sit, all front o' the bus, and insist it's just business. Fucking business!"

She threw a screwdriver at him as if it was a knife. Her hand shook so badly that the screwdriver missed its mark by a wide margin. "Demented goddamn motherfuckers, the bunch of you."

Captain Perfect rose, stepped close. Without warning, he backhanded Keko across the face, the blow hard enough to drop her to her knees. Lording over her, he sneered. "Fool. That could be. But we're very wealthy psychopaths. And I enjoy living above what was, in the past, my piddling corporate pay scale. Now I measure cash in how many inches thick the pile is. If I want a new sports car, I buy a new sports car. If I want a new yacht, I buy a new yacht. If I want women, I can buy them, too. Even with your skills, you are expendable. If we want a new one of you, we can buy one. Probably a quieter model."

Keko wiped the blood from her mouth with the back of her hand, stared at the red streak on her skin. "For fuck's sake, your overinflated ego defies description, you self-righteous bastard. I should have insisted that you shoot me from the get-go. That would have been preferable to listening to your brand of narcissistic lunacy."

"Too late now." His upper lip lifted to the side, and he sure as shit wasn't Elvis. "You should know these little beauties—the bombs *you* built—have a *very* special mission. If we don't kill you first, chances are you'll commit suicide over the sheer guilt that will choke the breath from your lungs over what you've done."

She rose to her feet, reached the end of her chain.

Even though she was secured and he had a weapon, he backed away.

"What the fuck are you talking about?"

"Meet the new companions, for however brief a time, of your incredibly naïve President and useless Vice President." The weird tone of the man's voice gave her goose bumps. And not the fun kind.

The scorn oozed from his words. "Hail to the Chief and his second-in-command. President and Vice President, gone, *poof!* The Speaker of the House will be totally consumed with running the country in the ensuing chaos. The American people, even the fucking doves, the bleeding heart peaceniks, will insist on retaliation. *Demand* retaliation.

"Our people will be moving the chess pieces around the world any way we please. Conflicts will continue. Our income is guaranteed for decades. New World Order? We *are* the fucking New World Order."

His mouth twisted in an ugly grin; he bowed from the waist. "And all thanks to you, my dear. All thanks to you."

Keko dragged her chair closer, sat down. Hard.

"Cocksucker. You can't be serious. It won't work. Number one, the Pres and Vice Pres don't hang out together, for that very reason. Number two, you'll never get these explosive devices past their Secret Service details."

He laughed, a harsh, cruel sound. "You don't need to worry your pretty little head over the logistics. We have it all worked out, down to the last detail. The Secret Service isn't infallible. The gaping holes in their protocols and procedures have been proven, time and time again. After all, how safe is our illustrious President when an air traffic controller in another country can announce Air Force One's flight plans on his damned blog?"

Holy shit, is that true? She closed her eyes, shook her head at the madness. *Is this lunatic for real?*

The sound of vehicles pulling into the yard coincided with the turn of the last screw on the second bomb. Keko closed the clear plastic covers, then banged her fist on the door for Captain Perfect, who'd gone outside.

"Your toys are done, asshole." Sweat dripped from her brow. Without electricity to the site, there was a limit to the amount of lines the small generator could handle; the lights and fans were directed at the components. With the workshop shut up tight, when she moved away from the directed fan breeze, the heat took over. The day that began cool and gray was now sunny and warm. The heavy tree canopy killed the breeze, trapped the humidity close to the ground.

As soon as the door opened, Keko pushed past Captain Perfect to breathe fresh air. "Damn, it's stifling in there."

She stretched the chain as far as it would go, giving her about six feet from the building. "Hey fuckface, don't touch anything!"

"Watch your mouth, bitch." He cocked his fist, as if he would strike her again.

Keko stuck her jaw out, daring him. "Oh golly gee whiz, what will you do, shoot me?"

Without warning, someone grabbed Keko roughly from behind, held her so she couldn't see his face.

She yipped in surprise. "What the—" All she had was a fleeting impression of a swarthy man with a need to shave. And bathe.

"Get your hands off me, you freakin' barbarian."

The man grabbed her hands. In a smooth move, he duct-taped her wrists behind her back again.

"Don't turn around, woman, or it will be my great pleasure to shoot you where you stand."

Captain Perfect unbolted her chain from the floor. He handed the shiny steel links to her new jailer, who apparently looped the chain over his shoulder to allow his hands to remain free. What felt like the muzzle of a pistol was shoved hard against the middle of her back.

"Move, American bitch."

All righty then, this boy's a far cry from a good ol' New England patriot. "Fuck off."

"Shut your filthy mouth, woman, or it will be my great pleasure to cut out your tongue." He pushed the muzzle between her shoulder blades. "I said move."

"And I said kiss my ass." She tried to dig in with her feet, which proved tough to do with the poorly fitted socks. "I want my jacket and shoes."

"What makes you think you will have any need for them?"

"Do you have *any* idea how long it takes to find the perfect Christian Louboutin stiletto half-boots in black suede? Do you know how much those suckers cost?"

He shoved her again.

Keko's body, stiff after working bent over the devices for hours, couldn't navigate the rough weedy terrain without difficulty. Dragging a length of the chain across the ground didn't help matters—not with the cuff cutting into her ankle—nor did her feet being swathed in oversized socks. The woolly weave picked up every thorn, plant sliver, and stick.

Moving her eyes, not her head, she did what recon she could. On the other side of the work shed were four small cabins arranged in a semicircle; they were obviously not in the best state of repair. Parked in the overgrown yard, between the cabins and the workshop, were two long-bodied, fifteen-passenger shuttle vans, with heavily tinted windows. White in color, fairly new, not rusted or beat up. No company logo. Nothing to identify them or attract attention.

From the far side of the vans, a spate of male voices spoke excitedly in what sounded like a Middle Eastern tongue, which Keko could not identify. They made no effort to keep the ensuing racket subdued. *They must feel awfully secure here. Not good for me.* She tried not to turn her head too far, but ended up twisting ever so slightly to catch any helpful intel.

The movement must have been noticed. Her captor rapped the side of her face sharply with the butt of his weapon. "Keep your eyes forward. Do not force me to take further action."

Keko stumbled, moaned in pain. *Well, that was fucking brilliant.*

He shoved her again, directed her away from his confederates until she reached the rear of the last cabin. Despite her previous bravado, chills ran up her spine. *Okay, does he plan on shooting me here?*

A small wooden shed with rotted slats stood about thirty feet closer to the edge of the woods.

Again with a fucking shed. I don't goddamned well think so!

Before she could do more than direct a kick his way with her free foot as her last hurrah, the man slung her over his shoulder. He carried her the last few yards with the chain cutting into her abdomen, then threw her down on the wooden floor inside the shed. With her hands still trussed behind her back, she cursed as bits of tree bark and log debris bit into her shoulders.

He secured the end of her chain to another newly installed ring on the floor. "I would rather whip you for insubordination for the enjoyment it would bring, then shoot you and be done with it. But we may need you alive. My compatriots argue to use you for their pleasure before you die. This may yet come to pass."

The jailer nudged the side of her face with his foot, but it was a halfhearted effort. "Pray to your own useless god during your last minutes on Earth, and know that he cannot save you."

She spit out a chip of pine bark.

"Kiss my royal white butt, fella. Maybe I like whipping, so stop teasing me with promises of a good time."

She didn't have time to protect herself from the next kick. That one had some effort behind it. She heard Kamaka's voice in her brain—*Miss Keko, when will you learn to keep your poi hole shut?* She could still taste the blood in her mouth from Captain Perfect's love tap; now her gut ached where her jailer caught her with the toe of his sturdy combat boot.

He jiggled the door latch from the outside, ensuring the door stayed closed. His boots crunched the tree debris underfoot as he marched away.

Buddy boy, not only do you smell like a goat, but you have no idea what you're letting yourself in for. My death will be avenged, you can bet your camels on it.

Pulling herself into a sitting position with her hands still bound behind her, Keko maneuvered her fingers beneath the hem of her ruined shirt, then under the waistband of her panties.

She took in a deep breath. Held it. *MacBride, baby, sorry we won't have the chance to duke it out in bed again. You certainly opened my eyes to new possibilities.* She exhaled. *Here goes.* Secured with duct tape to the skin above the crevice of her buttocks was a simple timer mechanism. She pressed the button, began the countdown.

Ten minutes, asswipes, until you all meet Allah. Ten minutes until you discover if the legend of the seventy-two virgins is true.

CHAPTER THIRTEEN

Thursday, late morning

ADAM GRABBED MAC'S arm in a death grip to prevent him from breaking cover from behind a collection of boulders as Keko's captor manhandled her, then tossed her into the shed.

"Stand down, frogman. Not yet. Our position is advantageous. Don't blow our cover. She's tough, she'll manage. Wait for Lucian."

Mac was forced to nod his agreement before Adam would release his iron grip.

Lucian appeared on cue, silent as a hunting owl at midnight. He kept his voice low.

"Quite a party, hoss. The SUV must belong to the dude in the spic-and-span field uniform. Smitty's old Jeep is parked next to it, so we're definitely in the right neighborhood. Each of the two vans unloaded six bearded, curly-haired yay-hoos. One of the jolly fellas took Keko to the shed, then returned to his scout troop."

Lucian shifted to a squat. "They all marched into the building Keko vacated, a baker's dozen, chattering like a flock of excited turkeys. One of them carried a pair of briefcases, with what looked like metal covers. Either he's bringing in something important, or expectin' to carry out the crown jewels. Don't know why *two* cases, though."

Adam kept his voice as low as Lucian's. "All inside the garage? No guards?"

"None that I can see, which is odd. Unless someone is hiding in the other buildings, but the cabins are in really rough shape. The covered porches are rotted through, the windows all broken out, so I'm thinking the cabin floors might not hold anyone."

Mac shook his head. "They must be feeling mighty secure to be this careless."

"Either mighty secure, or dumb as wooden fence posts. I'm tending toward the disposable cannon-fodder aspect. Possibly simple transporters. I don't know why two vans, though, unless they're using the buddy system. Go from point A to point B, fast-food drive-throughs, don't stop, rotate drivers. So, dumb as fence posts is good for us."

Lucian retied his long hair into a ponytail to keep it out of the way. He took his Marine Corps cap from his back pocket, then settled it on his head, brim facing backward. He held his M9 sidearm in hand, slung the strap of his M16 rifle over his shoulder. "Ready to go, hoss."

"Is there enough cover to reach firing positions?" Adam asked. It was his job to take out the insurgents.

"Absolutely. All sorts of usable overgrowth. Especially if we move now, while they're inside."

The men suddenly heard knocking and pounding, which appeared to be coming from Keko's prison.

"Shit, she's trying to escape. They'll hear her. Cover me." Mac crouched like a runner at the starting line, then sprinted across the clearing toward the shed before either of his friends could stop him.

Adam brought the M40A1 sniper rifle to his shoulder, locked and loaded. "His dick is going to get us killed."

Lucian broke out his firearm, checked the slide. "Hoss, you'd do the same if it were Lorelei."

"Shut up, Dr. Phil."

If I'd planned on being kidnapped, I would have damn well worn hiking boots. Her hands took a beating as she rolled around on the wooden floor. The metal shackle ripped into the flesh of her ankle. *Where are those nice padded leopard-skin cuffs when ya need 'em?*

Keko kicked the socks off her feet, so she had better control. She lay on her back, knees raised, aimed both bare feet to pound against the door again. As dilapidated as the building appeared, the latch on the shed door didn't seem to be giving way. She knew it was fruitless, but felt she should try something, anything, to escape.

Trapped in the shed, she guessed she had seven or eight minutes left before she gave up her life for her country. *I can take all of them out at the same time, the fuckers—as long as no one leaves in the next seven minutes. Probably five or six minutes, now. It will take them that long to finish congratulating themselves on getting their hands on the completed devices, then chanting, "Death to the American infidels, death to the American infidels."* They'd never expect an American woman to sacrifice herself as a suicide bomber. Americans didn't do such things. *Yes, and it will make the surprise so much sweeter. Won't that be a shocker!*

Still breathing hard from her efforts, it took Keko a moment to catch the slight rattle of the door latch moving.

Fuck, one might get away. Probably the same asshole who kicked me. She pulled her knees to her chest, her gut aching from the kick.

Could be they decided to party with me after all, have a little fun with the captive to take the edge off before they leave. Well, boys, my hoo-hah ain't available without a hell of a fight. And wag one of your sorry dicks near my mouth—I swear to all the gods that I'll bite it off at the root, then leave you writhing on the ground like a headless worm, bleeding to death.

She readied herself, her legs folded in the cocked and locked position, to slam her feet against her opponent as soon as the door opened.

Maybe I can wrap the chain around his neck with my foot. Choke the life out of him. Wouldn't that feel good! Hinges creaked, the door opened slowly. As she coiled to strike, the barest hint of winter-green reached her at the same moment as Mac's soft, low voice.

"Keko? Baby, are you all right?" He knelt beside her. Pulled her into his arms. Found her mouth, kissed her hard. Then, "Can't you manage to stay out of trouble?"

Hysterical laughter caught in her throat at his impossible, implausible appearance. *He's here! He's really fucking here!* Then she remembered what she'd done. *Oh no, he's really fucking here!*

"MacBride, you need to run—now. Get away as fast as you can. Go deep into the tree cover."

MacBride sliced through the tape that bound her hands. "Don't worry, I will. And you're coming with me."

He rose, pulled her to her feet, held her in his arms for the briefest hug. "Keep the shed behind you for cover. There's a good chance we can make it without being seen, if we hurry. Head toward your one o'clock into the trees. Adam and Lucian are waiting. Quick. Let's go."

She took a step. *He didn't see the chain when I crossed the yard. Too dark in here to see it. Too late, anyway. How do I get him out of here?*

"MacBride, we need to leave *now*! You're faster, you lead. I'll give you a count of two, then I'll follow on your six. Don't fuck-ing a-well look back or you'll slow me down. I'm right behind you. Go, damn it!" *No time, no time, no time.*

He kissed her forehead, nodded, pushed the door slowly until it was flat against the outer shed wall. He did a quick recon. "Clear. A two-count, no longer." He dove out the door, running fast and low.

One one-thousand, two one-thousand… Just long enough for him to clear the shed. "MacBride, I love you."

She launched out of the shed, hit the end of her chain. *Okay, folks, Elvis has left the freakin' building.* Dropped to the ground. Covered her head with her arms. Rolled herself into the tightest ball she could manage. *I wonder how long the hurt will last before I die, because without a doubt, this is definitely gonna hurt.*

Three, two, one.

The shockwave from the blast sucked away all the air, all the sound. The shed blew apart, rained splintered planks all around her—then the one-two punch of excruciating pain, followed by total darkness.

$$\perp \diamond \perp$$

The pain convinced Mac he was still alive. He tried to sit up, decided to give himself another moment to catch his breath.

Thick-trunked trees, ancient and sturdy, took the brunt of the shrapnel, but the concussion still slammed the three men to the ground.

Lucian, farthest from the blast, regained his feet first. He gave a hand to the other two, all three men spattered with their own blood from flying rubble. "Damn, now I know how a speed bump feels when eighty-thousand pounds of tractor-trailer runs over it."

Mac scanned the vicinity. *Where is she? Why isn't she next to me?* Without answers, the best he could do is hope that what he feared had not come to pass.

Lucian put his on Mac's shoulder as the men focused on the burning, debris-laden scene of complete devastation. "Mac, chief, I'm sorry." He cleared his throat. "Really sorry."

His rifle still at the ready, Adam walked toward the flattened shed, inspecting the surrounding area for anyone left alive who needed to be dead.

Mac followed Adam, his body stiff and aching, his gait mechanical. *This can't be. She said she loves me.* "She was right behind me. On the count of two. I know she was moving."

Lucian's voice came from behind. "Mac, she got out of the shed, I saw her. Right on your six, man. Then she dropped, rolled into a ball like a hedgehog, covered her head. Like she knew."

Like she knew. Like she knew what? What the hell did she know? What the hell did she do? "Wait a minute. Do you think *she* did all this?" The swing of his arm took in the enormity of the destruction.

Lucian shrugged. "Don't know, man. I'm just sayin' the girl ducked and covered like a pro. She knew something was comin'."

A deep, dark crater replaced the workshop and most of the overgrown yard. Fractured rocks and boulders, gnarled and torn tree roots were scattered without rhyme or reason. The crater's jagged edges reached what had been the line of crumbling front porches. Every building had been leveled.

Both vans had been thrown several car lengths away, morphed in a matter of seconds into twisted, smoldering hulks. The SUV lay on its side against a broken tree, the roof of the vehicle totally crushed inward. A bloodied arm hung out the driver's window; rags of sand-camo fabric clung to the torn flesh. The Jeep had flipped upside down on the far side of the tree.

Lucian took a quick look around what had been the work shed. "There's no way anyone survived the blast at ground zero. The FBI will be lucky to find a few bits and pieces." He glanced at Mac. "Man, I'm sorry. I didn't mean…"

Mac picked his way closer to the remains of the shed.

"Lucian, shut up."

He stepped around the smoldering debris, careful where he put his feet.

"Chief, I said I was sorry."

"Luce, will you shut the hell up? I thought I heard something." Mac lifted a couple of splintered boards, his arm muscles bulging with the strain. Cocked his head, listened again. Altered direction.

"Adam, grab the end of this plank."

When the wide, flat timber was moved aside, they all heard it—a low, weak moan.

Mac dove in with his bare hands, grabbed and slung aside broken and burning boards and smoldering rubble, ignoring the pain. "Keko? Baby, talk to me. *Keko?* Answer me, goddamn it!"

The men finally reached the flattened shed door, which had been blown off its hinges, but somehow survived intact. The sound seemed to come from under the door. Mac directed Adam and Lucian to each raise a corner, while he lifted the other end. "Slowly. Don't lift the door quickly—the wood underneath may flame."

"MacBride, is that you?" Keko's voice, fractured, raspy. "Can you...please...get this fucking thing...off me? Can't get...any air." She coughed, her breath sounding weak and thready. "Did I...did I...get...the rat bastard motherfuckers?"

Lucian laughed. "Oh yeah, whatever happened, she did it."

"Yes, baby, you got them. You got them all." Mac's voice cracked as he tried for cheerful.

"*Hallefuckinglujah.*" The whispered word was barely audible. "Lost my favorite heels. My best...damned...jacket..." Her voice faded, weaker yet. Then silence.

"Keko?"

Nothing.

The men carefully lifted the door, laid it aside.

Mac forced himself to pull air into his lungs as he looked at the bloody, unconscious mess that had been Kailani Holokai Larsson. *How the hell had she survived the blast? How long could she hold on?*

"Call..."

Lucian turned from the satphone. "Already on it, chief, already on it. Joe and Abigail heard the explosion, Joe immediately called for backup. The EMTs are on the way, should be here in a matter of minutes."

He gave Mac a quick glance. "Look, man, I understand chain of command and everything, but you have much more important things to worry about right now. *Please* let me call the FBI when we're finished here. I know it's your bailiwick, but I love it when they hear Sanctuary is involved. They chatter and jump up and down like crazed squirrels on moonshine."

Adam shook his head at his partner. "You're a seriously twisted sonofabitch."

He crouched next to Keko, whose lacerated face rested against Mac's blood-smeared thigh. He pressed his fingertips against the artery on the side of her neck. He shook his head, laid his hand on Mac's shoulder.

"The lumber is still burning, and there's no water supply to wet anything down. Mac, we need to lift her onto the door or a section of boards, carry her out of the debris. Are you up to it? If not, Lucian and I can handle it."

Mac, who wanted nothing more than to hold his lover in his arms so she could die in peace, grimaced. "Let's do it."

Then they found the chain.

CHAPTER FOURTEEN

Friday, early morning

WITH NO FRAME of reference, Keko drifted in and out of fuzzy consciousness that alternated with pain and more pain, for what seemed like forever. When her eyes finally managed to stay open, the world slowly came into focus again. She tried to move, but agony rippled everywhere. A whimper escaped her parched, cracked lips.

"Hey, baby."

She heard the soothing tones of MacBride's voice, but wondered how that was possible.

He freed his gentle hold on her swollen fingertips, then brushed her forehead with the back of his hand. "Welcome back to the land of the living. Sweetheart, you scared the hell out of everyone."

Keko attempted to push herself up in the hospital bed, but only struggled weakly without results. She looked down. Both hands and wrists were encased in bright purple resin casts from the middle knuckles of her fingers to the top of her forearms. She wore a blue cotton hospital gown with a diamond pattern. An IV line punctured each arm.

Someone had loosely plaited her hair, probably to keep it out of the way. The single long braid hung down her shoulder. She couldn't imagine why it mattered, but she was glad no one had cut off her hair.

"Oh, this is attractive." At least, that's what she meant to say. Her throat burned, and she sounded like a frog. She wasn't sure she was coherent enough to be understood.

MacBride pressed buttons to raise the head of the bed, then gently lifted her to a more upright position. A tent had been placed over her feet. She moved her legs experimentally. One foot felt much heavier than the other. *Oh, crap, that can't be a good sign.*

"There. Do you feel better sitting up?"

"Not sure. Bring…gallon…pineapple juice…crushed ice."

Focusing on MacBride's face, she didn't want to be the one to tell him that he looked like hammered shit.

He brushed her cheek lightly with his fingertips. "Baby, really, how do you feel?"

She spoke slowly, so she wouldn't cough.

"Seriously? D-9 bulldozer…giant iron treads…rolled over me—then rolled back and forth…to finish job." She took another breath. "Everything…hurts. Freakin' hair hurts."

"Splinters, no doubt. Although your arms and shoulders took the brunt of those. Your body looked like a pincushion with toothpicks sticking out from everywhere. Your phoenix is perforated. Blind luck that the nails missed you."

She tried to shift her butt over, which resulted in another groan. And not the good kind. "Throat…hurts. Can't…breathe…well."

"The rubble was burning. Fire got a bit close before we were able to carry you out of there. You suffered smoke inhalation. Plus, your gut is bruised from being kicked, looks like."

"Other…damage? Foot…?"

"You want the full inventory?"

She managed half a nod.

"It will probably be better if you listen, not talk. Lacerations and bruises from the back of your head on down. Your face is scraped up. Minor burns, mostly first-degree, a few second-degree blisters. Smoke inhalation. Concussion, but covering your head with your arms saved your skull from serious injury.

"Multiple fractures, both hands and wrists, from the door coming down on you. Left hand worse than the right. Good news is that the fractures are simple, not compound. Hard casts to stabilize, no surgery. The worst damage happened to the ankle chained to the shed floor."

Her mouth skewed in a grimace. "Afraid…to look. Do I have…one foot…or two?"

He lifted the sheet to show her the matching purple cast that covered her left foot from her toes to halfway up her shin. A light gauze bandage wrapped her right foot.

"As Kamaka would say, you're one lucky little coconut. You still have two feet. Ligaments and tendons damaged, lots of little bones fractured, skin ripped—you're damn lucky your foot wasn't torn off. The blast blew the door from its hinges. It came down on top of you, protected you from being sliced and diced to death by the big stuff. Physical therapy down the road. For you, not the door."

He attempted a smile, but it got caught halfway. "We should probably salvage the damn door. Make a coffee table from the wood."

She withheld comment.

Mac moved his chair closer to the bed, gently caressed the lacerated fingertips that weren't covered by the cast.

"Baby, why didn't you tell me about the chain?"

Keko shrugged without thinking. It hurt. She winced.

"No time," she croaked. "If you didn't leave…you were dead."

MacBride lifted her fingers to his mouth, kissed them gently.

"There wasn't a backup timer, was there?"

Surprised, she cocked her head ever so slightly.

She spoke slowly, used as few words as possible. "Who… discovered…flaws?"

"Kamaka. The boy is a genius. He knew you'd catch on. What we didn't know was what you would do, or could do, about it." He looked away for a moment, couldn't meet her gaze. He finally turned back to her, attempted a smile.

The smile didn't work well, but she declined to mention it.

MacBride cleared his voice. "Apparently you chose the path of suicide bomber, which was not one of the options we considered. Silly us. An ER technician found the trigger device taped under your knickers when he took you to X-ray. Clever plan, that. Kamikaze, but clever. Insane, but clever."

Ignoring his observation, she hit what she devoutly hoped was the morphine button. It took a few minutes before she could continue. "Hey, they wanted two bombs...I gave them two bombs. I was able to coordinated the timers...to blow...at the same time. Might have been...just a tad...overkill. How... did you find us?"

MacBride actually chuckled. "Heaven protect small town busybodies. We owe everyone a huge pizza party in the town square when this is all over. The short version: a group of us canvassed the entire town, then we compared notes. The only place that fit the 'anything unusual' criteria was ol' buggy Chet Adderson's dilapidated hunting camp."

"Brilliant lads." Keko coughed, winced. "You, Lucian, Adam... quite the team. Y'know, you...awesome...SEAL. Navy dudes, fools to let you go..."

The world suddenly became all warm and fuzzy again as the pain receded. She slowly sank into a soft, fluffy, drug-induced cloud.

"Never...let you...go..."

Will Chandler strolled into the hospital room, two fancy cardboard containers of coffee in hand.

Keko was awake and coherent, which she felt was a definite improvement over her earlier, somewhat hazy meeting with MacBride.

"Gee whiz, FBI Special Agent Will, what a surprise to see you. Who woulda thunk?" Her voice still croaked, but was somewhat improved.

He looked rumpled, as if he'd slept in his clothes again. "Hey, kiddo. How are ya doin'?"

"Better than you look. At least I have excellent drugs. Haven't you heard? Morphine is my friend." She tried to grin, but it didn't work well. "Damn, my face still hurts. Sorry."

Chandler pulled up a chair, set the coffee on the bed tray, settled with a deep sigh.

"Don't apologize to me. You're the hero of the day. Well, heroine. A faceless, nameless heroine, never to be identified. To be honest, I don't even know how or where to begin this crazy-assed report. Are you up to telling me what the hell happened? The short version, and please use small words."

"First things first. Is that hazelnut coffee I smell?"

"Yeah. I thought a bribe might help."

"First, I gotta know—how did you guys explain the explosion?"

"That part was actually easier than we thought. Mac reported to the little local newspaper that a person or persons unknown shot up a partially-filled propane tank out at Buggy's place, and the subsequent explosion took out everything. A substantial reward was offered, which will, of course, never be collected. Our guys set up a perimeter to keep out the locals, took whatever samples we needed. Got a bulldozer out there as soon as possible, pushed everything into the crater so the vehicles and body parts were covered, and the hole didn't look so huge.

"Everyone is speculating about the perpetrators being a bunch of kids or a wannabe hunter from the city. One helpful visitor even suggested the crater could have been left by an alien spaceship's thrusters. We should take samples, examine them for traces of non-terrestrial fuel meant for interstellar travel. However, across the board, the general consensus is how lucky no one was injured or killed. That's the bottom line. I think we pulled it off."

"Clever."

Keko had devised a simple method for holding a cup in her currently immobilized hands. Like a robotic device, she interlocked her fingertips and captured the container between the casts.

"Mmm. Boy oh boy, that tastes great. Thanks. So, you want the simple version, or the technical version?"

"The simple one, please. It's about all I can deal with at the moment."

"Okay. I was drugged at The Woodlands' parking lot in beautiful downtown Catamount Lake by a fake history teacher, Professor Simms, aka Captain Perfect. He whisked me away to some moldy, disintegrating camp, forced me to assemble two of Smitty's bombs at gunpoint. If I didn't do it, my asshole captor planned to shoot me, then snatch up Kamaka to complete the job."

"Okay, so far that jives with MacBride's account. Let's get to the explosion part of the tale, if you would be so kind. Did you say two bombs?"

She nodded, then gave him a curious look. "Aren't you gonna take notes or something?"

"Nope. Nothing gets recorded. Not until I hear the full story. Then, and only then, can I decide how best to handle the sheriff's 'unofficial' activities and his complete disregard for proper protocol, as well as explain the able assist from our lads at Sanctuary—as well as half the damn town. I trust you're okay with that?"

The small shrug that followed hurt, but she managed. "I stalled as long as I could, until Captain Perfect pointed his weapon at my gut. He said he'd shoot me if I didn't cooperate, then haul in my second-in-command to take up the slack. I told him my partner never saw the original device, but he didn't care. I couldn't let that happen."

She tried to get comfortable, but it was a lost cause. "We began to chat. I found out who our bad guys were. Then I learned what they intended to do with Thing One and Thing Two."

"You began to chat? Just like that?" Chandler shook his head. "Why do I believe there's more to the story? Okay, I'll bite. Who were they?"

"Businessmen."

"What?"

"Hey, you asked. A consortium of businessmen. Short and simple. A syndicate of manipulating financiers. Men in high places with boatloads of money who wanted more boatloads of money. Men who didn't want their fortunes to dry up if the conflicts around the world ended."

"I don't fucking believe it." Chandler rubbed his forehead, as if he was working on the granddaddy of all tension headaches." I just don't fucking a-well believe it."

She felt deflated, sank back into her pillows. "Sorry, that's all I have for you. I didn't get names and addresses, but I did get the plan. No proof, other than what the wannabe blabbed to me—since the egotistical idiot assumed I'd be dead shortly. The upshot? No *jihad*, just greed."

"Keko, I *do* believe you. That's the problem." He stared toward the window for a few moments. Took a gulp of coffee. Arranged the cardboard cup on the tray, just so. Rearranged it twice more. "Damn, I could lose my job—but you deserve the truth. If this gets out…"

She crossed her heart. "To the grave, Will. Nothing will ever pass these lips. Not ever. I swear."

"I'd like to say it's over, but that would be foolish and short-sighted. Your timely explosion apparently put a definite cramp in a really bizarre scheme to take this country down—which our security experts said actually could have worked. Could still work, I guess. Maybe not this time, or the next time, but eventually."

"NCS Special Agent Randall nearly lost her life a few months back, trying to deliver a flash drive containing details of what sounds like the same or similar plan. She wasn't aware of the data encoded on the drive. She'd be dead at the bottom of a gulley if it wasn't for Adam Stone and Lucian Duquesne. Your Sanctuary hosts."

"Lorelei? She almost died?" There was definitely a clench to Keko's gut. No one had said anything, Mac included.

"Yes."

"So, Captain Perfect actually told the truth? About taking out the Pres and Vice Pres, leaving the country in the middle of a total clusterfuck?" Keko pressed the lever on the bed to raise herself. "The war in the Middle East, the conflicts around the world—you expect me to believe it's all just business?"

"No. And yes. Take the real conflicts around the world, usually over territory or religious beliefs that have been ongoing since Man began to walk upright, then add instigators.

"We identified your Captain Perfect as George Ritter, a deposed financier, who had a reputation for spending much more than he ever earned. Guys like him are easy to turn—flash large wads cash or whatever lights their fires, they'll sit up and beg like trained poodles. As much as I hate to admit it, our intel backs up his story."

She began to tremble. "Damn."

"Yeah, I know. We were *that* close to worldwide chaos—then you managed to blow up old Buggy Adderson's camp, a dozen loyal jihadists, and one greedy turncoat."

"I couldn't have gotten all of them. Even I could tell they were just drones, grunts."

"Correct. The devices were the linchpins to the plan, not the men. The guys you took out appeared to have been the delivery crews. The vehicles were mostly burned, but in the glove boxes we found lightly-toasted tour maps for D.C., where the President was due to speak, and city maps for San Francisco, where the Vice President was scheduled to attend some sort of political rally. The maps were marked with times and routes.

"After the blast, we immediately leaked a careful trickle of false data. The bombs were too sensitive, too unstable, the special timers failed, *blah blah blah*. With the device designer dead—the killing of whom the members of the consortium are probably kicking themselves in the butts over—the only other person with hands-on experience was unfortunately critically wounded in the blast and is not likely to survive."

Keko gave him a wide-eyed look. "I'm critical? At death's door?"

Chandler nodded. "For the moment. Until we come up with a plausible cover story to keep you safe, to prevent some other jack-hole from trying to snatch you off the street again. Or take you out. Like they took out John, then Smith." He twitched uncomfortably for a moment. "By the way, sorry about your dad. I didn't know at the time that you were John's daughter. That intel didn't catch up until later."

Keko sucked down another swallow of coffee to keep tears from forming. "Thanks." She grimaced as she shifted her bad ankle for the sake of illusive comfort. "You *do* know the other side has their own explosives experts, right?"

He made a face at her. "Of course. We have quite the international list, built up over too many years of doing this stuff."

"So, what's to prevent them from building their own version of Smitty's Doomsday Device, then trying it again?"

"Nothing. Nothing at all. Except now we know the plan, but the bad guys don't know that we know."

Keko shook her head. Carefully. "Okay, this is beginning to sound like a really bad Inspector Jacques Clouseau spy plot."

Chandler chuckled. "Yeah, I guess it does. Glennon Garrett is our brilliant go-to surveillance and intel guy, former Marine Force Recon, now a freelancer. He decoded the data on the flash drive after it was spirited safely out of the country, thanks to an assist—albeit an unwilling assist—from Sheriff MacBride.

"Mac was conscripted against his will by Stone, Duquesne, and Special Agent Randall. Garrett, aided by Duquesne, has been working nonstop to direct subtle streams of misinformation to the right places, working with various government intel sources to heighten the level of believability.

"You've given our boys enough ammunition, if you'll pardon the expression, to have the bad guys chasing their tails for months, at the very least. If not longer."

"MacBride?" Keko's tummy tumbled again. "Our MacBride?"

"The very same. Mac handled the transfer of the flash drive. Stone, backed up by Duquesne, took out Agent Stanford, the NCS wannabe who attempted to murder Lorelei. Stanford actually tried to take her out three times. He ended up very dead. Harry Robson, a minor NCS supervisor and also Stanford's handler, managed to get himself assassinated within hours of Stanford's death for failing to grab the damned flash drive. We now assume the consortium was responsible.

"The intelligence community couldn't understand why no one, at least none of the usual suspects, took credit for the hit on Robson. What Garrett ferreted out in the last week or so meshes with what you were told by your chatty abductor."

Stunned by the news, Keko hit the morphine button again, then lowered her bed. "So, as Captain Perfect said, it wasn't personal—just business."

Will Chandler rose to leave, patted her hand as she drifted off. "Yup. Nothing personal, just business."

Well hell, Keko thought as the morphine kicked in. *Well hell.*

"Kailani. Kailani, can you hear me?"

Boy oh boy, that stuff is stronger than I thought. Now my mother is appearing to me, in full surround sound.

Someone patted her scraped cheek. *Ouch.*

"Kailani?"

Keko tried to respond, but her voice wasn't working much better than her vision. "Mother? Really?" *Is that me? I still sound like a crow.*

"Oh, Kailani, thank goodness." Her mother broke into a sob.

Keko tried to clear her voice, but the effort hurt. "MacBride? Chandler? Drifted off, sorry. Rude of me."

A new voice entered her room, accompanied by the faintest scent of wintergreen. *Mmm. I could get accustomed to waking up to that.*

"Baby, not to worry, you needed your sleep. Sleep helps the body heal. Trust me—I speak from experience." MacBride leaned carefully over the bed, placed a gentle kiss on Keko's forehead. He put a straw to her parched lips so she could sip iced water, but the skin around her mouth cracked and oozed a drop of blood.

"Keep still. Your skin is still dry." He dabbed at the blood with a tissue, then applied soothing lip balm to her mouth. "Aftereffects of whatever inhalant was used. They must have hit you a bunch of times."

He offered her the straw again, with slightly more success.

When the cold water eased her parched throat, she sighed. *I may live after all.*

"And who are you, young man, to take such liberties with my daughter?"

Keko saw her mother's indignation rise as much as heard it in her tone of voice. *Damn, here we go, and I am so not in the mood for this.*

"Mother, may I introduce Brian MacBride, sheriff of Catamount Lake, Maine." The words barely clawed their way out of her throat. "MacBride, this is my mother, artist Aolina Hualami from Maui and Honolulu. She paints and sculpts primitive Hawaiian tribal art. Mother, say thank you to the nice man. MacBride was one of the three heroes who rescued me."

Aolina walked to the windows, turned to face them. Her delicate features always reminded Keko of an exquisite porcelain doll. About the same height, but even slimmer than Keko, the stunning beauty wore a tailored skirt suit, navy blue with gold stripes. The skirt reached mid-calf which, when combined with navy-blue nineteen-forties-style peep-toed high heels, accented her tiny feet and slender ankles. Jet-black hair almost shimmered in an *über*-fashionable feathered cut that barely touched her shoulders. Her strikingly beautiful Kahlúa-colored eyes were not friendly.

"And why, Kailani, why did you need to be rescued? I understood you ended that horrid life after your father died. How could this happen?"

MacBride rose from his seat, took Keko's hand in a protective gesture.

Keko's heart gave a little lurch of pride that MacBride would take on all comers in her behalf, including her daunting mother. However, she needed to deal with this, up front and personal. "Sheriff MacBride, would you give my mother and me a few minutes alone? Please."

"Keek, are you sure?"

"I'll be fine." To her surprise, she actually believed what she said.

As soon as the door closed, Aolina turned on Keko. "Kailani, I do not know why everyone insists on calling you that ridiculous name. Keek. It's worse than Keko. That man acts as if he owns you. Much too possessive. I shall speak to him about his attitude."

"Mother, there's no need for you to speak to anyone. MacBride and I are…well… involved."

"Involved? Is that a polite way of saying you are sleeping with him?"

Keko sighed. *Okay, for the record, I tried to avoid this.* "Yes, mother, I'm sleeping with him. We have wild kinky sex. We shag like rabbits for hours, for days. As often as possible. In as many places as possible. There, do you feel better now?"

"Kailani, there is no need for you to be vulgar."

Oh yes, there is. It makes me feel better.

Her mother's carefully cultured voice and mannerisms had annoyed Keko when Keko was younger. After meeting people from around the globe during the course of Larsson Demolition jobs, she'd finally realized it wasn't a pretentious affectation on Aolina's part—her patterns of speech were the product of an educated person for whom English was not her native language.

"What MacBride and I do is our own business. Believe it or not, I'm an adult—and I've been an adult for a long time. Probably since I was twelve. I suppose you should be forgiven the gaffe, since you missed all those silly in-between years."

"He is a sheriff. Law enforcement. As bad as the military." Aolina's voice rose, became shrill. Unusual for her. *She must really be torqued.*

"Then, Mother, you'll be sorry to hear that MacBride *is* military. A former Navy SEAL. A demolitions expert, as well." She cocked her head. "Wow, it didn't connect before—he's just like Dad."

Her mother hurled an empty plastic water pitcher to the floor. "Why are you doing this to me? Why do you torture me?"

Damn. I haven't seen her throw anything since I was about five. Keko tried to sit straighter, but pain drained what little strength she had. "Why am I doing *what* to you, exactly? We don't see one another, except at your rare command. You didn't attend Dad's funeral. You do not acknowledge me as your daughter. We don't even live on the same land mass. As a matter of fact, why *are* you here? I'm not dead. A get-well card would have sufficed, or, better yet, an Edible Thingy Get-Well Bouquet. Love those chocolate-dipped strawberries."

Aolina's radiant golden color turned ashen, her brow furrowed. "How can you say those horrible things to me? *You* insisted on going to your father—I gave you what you wanted. How am I *hoa paio*, the enemy?"

"*Jeez*, Mother, you still don't get it, do you? I was five freakin' years old and tired of being handed around like a piece of old luggage!"

"And you believed it caused me no pain to give you up? You were my own child."

Keko needed to press the morphine button again before she could continue. *Ahh, blessed drugs.* "Wow, your child? I do believe that's the first time I ever heard you admit you gave birth to me."

Her mother's hand went to her throat. "Kailani, those are horrid, hurtful words. Of course you are my child, my daughter."

"No shit."

"There is no reason to be rude."

Exhaustion—or morphine—suddenly sapped Keko's energy. "Mother, what do you want from me?"

"I came to see how you are."

"Well, now you've see me. I'm sure Kamaka shamed you into flying out. Your guilt is assuaged. You can leave now."

"Kailani, how can you say such things?"

Keko made the effort, sat a bit straighter. "Long years of experience."

"What long years? You were five…"

"Oh yes, I was five years old, the magic number."

"It must be the drugs. You speak nonsense."

"Mother, do you remember what happened before I was shipped off to Daddy?"

"Of course. You wouldn't stop crying for days. Your *kupunawahine*, your grandmother, had no choice but to call the Red Cross to bring your father home on, what did they call it, hardship leave."

"Yes, my grandmother. Your mother. Grandmama Iekika called for intervention because you were off again. Do you remember what you told me before you left?"

"Kailani, I have no patience for your games."

"Yes, Mother, I know the drill, believe me, I know the drill. You have no patience for me now, as you had no patience for me then."

"Kailani…"

"Well, you may not remember, but I do. Even though I wasn't quite five, I remember that evening like it just happened."

"Which evening? Of what do you speak?"

"The evening of the big party, a celebration of the first-ever showing of your work at a mainstream art gallery."

"What of it?"

"I hadn't seen you for days and days. I missed you. You promised you would tuck me in at Grandmama's so I could see your pretty new dress before you left for the exciting party that everyone was talking about."

A frown marred Aolina's flawless face. "I still do not understand."

"You finally came to me, but you were in such a hurry, you were worried only about being late for your opening, not worried about seeing me. I begged to go with you, begged you to take me."

"That was silly. I could not take a young child to the gallery showing."

"You could, if you so chose. Instead, you sat on my little bed, and said you would tell me a magic secret."

"A magic secret? What sort of secret is that?"

"The lying sort. You leaned down and said that you would always be there for your good little Kailani. However, I mustn't cry and carry on any longer, or the magic secret wouldn't work. When I wanted you, all I needed to do was whisper your name, quietly, so no one else could hear me. Just whisper your name, and you would come for me."

Her mother stared at her, obviously not comprehending. "I did no such thing."

"Yes, you did." Keko's snarl was clear and concise. "You were in such a damn hurry to leave, you told me whatever it took to shut me up, to stop hounding you to stay with me."

"Kailani…"

"After you left, the family finally went to bed. Everyone settled, the house became really quiet. Believing the magic secret was true, I began to whisper your name. I whispered and whispered and whispered, but you didn't come for me. Then I whispered louder, but you still didn't come.

"I got frightened. I thought I did something wrong, because the magic wasn't working. That's when the crying began. It's tough for a little kid to whisper and cry at the same time, so I sobbed and hiccupped. The crying and hiccupping finally spiked out of control, which frightened me even more—that's when I began to call for Daddy."

"I have no idea to what you are referring. You were very young. You probably dreamed it all."

"No, I didn't dream it all. You know it's true. You didn't come back to the house, not even when Grandmama called you. That's when Daddy came for me, when he finally took me back to the States."

Her mother's hands were at her own slender throat, as if she were choking. "Lies!"

"No. Truth!" The tears were no longer contained. "That's when I became, as Dad called me, an independent little cuss. No magic, no secret wishes. The only magic I learned was the trick of the disappearing mother."

"I promised your father I wouldn't speak of our arrangement to anyone. I kept my word."

Keko's jaw dropped, then her words came out as a croak. "You did what? Arrangement? What arrangement?"

"John is gone now. It cannot matter to him." Aolina stepped closer to Keko, both hands flat on the hospital bed. Her dark eyes blazed.

"I loved him so much. That's right, I loved your father. Is that so difficult for you to believe? I loved him more than you can possibly imagine. Yes, I knew he was a Navy SEAL. I was young and foolish, too much in love to realize what that meant, him being a SEAL. In the end, I could not be the dutiful Navy wife he needed me to be. I did not have the strength to hold us together."

The tears pooled, then raced down her golden cheeks. "The panic every time he left. The fear when I realized I was pregnant and alone at the Navy base. I could not be brave, was not strong enough to join with the other wives. I went home to my family. John understood. He agreed."

Keko slumped against her pillow. Stunned. "Why didn't he tell me any of this? I thought you just dumped me."

"We agreed to never speak of it. After you were born, I continued my art studies with the full support of my family—as well as John's support. We didn't divorce while he stayed in the Navy, so you and I could receive benefits. When he finally left the SEALs to join the private sector, I agreed to send you to him.

Then we divorced, and I signed over full custody. That was our deal. I kept my end of the bargain."

"The bargain? What was I, a chess piece? The freakin' pawn?" Totally deflated by her mother's admission, Keko felt no emotion. Maybe it was the morphine—maybe not. "Mother's bargaining chip against future needs?"

Aolina moved to Keko's bedside, gently took her damaged hand. "Kailani, darling, it was not like that. We loved you, hoped to do the best we could for you. You wanted to be with your father. So young, so stubborn.

"You would accept no compromise—so much like your father. He promised to leave the SEALs, to keep you safe. He kept his word by leaving the Navy. I did *not* agree to allow you to be brought up with demolitions and devastation. That was *not* part of our arrangement."

"You can't blame Dad for that; that's how he made his living. That's how he paid for a beautiful home for me, paid for the finest tutors. I had an aptitude for his work; everyone said I was a natural." *At least, that's what I've been told since I was twelve. By everyone who mattered to me.*

"So, now you lay in a trauma unit after an explosion nearly takes your life, and may leave you permanently crippled. Excuse me if I do not consider that to be a fair trade."

What the fuck? Permanently crippled? MacBride forgot to mention that part.

"Mother, do you have any real notion of what that explosion accomplished? No, of course not—and I am not permitted to tell you. Just understand that I would have gladly given my life, if that's what it would have taken to stop the horror intended if those devices reached their targets."

Keko was fading, fast. "Don't you understand? I *need* to do what I do. I'm good at it. Actually, I'm great at it."

"And your *kane*, Kailani, your young man? Where does he fit in? An officer of the law? Every time he leaves, it could be the last time you see him. Are you prepared for that?

"And if you have children? Imagine telling them, through your tears of grief, that their father was gunned down in the line of duty, he will not be coming home ever again. Or imagine your sheriff gathering up your own daughter, your own son, in his arms. 'Oh, I am so sorry, your mother will not be coming home. She was just blown to bits, and I am afraid there are not enough pieces to bury her decently. Closed casket, of course.'"

Aolina had worked herself into a real frenzy, her usually soft, melodic voice oddly sharp, harsh. "Do you love him enough? Will he love you as much when he realizes the both of you cannot stay in bed forever? The sex and passion will wane; reality will rear its hideous serpent's head. Will the love be strong enough to hold you together in the harsh light of truth?"

The door opened. MacBride closed it quietly behind him. He moved to Keko's side, laid his hand gently on her shoulder. "Sorry for eavesdropping. Ma'am, I think those are our decisions to make. And yes, I love your crazy daughter enough to make our weird relationship work."

Aolina backed away, wiped the tears from her face with a delicate handkerchief. She gazed at the pair before her, shook her head once, then went silent.

"Mother, I believe our discussion is over. *Aloha*, I wish you well. May your trip be peaceful and uneventful. I don't believe we need to see each other again." The pain ramped up. The morphine drip kicked in, then Keko began to sink once again into blessed oblivion. "MacBride, did you just tell my mother that you love me?"

"I thought I should, since you admitted it first when you tricked me into leaving you. As my ass bolted from the shed you deemed necessary to destroy."

"I couldn't remember if I said it out loud. The words needed to be released into the universe, if I was going to be blown to kingdom come. Although I'm sure one device would have done the job, I sorta had to use what was at hand, in case the bad dudes split up the bombs. Both or none."

Aolina Hualami—acclaimed artist, brilliant sculptor, failed mother—shook her head, her expression sad. "Both of you are insane. As was Keko's father, who shall remain, for eternity, the love of my life."

She gently took Keko's hand, kissed her daughter's abraded fingers. "I hope it will be enough to see you through when the passion fades. *Aloha*, my child."

She removed herself gracefully from the room.

Aloha, Mother. Goodbye.

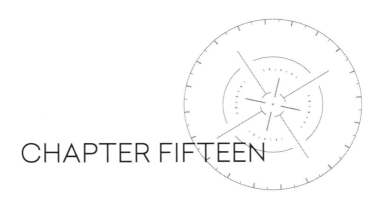

CHAPTER FIFTEEN

Friday morning, a week later

"HOW IS THIS going to work, if I stay here?"

Using the resin cast on her right hand and wrist, Keko pressed the joystick on the motorized wheelchair, took the chair for a lap around the leather furniture groupings in Sanctuary's great room like she was a road rally driver. She bumped into only one sofa, two chairs, and an end table.

"I have a business in Boston," she insisted. "We have projects on hold. I have employees who expect me to look out for them so they can pay their bills. I need to bring new jobs in so I *can* pay them, so they are *able* to pay their bills."

"Not to worry. Kamaka's been holed up in the comm center, has everything under control." Lorelei placed a glass of cold lemonade with a straw in the wheelchair's cup holder. "Lucian is working with Glennon Garrett to integrate your communication system with ours, so you and Kamaka can video stream to your Boston office in real time. It will seem as if you were standing in your own office."

"Wouldn't it be easier for everyone if I went home, so I *was* standing in my own office?" Depending on others grated on Keko's sense of independence, made her restless.

Lorelei chuckled. "Like it or not, you're not ready to go home. It's either here, or rehab. You might as well give in to it. Relax, enjoy being spoiled while you can. The royal treatment won't last forever."

She walked over to a wide door tucked cattycorner under the balcony, slid the pocket door into the wall. "Check this out. Here's your ride."

When Lorelei stepped aside with a Vanna White sweep of her arm, Keko saw a motorized lift, an elevator to the gallery level.

"Neat, isn't it? Apparently, when the camp was in full swing, broken legs were enough of an issue during ski season to have this beauty installed. It will certainly help as my belly grows and I'm waddling around like a water buffalo."

Keko couldn't imagine Lorelei ever waddling under any circumstance, but she appreciated the other woman's attempts to make her feel comfortable with the situation.

With her left foot in a cast and both hands still out of commission, she couldn't even manage crutches. She had to admit that, although her dad's house was spacious, the floor plan wasn't as conveniently set up as the lodge's.

Lorelei headed for the kitchen, spoke over her shoulder to get in the last word. "And then there's MacBride."

Yes. And then there's MacBride.

Thursday morning, a week later

AND THEN THERE'S MacBride. When Keko woke, the refrain would not fade away. What to do about MacBride? She parked her wheelchair by the knee-to-ceiling windows that allowed magnificent light, as well as a magnificent view, into the great room. *Next best thing to being outdoors.*

No one shirked duties at the lodge, so chores kept everyone busy. Apparently, a new roster of clients would overtake Sanctuary in a few days. Keko felt useless, but there really wasn't anything she could do with one foot still in a cast. Her wrists had been freed from their resin traps, but they were still in braces. She forced herself to be as self-sufficient as possible by using the wheelchair. Adam offered his giant open shower with the spray handle so she could rinse off and do her hair. After plastic bags were taped over the cast, of course.

And then there's MacBride.

Keko managed to stand, using the back of the wheelchair seat as a support for her bent elbows. She gently swung the casted leg fore and aft, doing thirty reps at a time, to keep the circulation moving.

It had been a real eye-opener to realize that, other than Kamaka, Lorelei Randall had stepped up as a real friend. And her only female friend. A woman she'd only known for a few weeks. *I must be a pitiful choice as friendship material.*

It was a no-brainer to realize Lorelei stood firmly in MacBride's camp, as did Adam and Lucian. *So, what's the problem?* Keko settled in the wheelchair, raised the leg support for her injured foot when it began to throb. *The guy is handsome, intelligent, totally buff, employed, comes without girlfriend baggage.* Her hoo-hah tingled as she mentally added his bedroom skills to his list of attributes. *And he certainly does have skills in that department.*

Aolina's comments circled Keko's brain, like Santa's Express train stuck circling a Christmas tree. *Will he love you as much when he realizes you cannot stay in bed forever? The sex and passion will wane, reality will rear its hideous serpent's head. Will the love be strong enough...?*

Do I really love him? Do I love him enough?

Mac had been hangin' tough since the explosion, keeping himself in SEAL Tactical Yellow Alert mode, for the sake of self-preservation. He didn't consider the what-ifs or why-fors, didn't think of the could-have-beens. SEAL alert meant that he didn't imagine how Keko's body would have looked, had the wooden door not protected her.

He kept all and sundry under surveillance; everything and everyone out of the norm was suspect, no matter how inconsequential. Tactical plans of offense and defense ran through his head, and he planned accordingly. He automatically scanned areas where an enemy could hide, could attack, or support a firing position. He had a keen interest in alternate offensive and defensive positions.

Being in SEAL mode safeguarded his sanity. But he wasn't in the SEALs any longer. He didn't have his team.

After surprisingly tender lovemaking in her bed at Sanctuary the night before, Keko had curled against him, instead of their usual spooning. He was on his back; her face snuggled against his shoulder, her damaged hands folded against her own chest. Her casted foot was out of the way, on a flat pillow. He'd slid an arm under her shoulders to hold her close; his fingers played with her hair. He folded his other arm under his head.

Mac had moved to Catamount Lake to get away from the horror of death. Away from war. Away from the 24-7 conflict. Moved to this quiet community with its forthright people, people who accepted him even though he wasn't a born and bred New Englander. A quiet place where there had been no capital crimes for over a century.

Keko is safe. That's all that matters.

He knew it was a lie. There was so much more that mattered. The leviathans of his memory, monsters that had once sounded and gone deep, were returning to the surface, breaching the surface into the light of day.

Sunday morning

After MacBride slipped out early for work, the sound of voices drew Keko downstairs to the kitchen.

"This is so totally unlike him, and you know that as well as I do." Abigail lifted a coffee mug to her lips as she saw Keko. Lorelei sat across the table from Abigail, her back against the dish cupboards.

Keko headed for the coffee pot. "I'm coming late to the conversation. Unlike whom, exactly?"

Lorelei hesitated. Abigail did not.

"Mac."

Keko felt her gut clench.

"What about him?"

Abigail kicked back in her chair. "He's wandering around with his head so far up his ass that he'll never see daylight again, that's what. I...we...strongly suspect it has something to do with you."

The mug didn't spill a drop as Keko carefully placed it back on the counter. "Me? Why me?"

"Girl, you can deny it until the cows come home—if we had any cows. The man is smitten. When you're both in the same room, the air crackles with sexual sparks like you guys were Tesla coils. He hasn't been right since he came back from LA."

"But..."

Lorelei tapped her fingernails against the table. "Keek, I hate to jump in here, but Abby's right. Mac is absolutely bonkers, head over heels in love with you. Well, at least, in lust. I'll withhold judgment on the love part. He might still be in denial over that. He's even making Adam and Lucian edgy, and they're usually of the live-and-let-live camp. Lucian slipped up once, so I know the three of them partied together for years. *Seriously* partied."

Keko pulled out a chair, slumped into the seat. "So, what can I do? You both know him. What *should* I do?"

Abigail shrugged. "Fuck his brains out. Go home to Boston. Pick up the pieces of your life, then get on with it."

Lorelei looked surprised at her friend's comeback. Wide-eyed surprised. "Damn, girlfriend, that's a bit harsh even for you, don't you think?"

"Yeah, well, it might be. But the simple plan saves time, not to mention heartache and emotional wear and tear."

Abigail headed for the refrigerator. "Is there any of Lucian's key lime pie left?" She turned to Keko. "Nothing like the real thing. Lucian is a purist. He refuses to use anything except genuine Mexican limes that his mother sends up from the Carolinas. Mama Duquesne has a secret supplier across the border—she trades quilting patterns in exchange for the little green fruit."

"Abigail," Keko responded, "you can't drop a bomb like that, then segue to key lime pie recipes."

The game warden sliced the pie into sections, pulled out plates from one of the dish cupboards, grabbed dessert forks from a drawer. "Look, all I'm saying is that you need to face up to the attraction. Then either embrace it, or end it. Get the fuck rid of it."

Abigail hit Keko with a direct gaze. She ticked points off on her fingers. "Are you attracted? I'm guessing, yes. Do you want to shag like super-rabbits? Again, yes. Superb shagging aside, will you leave your business in Boston, move to Maine to be with Mac? Do you plan to relocate to Catamount Lake? Is he going to jump ship to join the Boston PD?"

Words would not come forth as Keko's throat tightened up. *Give up her business? Relocate? Nothing was said about relocating.* "Abigail, I think you're reading way too much into the situation."

"Am I? Can you honestly deny your attraction to Mac?"

"Attraction is not the point."

"Attraction definitely *is* the point. Mac can't function when you're around, and it appears you have the same problem. At least, according to Chandler."

Keko covered her face with her hands, then peeked at the two women between her fingers. "Oh, crap, please tell me you're not serious. Chandler knows?"

A forkful of pie poised halfway to Lorelei's mouth. "Everyone knows."

"*Aw*, hell's fuckin' bells." Keko's sigh couldn't be helped.

Abigail shoveled another piece of pie into her mouth, chewed while she considered. "I mean, Mac is a total fox, so it's perfectly understandable. I'll bet even Kamaka has the hots for him."

Keko shook her head, looked up. "This is going from bad to worse. And yes, Kamaka agrees with the whole fox thing, since L.A."

She tried the pie, more to buy time than because she had the urge to choke down dessert. "Okay, Lorelei is obviously not up for grabs, but what about you and MacBride?"

Abigail grinned. "Nope, not happening. As Grandma O'Connell is fond of saying—bless her blue-haired heart—don't shit where you eat. Of course, my mother loses her mind every time Gram says it, since it's usually at the dinner table when tons of guests are present."

"Christ in a sidecar, that's freakin' helpful. How do I interpret those words of wisdom, or is it a secret Maine phrase that I need a special-agent decoder ring to understand?"

"It means," Lorelei explained, "do not become involved with anyone too close to home."

"Oh."

"Mac and I made a pact early on," Abigail said. "No dating, no casual boinking. We work together too closely. If our lovey-dovey relationship went south, it would result in a very uncomfortable operational environment."

"An *uncomfortable operational environment.* I see."

"Mac and I meet in town on occasion and hoist a beer or two. Since we were friends of Adam and Lucian first, we shamelessly horn in on Lorelei's territory here at Sanctuary to work out, hone our skills with weapons, or play cards. That's it. I'm just one of the guys."

"And don't forget Garrett." Lorelei went for another forkful of pie. "Damn, this stuff is great."

"Garrett?" Keko asked. "Who the hell is Garrett?"

"Lorelei, no need to bring Glennon into this discussion."

"Oh, Glennon. That name I've heard. Who is he?"

"Go for it, Abigail."

"Glennon Michael Garrett. GMG surveillance and security guru. He was here for a special op. When it was over, we hooked up. That's all there is to it."

"And where is Mr. Garrett now?" Keko asked.

"At his headquarters in Jersey. He was somewhat damaged in, hmm, an accident, the last time he was here. He's back home, recuperating. Catching up with business."

"So, Garrett is your guy?"

"I don't know whether I'd phrase it like that, but yeah, okay. When he's here, we're together."

"Are you going to move to New Jersey?"

"Move to Jersey? Me? Not fucking hardly. If Garrett wants me, he knows where to find me. I like my life. I like my job. Why should I give up everything for occasional hot sex?" Abigail chuckled. "Although, I must admit, sex with Glennon sizzles."

Lorelei gave her friend a look. "Abbs, Glennon with a full leg cast and his shoulder in a sling? I don't even want to know how you guys managed."

"Trust me. Where there's a will and the promise of such rewards at the end... Let's say we manage just fine and leave it at that."

Keko didn't have an answer. *If I did, I'd be able to deal with my own damned dilemma.* "I can't give up my life, either. I have people who depend on me for their livelihoods. I just took over my father's company, and I need to make the business work. We have jobs lined up. How could I justify bailing out on my responsibilities? MacBride can't expect me to drop everything."

Lorelei spoke, her voice soft. "Those are the choices we all face, Keek. Women living and working in a man's world—strong women who are good at our jobs."

"Yeah, but you *are* managing. You live here, in this awesome place. You have two incredible men who would die for you. Literally. You're gonna be a mom and *not* give up your profession."

"I'll admit I'm one of the lucky ones, Keek. Nothing held me in D.C. that I can't do here. If the NCS cuts me loose after the baby is born, I'll freelance with the boys. And I made those decisions in the clear light of day. We hammered out our decisions together. I'm as anchored to Sanctuary as are Adam and Lucian. This will be home to our children."

Abigail picked up a section of piecrust with her fingers, ate it. "Yeah, and not all of us are headed for the mommy track. I'm not looking for a permanent relationship. Don't want babies. No offence, Lorelei, but I don't need the whole domestic scene to feel complete. At least not now. I like the way I live. Come and go when I please. When Glennon's here, there are excellent bonuses—but that's all."

Keko's coffee grew colder, the pie forgotten. *And no one has answered the question: what am I supposed to do?*

Sunday evening

The scene at dinner had grown ugly. Reactions ranged from curiosity to anger. Keko continued to offer her point of view. "Look. I appreciate everything you folks have done for me. Everyone has gone above and beyond. But John left me a business that won't run itself. Larsson crews depend on me to keep the jobs on schedule and the company solvent."

Mac slid his chair back, got to his feet. "Kamaka has the talent and the skills. Let him take over."

Kamaka shifted in his seat, held his hand up. "Whoa, hold on. That's not my gig, dude. I'll do whatever Keko needs me to do, but I didn't sign on to run the company."

He glanced quickly at Keko, then shifted his focus to his dinner plate.

Keko met MacBride's eyes. "Come to Boston with me. I'm sure the Boston PD would happily make room for an ace sheriff with SEAL bona fides."

"No can do. I settled here to avoid big-town crime and bloodshed, not to jump back into the fray. I saw enough of that in the Navy."

"Understood. You've chosen your career. I have a business to run. Neither of us can leave. Let me rephrase that. Neither of us *chooses* to leave. Have I missed an option?"

"You can run Larsson Demolitions remotely. I don't have that luxury as sheriff."

Keko rose, leaned forward on rigid arms, her wrists still wrapped. "I see. So, your job is more important—"

Lorelei jumped in. "Okay, people, calm down. Let's ratchet this discussion back a notch. Neither career is more important than the other."

Lucian leaned back in his chair. "What if you both took a leave of absence, took some time off to try to sort through the issues. Take the situation out for a test drive. See what works for y'all."

"Won't work," Adam grunted. "Too soon."

"And there we have it. Pared down to the bare bones." Keko gave Adam a nod. "Short, to the point. And, while I do appreciate everyone's input, the arguments are moot. I booked tickets for Kamaka and me. We leave in ten days."

The stunned silence immediately ramped up from zero to sixty with everyone talking at once. The look Mac gave her mirrored such pain that Keko dropped her eyes. She didn't see him leave, but she heard the back door slam shut.

Oh, hell.

"Uh, Miss Keko, Boss Lady. I have some news."

Keko whipped around to Kamaka.

Now what?

Sunday evening, later

"What do you mean, you're not going home? When did all this happen?"

Kamaka actually blushed. "We were just, like, batting it around for fun while you were in the trauma unit. Lucian said I could stay at Sanctuary. I can cross-train, study other disciplines. Learn to use and control my strength. Lose the whale blubber."

He grabbed his love handles, which resembled the Michelin Man's spare tires. "I thought we'd have more time to, y'know, discuss it."

Flabbergasted, Keko's jaw dropped. "And Adam? Adam Stone agreed to this?"

Lucian jumped in before Kamaka could speak. "We talked. He's good with it. Kamaka can actually earn his keep. We have a full schedule of clients for these next few sessions, so he can assist as he trains."

"But who's going to be my second, if you leave me?"

"Boss Lady, I'm not leaving forever. Think of this as on-the-job training, or like you're sending me off to college. If I were you, I'd tag Freak to take my place—that crazy fella eats, sleeps, and dreams explosives. Has a good nose, too."

"Oh, goody. Freak lives on Cocoa Puffs drowned in Yoo-hoo, peanut butter wafers, and diet Coke. *And* keeps giant hairy spiders as pets."

"Tarantulas."

"Whatever. Giant hairy spiders."

"Trust me, Freak's your best go-to guy. Just keep him away from coffee. He gets enough caffeine with all the chocolate and soda pop, and you don't want him awake for seventy-two hours at a time."

Keko suddenly realized it was a done deal. She could raise a huge fuss, but all that would accomplish would be to make her friend feel more guilty than he already did. She wasn't going to make any headway. *Might as well accept this graciously.* "All right. But he's not moving in with me. Especially with the spiders."

"Tarantulas."

"Whatever."

Kamaka lifted Keko from the wheelchair, gave her a huge hug.

"Makaha, you're breaking my ribs and flattening my tits. I can't breathe."

"Kamaka, not Makaha. *Oops*, sorry, Boss Lady." He sat her down again, kissed the top of her head. "I'll e-mail every day."

"See that you do, Pineapple Man. I'm not sure when we'll see each other. I love ya, dude."

Kamaka hugged her again, gently. *"Aloha, Kailani Holokai."*

"Aloha, hoaloha, Kamaka." Tears pooled, then spilled down her cheeks. *Goodbye, friend.*

Monday evening

Kamaka was leaving her. Well, actually, she was leaving him. Returning to Boston without him. Leaving Sanctuary, which had become more of a home than the dwelling she'd lived in since she was five years old. Leaving friends. Real friends. Friends who'd saved her life—emotionally as well as physically.

And then there's MacBride.

MacBride *was* Sanctuary to her, as much as Adam and Lucian and Lorelei. *Be honest. More than Adam and Lucian, who helped to save my life, and Lorelei, my new second best friend.*

So, what about *MacBride?* She snorted at the phrase, which rattled around in her brain while she spent the day organizing and packing. *Look, Jiminy Cricket, get out of my freakin' head, will ya?*

Adam and Lucian disappeared into the workout room after dinner. Lorelei simply nodded when Keko asked to borrow Lucian's Explorer, which had become Keko's truck-away-from-home since arriving on Sanctuary's doorstep. It was her first time behind the wheel since the explosion. The SUV was an automatic, so her black-leather-laced ankle brace made things awkward, but not impossible.

Lucian had scoured the antique shops a couple of towns over and found a walking stick just the right height for Keko. The stick was black lacquer, festooned with a hand-painted garden of flowers and dragonflies. Instead of standard hospital wraps, she wore fingerless black leather Harley Davidson gloves, paired with leather HD wristbands. Padded, rolled gauze protected her mostly healed hand fractures.

Keko had dressed in the blue backless halter top that showed off her phoenix tattoo. Her black stretchy hip-hugging capris went well with her Harley accoutrements. Her favorite black leather heels had been blown up, along with her bomber jacket—plus, her foot and ankle weren't anywhere near ready for heels yet—so she made do with black suede flats decked out in blue metallic sparklies. The black ankle brace also matched her capris, so she thought she was doing well as a fashion-conscious convalescent. Her hair was gathered in a high chignon, skewered in place by long bamboo hairpins. She borrowed a blousy blue jacket from Lorelei.

The closer she got to town, the more nervous Keko became. There was no reason *not* to see MacBride, unless she counted on screwing up his life even more than she already had.

She parked the truck in the driveway, just sat there. Then sat there longer. *I handle high explosives, rigging equipment, and thirty-odd hard-boiled powder monkeys. This is ridiculous.*

She knocked. When MacBride opened the front door, she couldn't read his expression. He just stood there. Tall. Strong. Silent. Looking down at her. He stood long enough that she began to fidget, leaned on her cane for support.

Oh god, this is stupid. I was so wrong to come here. Lorelei, why didn't you talk me out of this? Why didn't you act like the adult and snatch the keys out of my hand, then send me to my room? Threaten to ground me until I was thirty-five, like my father did in the good old days?

"Uh, look, this is stupid, I'm sorry to have disturbed you." Totally humiliated, she dropped her eyes, turned to leave before she embarrassed herself further.

MacBride grabbed her arm, spun her toward him, shocked her speechless.

"You're sorry to have disturbed me? Woman, you've done nothing *except* disturb me from the first damned moment we set eyes on each other. Oh yeah, you definitely disturb me—on so many levels I can't keep count, and on both coasts."

He pulled her into the house, closed the door behind him. Still holding her arm, he forced her to make direct eye contact.

"What do you want?" His voice came out as a snarl. "Shouldn't you be packing?"

She stammered, cleared her throat, tried again. This was not going the way she imagined. "Um, maybe a hello?"

"Larsson, don't fuck with me. You made your choice. Kamaka is staying. You're leaving. So, exactly what are you doing here? Trying for another goodbye? I think you already said that. Very clearly."

"I…"

"You what? Forgot something?"

She pulled her arm loose, set her cane against a chair, rubbed away the depressions in her skin made by his fingers. "Damn it, MacBride, you're not making this easy."

He cocked an eyebrow. "Why should I?"

She lowered her head, muttered. "I don't know what to do." *There it is, chief, the bald truth of the matter.*

"What was that?"

This time her voice was stronger. "I said, I don't know what to do. Did you hear me that time?"

"I'm not your Dutch uncle. I can't tell you what to do." He paced the room, came back to face her. "Do I frighten you? Or, is the thought of staying with me so damned repulsive that you'd rather scurry back to Beantown?"

"Of course not. How could you even think that? But you're not the only one to consider. I have a company to run, employees to care for. They depend on me, and I'm not there."

"Then sell out."

She took a step back. "I beg your pardon?"

"Larsson's is a viable international enterprise. John always had offers on the table—scuttlebutt like that gets around. Hell, you'd have top-shelf competitors hammering at the gates. Throw the business into the hands of a broker, get the best deal. If you play your cards right, you could be set for life."

Keko was fair gobsmacked.

"You can't be serious. I *like* my work. I'm *good* at what I do. My crews are the best in the world." Her heartbeat rose as quickly as her temper. "How dare you!"

MacBride crossed his arms over his chest, stood spread-legged. He seemed taller. Looked meaner. "Your crews? Those are John Larsson's men."

"*Ooh, you bastard!*" She picked up a tall, fat, pillar candle from an end table, hurled it at MacBride with a good, strong, overhand pitch—and she didn't throw like a girl. "*How dare you!*"

Even though he moved quickly, it wasn't quickly enough. The heavy, spice-scented wax column glanced off his thigh, hit the coffee table with an audible *thud* before the candle landed and rolled on the rug. "*Shit! What the hell is wrong with you? That hurt!*"

She scanned the room for another weapon. "Sonofabitchin' *cocksucker*. Those are *my* men! *I* earned the right. *I* paid my fuck-ing dues. My father believed in *me*! My crews trust *me*!"

The tears came, and they weren't crocodile tears. They were tears of righteous anger. She balled her fists up, screamed with pain from her damaged hands, which added to her outrage. "How fucking *dare* you!"

MacBride strode toward her before she could rearm.

She fought him, but he managed to overpower her without inflicting further damage to either of them. He pulled her close.

"Ahh, here's the Keko Holokai I know. I thought I'd lost you. Here's the bombshell raised by the great John Larsson to be the toughest, the best, the baddest, the boldest. With all the talents of the son he never had, packaged in a killer sexy body."

"MacBride, you are *such* a humongous shit. You did that on purpose?" She struggled in his arms. The adrenaline still high, she freed a hand and without thinking, pounded her fist against his shoulder. "*Ouch*, sonofabitch, that hurt."

"You needed to remember what was important to you, instead of waffling back and forth like a debutante picking her choice of beaux."

"Oh, and you think pissing me off helped?"

"It worked, didn't it? You realized that you don't want to give up your business or your career. That's part one."

He gently took the hand she used to punch him, removed the protective Harley Davidson glove, unwrapped the gauze. He began to massage the top of her hand and her wrist with his thumbs. "You may have fractured the bones again."

"I don't care. I'll live."

His touch felt so good, her eyes closed of their own volition. A soft groan worked its way from her throat as her tense body began to relax.

"Part two is the problem." His voice sounded closer. Actually, his voice sounded very close. Like next to her ear. She opened her eyes again to find them nearly face-to-face.

"Part two?"

"Yes. Part two. What about MacBride."

That got her attention. *Did I say that out loud? Or did he read my flippin' mind?*

Just as quickly, she felt the trap close again, the threat of being confined, of being caught, attempting to choke her.

"I-I-I don't know what you mean."

"Keko, dear heart, you may not be the world's most usual woman, but you're not an idiot, and you're not a liar. You know exactly what I mean." Finished with her hand, he pulled her closer.

Her good sense rebelled, but her body began to melt with the desire to form itself against him. To fit them together as she knew they could.

"Keko, I want us to have a future, but you panic so quickly that you won't even discuss it. You break out in a sweat, your emotions lock up, every time the subject comes around. You care, I know you do."

He pushed his hips forward. "We were meant for each other. No two people are as perfect together as we are, even when we're disagreeing. And, if I dare say it, especially in bed."

"B-b-but, you heard my mother. That was probably the only thing she got right, and you know it. There's a real world outside the bedroom."

"I don't deny that." He pressed closer.

Her body responded, but she tried to push him away. "MacBride, I can't think when you're close to me. My brain shuts down."

"That's another thing. Why won't you call me Brian, my given name? My mother likes it, she chose it. Or even Mac? Why MacBride? No one else calls me MacBride, unless it's preceded by Sheriff."

She felt the warmth rush to her cheeks. "If I tell, you'll laugh at me."

Backing up a step, he held her at arm's length, his big hands warm on her shoulders. "Will you tell me if I promise not to laugh?"

She looked away, but he coaxed her face back with gentle fingers under her chin.

"I swear, I will not make fun of you. Really. Cross my heart."

"Just remember—you promised." She sighed, and her shoulders drooped a bit. *This is going to be a mistake, I know it.*

"When I went to live with my dad, he called me his little five-year-old hellion, way before I knew what a hellion was. One-on-one, the two of us alone in the house, he didn't exactly know what to do with me. I clung to him like Velcro-kid, afraid I would be left behind again. So, he began to read to me every night. Well, every night that he made it home.

"I wouldn't let my nanny read to me, just him. He read stories of knights and kingdoms and warriors who had the most awesome adventures, who had special powers, who wielded magical swords. Vikings, Celts, Scots, Knights Templar, King Arthur and the Knights of the Round Table. I knew them all.

"I could listen to his wonderful voice for as long as he would talk. After he finished each book, we cruised through the model shops for toy soldiers. He helped me to pick out little figurines. We painted each one, then I named them. He put up special shelves in my bedroom for my warriors, my heroes, and my storybooks." She stopped, lost for a moment in the memories—and missed her father all the more.

He lowered his voice as he gently urged her to continue. "Go on."

"For whatever reason, one of the warriors became very special to me. Angelus MacBride. When I was old enough to do my own online research, Dad seemed impressed when I told him that Angelus was a Latin name. Well, Roman, actually. The masculine form of Angel." Her eyes closed for the briefest moment. *And how Dad smiled, he looked so proud.*

"In the MacBride illustrations, there was a real feel to the art, like the *Conan the Barbarian* covers by Frazetta. Angelus was tall, incredibly strong, with hair and eyes just like yours. He was dressed in a black kilt, leather arm cuffs, a leather tunic with chained mail, fur-lined cape, and boots. He wielded a mighty, magical sword, fashioned with a hilt covered in rubies, and rode a huge black warhorse, Goliath.

"As I got older, I dreamt more often about my MacBride. Sadly, the other heroes went by the wayside. Only MacBride remained. As I got older yet, those dreams became more vivid, more intense." She could feel the blush warming her cheeks.

Finally, she raised her eyes to meet his. "Twenty years from our first meeting in the pages of an adventure book, there you were. In Los Angeles. Angelus, in the City of Angels. My warrior. My own MacBride. Only, I didn't know who you were until we landed in Maine. When I saw you again, when you said your name, I didn't know if you were real or an image my jet-lagged brain cooked up. I didn't know what was right, what wasn't."

True to his word, he didn't laugh. Rather, he pulled her into his arms, nearly smothering her with kisses. At first, soft, gentle kisses. Then not so soft, not so gentle. He lifted her in his arms, carried her to his bedroom.

Keko's arms wrapped around his neck as she inhaled the fragrance on skin left bare by his unbuttoned shirt. *Wintergreen, damn him.* She didn't complain. Didn't argue. Didn't fight him off.

When they reached his destination, he settled her on the edge of his bed. Without speaking, he freed her of shoes, worked around her protective leather until she was nude, except for those coverings.

"Mac…"

"Just hush, and let me work."

He spread Keko's arms and legs out like she was a snow angel.

"Stay." Fully dressed, he crawled onto the bed, then positioned himself between her opened thighs. With gentle licks, he tongued her from her knees to her throat.

Restraint took everything she had to keep her body still, but she could not prevent the soft moans that escaped.

Mac assumed a prone position, slid his arms under her thighs. He covered her mound with warm, gentle kisses, worked his way to the doorway of paradise. Using only his mouth, lips, and tongue, he slowly brought her to such a state of ecstasy that he could barely keep her thighs under his control. With her first cry of release, he slid two fingers into her, pinned her against the mattress like a butterfly to a board.

Arching nearly off the bed, her whimper bloomed into a cry that sounded suspiciously like *MacBride!* as her fists tangled in his hair.

Omigod, omigod, omigod, that feels like heaven! She stretched out on the mattress, gave herself into his care.

Angelus.

When the smoke cleared, comfortable silence filled the dark bedroom. Earlier, Mac had divested himself of all clothing, pleasured

Keko again, and gave his aching cock the relief it demanded. He finally slid under the bedclothes, pulled her into his arms.

Keko wiggled, stretched.

"Mmm. Nice." She wiggled a bit more. "I should go."

He lifted his head to check out the digital clock on his dresser, then murmured against her skin. "It's three in the morning. Go where?"

"Back to Sanctuary. To my own bed. Lorelei will be expecting me, and I have Lucian's truck."

"*This* is your bed. *Our* bed. *This* is where you belong. Here. With me. Secure. Warm. Comfortable in my arms. Sated. Deliriously happy after the most incredible lovemaking."

She stiffened.

Mac enveloped her. "Yes, lovemaking. It's not such a terrible word."

After a moment, he felt her relax, grow softer in his arms.

"Keek, don't you get it?" he whispered to her. "Being with you is so much more than just sex. It's about the electricity that fair hums through the air between us. Can't you feel it? There's no other woman who lights my fire the way you do—and no woman who ever did. When we're together, my body is on total sensual overload."

He kissed her ear. "Our friends know you're safe." Kissed her neck. "Protected." Kissed her cheek. "Out of harm's way." Kissed her shoulder. "And Lucian doesn't give a good goddamn about his truck."

"I can…"

"Yes, I know you can take care of yourself. You've proven it, over and over. You blew a crater in the earth big enough to see from orbit. Baby, I don't want to own you—but let me at least care for you. And not only until you finish recuperating. Even on the rare occasions when you're not bashed and battered."

She became very still.

"You can say it, y'know. Not just when you think you're going to be blown to smithereens. Here and now, in the security of this nice, safe, quiet room, you can admit it. Again. You can admit that you love me."

He rubbed his chin against her soft, sleek hair. Ran his hand down her hip to caress the smooth skin of her thigh. "Is it so difficult to accept the fact that I love you? I want to do things for you because I care, not because I think you incapable. I enjoy your company. I'd like to share more of my life with you."

How can I get through to her? "We don't need to duel for dominance if I bring you a cup of hazelnut cream coffee while we're in front of the fireplace at night, watching the dying glow of the embers. I'm not your master, not your boss. I don't want to dominate or be the leader of the pack. I don't want to own you. All I ask it that you let me in."

"*Aloha Au Ia 'Oe.*" Her voice was soft, low. Almost too low.

"What was that?"

"I said, I love you."

"And?"

"And, I want to be with you."

"Hallelujah." He smiled. "See, the heavens are still above us, the earth below, and the world did not come to an end."

"But what if—"

He cut her off, stroked her soft cheek with his finger, looked into her compelling green eyes.

"Let's not do *what if.* Let's see how we handle *right now.*"

~The End~

ABOUT THE AUTHOR

Danica St. Como, a former Jersey girl, writes at her farm in central upstate New York. Surrounded by a gaggle of Whippets, St. Como puts her pen to several romance sub-genres: erotic contemporaries including m/f/m, m/f, m/m/f, and m/m relationships, erotic historicals, and paranormals—all hot, all steamy, and all sexually explicit. Learn more about Danica online at http://www.danicastcomo.com/ or on Facebook. Readers may also contact her at DanicaStComoAuthor@gmail.com.

OTHER TITLES BY THE AUTHOR

Men of Sanctuary Series:
Book 1: *A Strength of Arms*
Book 2: *Hunting April*
Book 3: *Bombshell*
Book 4: *Above the Law*
Book 5: *Aloha Man*
Book 6: *Saving Nico*
Book 7: *His Brother, Her Lover*

Other Contemporary Novels
A Feast of Tides
Logan's Girl: A Novella
Imala's Heart
Blade Dance

Paranormal Wolf-shifter Series
Loving a Wolf: Books 1 & 2

Victorian Novel
In Her Lover's Arms (watch for re-release)

~~~~~~~

**St. Como also writes under the pen name
SOPHIA ROSLYN.**

Sophia Roslyn Novels
Dragonetti's Mountain (watch for re-release)
Her Special Forces

Made in the USA
Middletown, DE
15 May 2020